THE WYKEHAMIST

This book first published in 2025
By The Black Spring Crime Series
Black Spring Press
An imprint of Eyewear Publishing Ltd
BSPG
London, United Kingdom

Interior design by Edwin Smet

All rights reserved
© 2025 Alexandra Strnad

The right of Alexandra Strnad to be identified as author of this work has been asserted in accordance with section 77 of the Copyright, Designs and Patents Act 1988

ISBN 978-1-915406-89-7

BLACKSPRINGPRESSGROUP.COM

Author's Note

This novel is a work of fiction. Names, characters, and incidents are either the product of the author's imagination or used in a fictitious manner. Any resemblance to actual persons, living or dead, is purely coincidental.

THE WYKEHAMIST

ALEXANDRA STRNAD

THE **BLACK SPRING**
PRESS GROUP

'Moderation is a fatal thing, Lady Hunstanton, nothing succeeds like excess.'

—*A Woman of No Importance,* Oscar Wilde

PART I

Hong Kong

Lucian Dorsey walked to the hardware store a few blocks from his apartment building. He was wearing a grey Sunspel polo shirt and matching jogging shorts. Two large sweat patches had expanded beneath his armpits, and another was beginning to appear in the middle of his chest. His square, buffalo-horn Maison Bonnet spectacles were moist from his exertion.

It was early October and the weather on Hong Kong Island was approaching perfection. The rainy season was over and people were enjoying the pleasantness of being outdoors: from the hawkers selling plastic toys on Tai Yuen to the customers at the wet markets in Wan Chai. The city beckoned the senses with a fragrant medley of spice from the snack vendors' stalls, which hovered like a top note over the scent of butchered meat and exhaust fumes.

Lucian continued to sweat through the mild weather that afternoon. His increased body mass and the cocktail of drugs he had taken an hour before were putting a strain on his system, and now even the mildest form of exercise made his forehead trickle.

Lucian could hear the sound of megaphones. It was another pro-democracy rally organised by students. There had been a series of blockades around Wan Chai preventing government workers from accessing buildings. Many of the students Lucian passed on the streets were wearing masks and goggles to protect their eyes from pepper spray. They were no doubt on their way to the blockades in Admiralty. He had read online that Mong Kok and Causeway Bay were also being occupied. He watched a group of twenty singing the new anthem "Raise the Umbrella" as they walked down Johnston Road, faces covered, banners held high. It was a perfect clear-skyed day, but the city was in turmoil.

As Lucian opened the door of the hardware store, a rush of AC made him shiver. The store was lit with white strip lights. Its shelves were lined with drills, leaf collectors, spools of wire insulation and measuring tape. Three models of lawnmower were artfully displayed in the window. *Who fucking needs to buy a lawnmower in Wan Chai?* Lucian thought to himself. It was true that Wan Chai was a built-up area, in which most inhabitants lived in apartments with small balconies. Few people owned gardens with lawns. He made his way unsteadily to the clerk at the back of the shop and smiled, putting his wet, marbled hands on the counter, leaving a damp mark on the Formica top. He steadied himself.

'Can I help you, sir?' asked the clerk behind the till.

'Yes,' Lucian replied, 'I have quite a list.'

The clerk nodded. He was small, around fifty, with a wispy comb-over. He seemed affable enough. Lucian looked at him hungrily.

'First,' said Lucian, 'I'd like some sandpaper. Do you have extra coarse?' Lucian spoke in the confident and sonorous tones of a well-born Wykehamist. It was an expensive voice, cultivated in the halls and classrooms of his youth, burnished by his time at the University of Cambridge.

The man nodded and brought down a few small sheets.

'I'm afraid I'm going to need a bit more than that,' Lucian chided but still keeping a note of cheeriness in his tone.

The man obliged.

There followed a list of items that Lucian reeled off, as if going through a meticulously rehearsed mental checklist, including gaffer tape, power drills, nails, pins, clamps, electrical cables, a blowtorch and a power sander. The clerk explained regretfully that blowtorches were currently out of stock. Lucian looked disappointed. He wanted the clerk to feel that he had let him down. He shook his head solemnly, rested his elbows on the Formica top and covered his eyes with his hands.

'One moment, sir, I'll go to check with my wife at the back.' The assiduous Hongkonger ran through the beaded doorway and was, for a moment, out of view. Lucian could hear him speaking in Cantonese to someone in the back room. A television was on above the counter blasting a drama on the Hong Kong television station Jade, so Lucian could only make out a few words of the clerk's conversation with his wife. The stark lighting in the shop was giving him a migraine. A fly that had been buzzing around the trowels and seed sachets committed suicide with a fizz and a pop in the electric flycatcher, spraying bits of its body over the sparkling displays.

The world was spinning in a steady oscillation. Every pore on Lucian's body oozed with torment.

The clerk returned. 'Sir, we have one left. Propane gas. Is that ok?'

'Good man, I'll take it.' Lucian made a show of looking for his credit card. He took his leather cardholder from the damp pocket of his shorts and flicked through it before selecting a black centurion American Express card. Lucian liked the coolness of the anodized titanium between his fingers. He was disappointed that the clerk, upon seeing the card, made no comment.

Lucian paid and carried his purchases out in two large plastic bags.

His apartment was on the thirtieth floor of a fifty-storey skyscraper, with views over the city. He took the elevator up, glad that he got a straight run all the way to his floor without stopping. The building was hardly inhabited during the day. This meant he could play music or video games as loud as he wanted, and no one ever complained.

Once Lucian had unlocked the door, stepped inside, set his shopping bags down, closed the door and locked it, he began to wriggle out of his t-shirt and shorts. His skin was crawling, and the only way to alleviate the itch was to be naked. He went to the bathroom and fumbled around in the cabinet for a tube of cortisone cream. It helped to stop the maddening itches, which felt like termites moving about below the surface of his skin. He squeezed the white cream onto his fingertips and gently dabbed it onto the most irritated patches.

Then he went to the drinks cabinet and poured himself a large measure of twenty-one-year-old Laphroaig in a Cumbria Crystal Grasmere tumbler. The whisky hit the spot. Lucian felt its warmth running through his blood.

Then, with a grunt, he lumbered back to the entrance of his apartment, where he had left the two plastic bags. His hands trembled with excitement as he took out each piece of equipment, examining it carefully before placing it on the large, glass-topped Newton coffee table, designed by Holm and Sunaga.

Lucian decided to arrange the instruments on an immaculate, white Turnbull & Asser pocket square in order of size. Then he rethought the assemblage and reorganised in order of use. Each piece was pleasurably new. The sandpaper had never been used, the plyers never gripped.

Lucian decided to listen to some music to maximise the experience. With "Sussudio" playing on his Bang & Olufsen sound system, Lucian imagined what each piece was capable of doing.

Through the windows of his apartment the city lights prickled into life, the conch pink of the sunset almost disappeared and the ubiquitous orange glow of the city at night became visible. Lucian's belly flapped against his pelvis; his moon-face had two days' worth of stubble shadowing its soft lines. He was heavy with flesh, drink, and uncut cocaine.

On the coffee table before him lay his remote controls. He had a remote to operate most things. He pressed a button on a sleek, white remote and the blinds slithered over the windows like sleepy doll's eyes. He had been working like a maniac for the past month: long days, long nights, training his mind to chow down on the task in hand. When he worked like that, he needed some serious release afterwards, and each month his excesses became greater, his need more urgent.

At that moment he wanted to know what pressure was needed for the pair of plyers to sever a little finger, and what it would feel like as the flesh and bone finally gave way to the greater force of the sharp steel.

He went to the fridge and pressed a round pizza-shaped magnet, which signalled his order to the takeaway downstairs. They knew his 'usual' by heart: meat feast with mushrooms, onions, sweetcorn, extra cheddar, two cokes and a chocolate-chip cookie.

Lucian slumped in his leather armchair with a copy of *Spear's* magazine over his eyes. His loneliness was deafening but he would never admit that loneliness was the feeling. He always identified the gnawing pang as something else: thirst, hunger, *tiredness, desire.*

Lucian slipped on a bathrobe when the delivery boy came to the door. He pressed his eye to the peephole just to check it was the pizza. The boy was adolescent and acne-pitted. Lucian opened the door, thrust a few dollars into the boy's hand and grabbed the bag with more force than required. So much force in fact that the paper handles ripped off. The boy did not notice; he had already turned his back, walked down the corridor, and pressed the button for the lift.

Lucian returned to the living room with the food. He sat in his leather armchair once more, feet elevated, pizza box on his thighs with a tea towel to stop his skin getting too warm. He flicked through porn sites on his widescreen. Nothing tasted good to him today. All this fantasy stuff was like imitation meat. He took a large mouthful of his pizza. Bacon, chicken, sausage rotated in his mouth, as he swallowed the fatty juices.

He stared at the line-up of instruments. Somehow that was more satisfying. More satisfying than girl-on-girl action, fellatio, anal. He thought about the sandpaper and what it could do to the insides of the human body. He had a magnum-sized dildo in his bedroom. He combined the sandpaper and the dildo in his mind; he thought a lot about that.

His mind floated about the room, swimming over the cream carpets, pinging from corner to corner like a pinball.

CHAPTER 1

Four months after the news of Lucian's crimes had broken, Clementine sat at a table for two at Yan Toh Heen, at The InterContinental in Hong Kong. She was waiting to meet a contact from *The South China Morning Post*. Clementine viewed herself as a hard-nosed journalist who stopped at nothing to get to the truth: she felt it was her duty to give the Western world the inside scoop, and as soon as she could she had been working with the authorities in Hong Kong to secure the story. She didn't say much to her Hong Kong contact about why she was pushing herself forward for this interview. But she knew the public wanted to know about the Wykehamist, the Cambridge graduate who had turned into a cold-blooded killer. Lucian was serving his sentence at Stanley Prison, a maximum-security facility built in 1937.

Over lunch, which consisted of braised abalone, imperial bird's nest soup and an array of steaming dim sum, Clementine's newspaper contact told her that Lucian was allowed two one-hour visits every month and that he had agreed to be interviewed by a journalist from the UK. Clementine had wanted to get this interview but requested that Lucian not be told the identity of his interviewer.

Apparently, he was desperate to tell all – he hated the wall of indifference that seemed to be growing since the furore over his crimes. Perhaps, thought Clementine, he was keen to offer more gory details or to relive the murders for his own pleasure. Lucian joined a long list of notorious murderers – Jeffrey Dahmer, Richard Ramirez, Ted Bundy – in his desire for the notoriety that came with publicity.

Over the exquisite Cantonese cuisine, which Clementine had offered up as something to sweeten the deal, her contact had agreed to her terms. She would be the sole interviewer for the two sessions, and her information would be used in an exclusive exposé of the murderer, Lucian Dorsey, to be published in the *South China Morning Post*.

But there was a whole side to the pending interview that Clementine did not and would never discuss. She was driven by an insatiable desire to know and to understand why everything had happened. And she needed to see Lucian again – it was like a reflex: uncontrollable and almost certainly disastrous.

Two days later Clementine took a taxi from Causeway Bay to the coastal town of Stanley. From there, she met the police driver, who took her to the correctional facility. To get to see Lucian, Clementine needed to undergo searches of her person and her possessions. Her leather satchel was put through a scanner, and she was patted down by a female prison guard. She was then led to a waiting room with no windows and two unsmiling guards standing in the corners. Her interview with Lucian would be conducted through glass, as prisoners were not allowed any form of physical contact with their visitors. A telephone was available on either side of the glass for communication purposes.

Clementine arrived first. She sat down on the orange plastic chair. She could hear her own pulse thumping in her head. She did not know how Lucian would react, worried that he might not go through with the interview, even though he had given his consent. A bell rang and all the doors on the prisoner side were opened. The prisoners were let out into their separate communication areas. In her hands, Clementine had a fresh pad of note paper and a pen. Recording devices were not allowed – she would rely on her shorthand to get the main points down.

Lucian emerged through the door a few seconds after it was opened. He looked healthier. His hair was close-cropped and his beige prison overalls fitted well. His waist was once again narrow. He was not allowed to wear contact lenses in prison, so he now wore his spectacles all the time. It was as if the old Lucian was back, from all those years ago at Cambridge, thought Clementine. His hands and feet were shackled, and the guard removed the lock from his own wrist and fastened it around a ring on the wall beside him. The chains were long enough that Lucian might reach the telephone. He raised his eyebrows upon seeing Clementine, and a genuine smile flicked over his face. It was a disarming smile, and she told herself that she should never presume to know Lucian. He was deeply secretive and cunning, an entity unto himself.

Lucian smirked – it was always like there was a party going on behind his eyes. He clicked his tongue. His eyes narrowed further in an expression of amusement. 'You can't seem to get enough of me, Clemmie.'

Clementine had practised what she was going to do in the interview. She had visualised it while staring at her own reflection in the bathroom mirror. But here with Lucian again, in this moment, she was transported back to the past. She was eighteen years old again and under his spell. She felt the heat rising in her stomach, then chest, neck and finally her face, which no doubt reddened.

'Yes,' said Lucian. 'There it is. The schoolgirl blush.'

'Do you want to waste time?' she shot back, trying to stay calm and professional – in control of the situation.

'Time?' said Lucian. 'I have bags of it.' He cradled the receiver in both of his shackled hands. 'It seems, Clemmie, that it is you who is in a hurry.' He shook his head. 'That won't do at all. I don't have to say a thing, you see. Whereas you, you need something from me. You can't seem to get over me, even though you know, to me, you meant very little.'

'That's not what I'm here for,' she said.

'Oh, you're here to get the scoop and to show the world how a person like me can become a monster.'

'Well, how does it happen? You tell me.'

Lucian changed the subject. 'You look good. Better than the last time I saw you.'

Clementine didn't know what to say.

'I mean, you're still not my type, but you are looking a lot more put together. The lipstick suits you – a more subtle shade than you wore last time we met.'

'This is not about me,' said Clementine, but it sounded all wrong. It was like her voice was being strangled.

'It's ok,' said Lucian. 'Baby steps.'

'If you get this right – maybe you could redeem yourself a little, if only in the court of public opinion.'

'Yes, you're right, of course,' he said. 'I should try. I'll start by saying I have remorse – isn't that where one always begins. I will go on and talk about my sense of compassion for the families whose loved ones died. Something of that ilk.'

'You are being glib,' said Clementine.

'Clemmie, do you go to bed at night thinking it could have been you?'

'Yes,' she whispered.

'Well, you should make your mind easy on that score.'

'Will you tell me why?' she asked.

'I'm sorry, Clemmie, I'm not sure you want the truth.' He whispered in his deep, silky voice.

'I can handle it.'

'Well, if I must tell you, first off, you're too big,' he said.

'What?'

'You're too large.'

'In a physical sense?'

'Yes.'

'Well, I guess I'm glad about that,' said Clementine.

'No, you aren't,' he replied, wryly.

It was so typical of Lucian, thought Clementine. He was actually trying to make her feel jealous of two dead women; jealous that he had chosen them as his victims rather than her. It finally proved that he was a complete narcissist.

'Is there another reason?'

'Oh, so many,' he said with a sigh, as if thinking about all those many reasons quite wore him out. 'Never forget, Clemmie,' he said with a twinkle in his eye, 'that you pursued me.'

'If that's what you want to believe, Lucian,' she shrugged.

'I remember you at Cambridge. The loner, the friendless one. Always turning up in the places where I was. Christ!' He ran his fingers over his close-cropped hair. 'You must have memorised my daily schedule like a deranged stalker.'

'I'm not going to deny that I liked you,' she admitted, 'but let's face facts. A lot has changed since then. You became you, and I became me. Now we have very little in common.'

'But I continue to fascinate you,' he snarled, his canines flashing for a microsecond, giving him the look of a caged wolf.

'Yes,' she replied simply. 'Even after the entire world has forgotten your name and you turn grey and old in prison, I will always remember you.'

'That's some power I hold over you,' he goaded.

'No, it's not like that anymore.'

'What is it like?'

She thought about it. 'Have you ever broken your leg?'

'No,' he replied.

'Well, I did, at ten years old, when I jumped off a climbing frame and fell at a funny angle.'

'Go on,' he said, seeming interested despite himself.

'Even after it healed and the cast came off, I still walked around carefully, expecting it to hurt at any moment. It is the same with my memories of you. I hold them carefully in my mind, trying not to poke them for fear of what may happen.'

'More psychobabble,' he sighed.

She laughed genuinely for the first time since she had laid eyes on him.

'So,' she said after composing herself again. 'Is there anything you want to tell me, for the article?'

Lucian rolled his head back and looked at the fan, spinning on the ceiling.

'Tell them that I am sorry for the victims' families, that I wish I could go back and not do what I did. I think about my actions every day and I can't understand why they made sense at the time. I was out of my mind.'

Clementine tried not to show her surprise at how genuine he sounded. Was it true, she wondered, or just another ruse to make him look like a more sympathetic character?

'I didn't intend to kill Sue-Lin. You might say she was collateral damage.'

Lucian tapped his fingers on the plastic table. 'And as for how I became what I've become. Well, that's a long story. So many little things had to happen. Maybe it was coincidence, fate. Maybe I was predisposed to violence – born a psychopath. You and the others can continue to speculate on that score.'

'They'll want to know about Cambridge,' Clementine suggested.

Lucian laughed. 'Boarding school, Cambridge, why are the elite institutions always deemed to be at fault? Oh, so I could blame all this on the selection process, or the lack of pastoral care that I received.'

Clementine could see that he was adamant, that there was no way he was going to let any institution take the blame for his crimes.

'No,' he shook his head. 'It won't do.'

'We have fifty minutes left,' she said.

'Then let's reminisce. You start by telling me your story, and then you will get mine,' he said. 'Take me back to when you first laid eyes on me. I want to know who you were back then and how it felt.'

'How it felt?'

'How it felt to be an adolescent girl suddenly infatuated with a beautiful stranger. And I was beautiful in those days, wasn't I? Humour me.'

Clementine was about to say no. She had a horrible feeling that any words or images that she described for Lucian would be used for his private sexual gratification.

Lucian looked at her intensely as she mused.

Suddenly, it came to her. Why not? If this was what she needed to do to get him to soften up a bit and disclose information, then she was going to do it. But she would do it on her own terms, of course. He would get nothing salacious from her unless she thought it would be useful in getting him to speak.

Lucian saw her eyes brighten, her resolve not to say anything about herself weaken. It gave him a feeling of dominance. He felt like a soft hand was massaging his neck, his temples, his eye sockets as she began to speak.

It was hard to speak of Cambridge while sitting in a maximum-security prison. It seemed they were a world away from the dreamy spires. Clementine closed her eyes and tried to think back. She tried to remember the girl she had been and the boy she had met, nearly a decade ago. Slowly it came back to her. The feel of a Cambridge winter morning, the endless miles you cycled to get around the city, the ever-present river, which was a source of most of their undergraduate merriment. Clementine remembered the smell of the books in the University Library, the fear of having to speak in a seminar, the people sitting in lectures at the English Faculty. Yes, she thought, she was ready to remember.

Hong Kong

It was Saturday. Lucian got himself ready and left his apartment that night, knowing he was looking for someone. A type of person. Of course, nothing had to happen immediately, but Lucian wanted the hook to be firmly in place. Some sort of guarantee that this person (whoever she was) would turn up for their future assignation.

Lucian had made himself look presentable. He had washed and gelled his curly hair back. He had trimmed his beard and dabbed Floris No. 89 on his face and neck. He loved the citrus notes and cedarwood that combined to form this quintessentially British fragrance. He dressed in a Hawes & Curtis steel-blue linen suit with a Turnbull & Asser shirt. On his feet he wore a pair of black English Oxfords made by his favourite London shoemaker Crocket & Jones. Before he left his apartment, he looked at himself in his full-length mirror. He practised smiling naturally, liking the way his mouth and eyes adopted a look of mischief. Then he left the apartment and sauntered out into the Hong Kong night.

It was almost Halloween. The shops and restaurants were full of polyester webs, plastic pumpkins and figurines of ghouls and witches. Lucian walked past stalls with red Chinese lanterns and cauldrons spilling out dry ice. It was then that the idea for the Halloween party came to him. That would be the hook. A Halloween party in his apartment.

After a few drinks at the bar of his favourite nightclub, he slouched at one of the standing tables outside, looking out onto the street. He had chosen to be alone. Occasionally a girl he knew would come over and try to engage him in conversation. He had to tell them all to leave him alone, but he sent each one away with a generous tip. The male expats who recognised him, men in their forties and fifties, in chinos with white shirts or wearing light-beige linen jackets, faces reddened by alcohol and the climate, would acknowledge him with a wave or a raising of their glass. None came over to talk to him. He was known in this area of Wan Chai as a rich man.

The pavements were so crowded that occasionally Lucian's leg would be brushed by someone passing. He resented this close contact with strangers. But he had chosen to watch the street that evening and find the girl he needed.

At the table across from him he overheard a conversation about some dogs that had been poisoned by eating contaminated chicken, on Bowen Road. Lucian had read about this notorious dog serial killer, whose penchant for death had resulted in the demise of over two hundred dogs, spanning a couple of decades. Lucian felt he understood this individual on some level. The man's (or woman's) hatred knew no bounds, and they were prepared to risk everything to annihilate the object of their disgust. Furthermore, the secretive perpetrator had never been caught — this also made whoever was responsible go up in Lucian's estimation.

Lucian sipped his pint and put it back down on the wet beer mat.

It was then that he saw her. A young woman, in a white crop

top, tight, black latex skirt and knee-high patent neon boots. Her face was heavily made up. She was walking up and down the same fifty-foot stretch, looking at the men that passed, exchanging a few words with some of the drivers who slowed down to comment on her looks. Over the hiss and honk of the traffic, Lucian could just about hear her speaking broken Cantonese. At this point, Lucian's Cantonese was pretty good. He had taken intensive classes, and he was also blessed with the ability to acquire languages without too much effort. It was another attribute that made him confident when conversing with locals.

He observed the woman for a full twenty minutes, trying to plan his move. He was also trying to ascertain whether her pimp was skulking in the vicinity. There were shady-looking men in doorways, milling around the club's entrances, and each had his crop of women that he was watching. Lucian hated the pimps who clamoured for money and dealt harshly with their women. They knew he was good for it, but they still hounded him like he was going to forget to pay. It was possible that the young woman was new to the trade, or that she was supplementing her regular income with sporadic night jaunts. He had met women like that before, and now he felt he had a sense for them, that he could tell the difference between a belle de nuit and a belle de jour.

It was not hard for a man like Lucian to get what he wanted out on these streets, and at this point in his life he had sampled most of it. He saw the young woman pull out a cigarette and ask a passer-by for a light. She cupped her hands sensually around the man's hand, trying to shield the tiny flame from the wind vortices that stirred around the buildings.

It was good that she was a smoker, thought Lucian. Smokers were always easier to strike up a conversation with. In his trouser pocket Lucian had a packet of Camels. They would be his icebreaker. He watched the woman as she talked and laughed with the men who walked by. From a distance she looked magnetic, irresistible, to Lucian. She made the trade she plied look glossy and admirable. A few times, as Lucian watched, he thought she would accept one of the rides she was being offered. But somehow, she always declined. The price had not been right, or perhaps it was the man who offered it. Had she sensed something untoward in the offers, or in the scent of an aftershave, or a wink. Or maybe fate had conspired to throw her in Lucian's path.

After Lucian had finished his drinks and paid his bill, he slung his jacket over his shoulder and walked over to her. She smiled her biggest smile and tossed her long, dark mane to one side. She showed him her best side, and in the half-light, Lucian liked what he saw.

'Hey baybee,' she said coyly.

Lucian could see that she was interested. She could smell the money on him: it was in his clothes, his shoes, his bearing. For girls like her, that scent was like a drug, he thought.

'Hey honey,' Lucian said, taking out the pack of cigarettes from his trouser pocket. He put one in his mouth, lit it, then offered it to her. She took it.

'So, what's your name, beautiful?'

She giggled and replied, 'My friends call me Jojo.'

'Where are you from, Jojo?'

'Jakarta.'

'No, really?'

'You know it?'

'Yeah, of course.' He gave her a wink.

'You like the wimmen there?'

'Yes, honey, who doesn't?'

Jojo laughed. She was warming up to him already.

Lucian almost felt sorry for her. It was so easy for him to lure these women.

'Nice to meet you, Jojo.' His voice was low and barely audible above the noise of the traffic. 'Listen, I'm having a Halloween party for some friends of mine tomorrow night. You want to join us?'

Jojo shrugged. She was weighing up if a night at a party would be more lucrative than a night on Lockhart Road.

'It'll be worth your while,' said Lucian.

'How much worth my while, baby?' she countered.

'Let's not talk business now, honey. Just come, tomorrow, 7 pm.'

'Where?'

'It's a secret,' said Lucian, winking.

She giggled again.

'Here, let me whisper in your ear,' said Lucian, pulling her towards him and putting his mouth close to her small, neatly formed ear, from which a large silver hoop dangled. He took a deep breath, breathing in the scent of her, before he began to speak. He could smell smoke, coconut hair oil, some cheap eau de toilette.

She nodded as he gave his instructions.

Then he pulled away and looked at her again in earnest.

'Don't let me down, ok, honey girl?'

She nodded.

'Oh, and when you come, be sure to...' here he leaned in closer and whispered something further in her ear.

She nodded shyly and smiled. He started to walk away but he made sure to look back at her once or twice, just to show that she was still on his mind, driving him crazy.

He saw her looking back at him. Would she turn up? Lucian

could not say for certain, but he felt like he had made an impression. He returned to his apartment and started what would be a four-day cocaine binge.

Later that night, Jojo found a client and went with him to a cheap hotel. The encounter lasted three hours, and then, because she was tired, she headed back to the room above a nightclub, which she shared with two other girls from the Philippines. Jojo had a day job working at a salon, sweeping up hair cuttings, but it didn't pay nearly enough. So, one week ago she had decided to try night work to see if she could make a bit extra. She knew she was risking a lot, and was aware of the danger of being alone on the street, but she hated the idea of a pimp and had thus far managed without one. She knew the pimps had noticed her but were unsure who she belonged to. It was only a matter of time before one claimed her. There would be nothing she could do about it.

Jojo asked one of the girls if she had anything to lend her for a Halloween party. The girl gave her a long white cape and a white witch's hat, which she had worn at Halloween the year before. Jojo also told her about the other things Lucian wanted her to wear. Together, they rummaged through the messy wardrobe and chest of drawers that all three girls shared and put together an outfit. Jojo tried it on in front of the girl. They both laughed. She told the girl she was excited about the Halloween party and that she would no doubt make some money. She told her about the handsome man she had met.

The girl asked if they could go along to the apartment together and give the man a surprise. She almost managed to convince Jojo to let her, but after thinking it over for a while, Jojo said no. The stranger she had met had chosen her, and she really needed the money to send back home to her family. She could not afford *to share her good fortune this time. Jojo promised the girl that she would get her something nice to say thank you for lending her the clothes. The girl called her a bitch – but not in a mean way. They turned off the lights and lay down on the mattress together, watching the reflections of car headlights moving over the ceiling and listening to the familiar cacophony of the city through the half-open window. Soon they fell asleep, their backs touching.*

CHAPTER 2

It was Michaelmas term and the rain and cold had set in for the long Fenland winter. The trees shook in the wind like nodding heads of hair. The Cambridge students sat in their rooms drinking tea or in pubs cradling their pints. The more industrious individuals were still busily flitting between lectures, supervisions, auditions, sports practice, libraries, bops and formals, never in one place or in one person's company for more than a couple of hours. Cambridge was, for some, the culmination of years of dreaming – a dream that they would live sumptuously, savouring every drop – while for others it was merely the steppingstone onto bigger and brighter things, things that they had long had in their sights.

The division was palpable, thought Clementine. She had already made a few acquaintances at her college who seemed incapable of ignoring the time ticking by. Every second spent in conversation with her appeared to be keeping them from far more worthy activity. It made her feel small, and then it made her annoyed. It was a subtle brush-off that hurt more than she would ever acknowledge. Clementine's friend Bea had tried to host a dinner in her rooms, for a handful of 'interesting types' – but only one had shown up. Bea and Clementine had sat awkwardly opposite him, at the expertly prepared table, for an hour, contemplating the mountains of beef and roast potatoes, which would now have to be stored in Tupperware and put in the fridge (much to the annoyance of the other students who shared the same fridge and got uppity when there was no room to store a berry smoothie).

Not everyone was in such a hurry – Clementine had already met a group that seemed keen to sit and smoke weed together, huddled in one stuffy set or another, talking endlessly about Nietzsche, or the Armenian mystic G.I Gurdjieff, or Wordsworth, or the films of Jim Jarmusch (in particular, *Coffee and Cigarettes*), while also smoking filter-less Woodbines and drinking Hawaiian Kona coffee – beans that some pretentious bastard had brought back from their gap year.

The music that they listened to was the usual melancholy playlist: Joni Mitchell, Nick Drake, Johnny Cash or Leonard Cohen. A conversation would take place where the students would bat around ideas, quoting Plato in ancient Greek, the work of the stoics, in particular, Seneca and Marcus Aurelius in Latin, or Descartes and Rousseau in French. Clementine was lost after one or two sentences. She listened to their beautiful monologues on Orthodox Christianity and the Gnostic Gospels, trying to bathe in the wealth of their accumulated knowledge. But she was secretly pleased when the topic changed once more, and they talked about Armagnac or how to correctly make a white Russian. She could, she reassured herself, at least understand food-and-beverage-related vocabulary.

It was new and challenging, but Clementine was not content to remain in the company of these people either – intelligent and interesting though they undoubtedly were. She told herself that she wanted an experience, something that would thrill her, someone with something she had not ever seen before. She would not admit to herself that her sense of estrangement from these cerebral students was in any way connected with her own ignorance on many of the topics with which they were so at ease, or her flagging sense of self-worth. Not being able to adequately communicate with her peers was yet another failing that she placed firmly at the foot of the comprehensive school system. A system that had, according to Clementine, been a comprehensive failure since the eighties. She felt angry and cheated, and unable to make up for all the lost time.

So, feeling dejected but with a slim thread of hope, she decided to do the rounds of auditions and see if what she was looking for might be found in the thespian circles.

It was a Monday morning and Clementine stood with the others in an audition room at Gonville and Caius, which used to have a large fireplace, now boarded up. The girls warmed their bottoms against the radiators. Clementine was not used to being upstaged, but here she was in the audition room, watching the performance of a lifetime. She could hear the whispers, along the line, 'She's got it', 'No point auditioning now'. The line of girls hid their mouths behind their audition sheets, but everyone could hear. The actress in question was a gorgeous blonde with a lithe body – she looked like a model. She was auditioning for the part of Blanche Dubois and had really perfected the southern drawl, the coyness and sexiness of the role.

Shit, thought Clementine, bloody little shit. Her heart had dropped into her stomach, as it had when she discovered at school that she had not been selected for a county sports event. Failure had never sat well with her, but here at the University of Cambridge it was hard to feel anything but a failure among these intellectual giants, these young gods and goddesses.

It was all because of the comprehensive – she believed the stench of it would never leave her, that people could smell it. No one asked directly, but it became apparent when others talked about their schools. Everyone who had been to a public school – Etonians, Wykehamists, Paulines – had come up with a cohort that they had already known for some five years or more. Clementine noticed that as soon as they moved into their rooms in college, they got dressed up and headed out to party. They did not wander around the buttery with their plates full of food wondering who to sit next to, or spend too much time clinging to their college parents, or stand around in the gyp making endless cups of tea hoping to strike up a conversation with someone on their floor, or go batshit crazy at a bop – drinking too many screwdrivers in plastic cups. No, those that had been at public school were poised and elegant and seemed to view all the other freshers with disdain. There was no way to enter their clique – like so many things, they were exclusive.

Clementine was always silent and evasive on the topic of school, as she did not want to be pitied. Some people thought that she had been to public school – she had heard that through Bea, but even Bea did not know the truth – those who thought this were others from comps or less-good private schools. Clementine was secretive. She did not like to overshare or give too much away about her background – what mattered was that she had made it, she was at Cambridge, and nowhere else mattered.

For camouflage she had learnt the difference between U and non-U words – she had studied the glossary compiled by Nancy Mitford and now she never called a lavatory a toilet, or a knave a jack, or a napkin a serviette, or a looking glass a mirror. It had seemed absurd to her at first, but it was one of the easiest ways to appear, at least on the surface, like an upper-class individual rather than a prole. She made sure to slip in a couple of words that would signify her belonging to their class; of course they all noticed immediately if she said something like 'sweet' instead of pudding or 'settee' instead of sofa. She could kick herself when that sort of thing happened.

The audition room buzzed with the murmur of mumbled lines. Nobody tried to strike up a conversation with anyone – if they did, there would be the awkward feeling that every person would be listening in. But not talking felt strange too – as here were some like-minded souls, all keen to perform. Clementine looked again at the blonde and back to the play's director, whose eyes kept darting back to her – their looks gave everything away, as if, for them, all the other girls had faded away.

Clementine perhaps did not need to worry. She too was a good actress and physically striking. She had the long, thin limbs of a silver-screen icon. Her hair was dark and carefully straightened, and although her face was not classically beautiful, no one could deny it was captivating, with its wide-spaced dark eyes and the small mouth always twisted to one side in an attitude of mirth or disdain.

The blonde's name was Claudia, and she was one of the freshers making a big impression on the university. She had attended Downe House – a hothouse-type establishment that squeezed its pupils for the best attainable grades and their parents for their money. Claudia was rich and able; she had found her common entrance exams so easy that she had completed each with half an hour to spare. Claudia had thrived at Downe House, becoming captain of the lacrosse team and taking them to victory in the national schools' tournament. She had skied, played tennis and won several cross-country championships. But Claudia's real love was the stage, and ever since she had taken the lead role of Maria in *West Side Story,* everyone had told her that one day she would be a famous actress. She completed her Trinity Guild Hall Awards, had been accepted to the National Youth Theatre and, because of her family connections, or rather patronage of the arts, she had been offered a minor role in a new film version of *The Merchant of Venice*. Claudia was to begin filming over the long vac – she knew it would almost certainly be her big break.

At her less illustrious school, Clementine had always been cast in the leading roles, Hedda Gabler, Titania in *Midsummer Night's Dream* and Miranda in *The Tempest*, to name a few. At school, acting had been her life. But now here she was at Cambridge, the old stomping ground of the likes of Emma Thomson, Stephen Fry and Hugh Laurie, and suddenly she was no longer special or unique. All these girls – Clementine eyed each one of them, along the line with their audition sheets and their looks of hope and excitement – all of them were well versed in Shakespeare, could remember lines and could act. Many of them were very pretty; Clementine started to compare their looks to her own, and to her dismay she decided that she was far from the prettiest in the room. Not that the actress who plays Blanche Dubois needed to be pretty – she was an ageing woman, who drinks and has psychotic episodes – but looking at the director and his team (four young men, all most likely heterosexual) she could see the role was likely to go to a pretty girl who they'd like to fuck.

Clementine had spent two weeks going to auditions for plays that were to be performed in the fourth and fifth weeks. She auditioned for Viola in *Twelfth Night*, Martha in *Who's Afraid of Virginia Woolf* and Haley in *The Pitchfork Disney*. Yet she had not got one role. Not one. She was on the edge of desperation. She began by questioning her acting abilities, and later, when she found out who had received the roles, she began to question her entire purpose in life. This was her last chance to secure a good role in a decent play.

When she talked to her father about the situation, he suggested that she try backstage work instead, something like lighting or sound, which could come in useful later in life, if the acting thing didn't work out. She baulked at the thought. Clementine had never seen herself as anything other than an actress, although she hated the over-the-top thespians of the ADC Theatre and would rather spend time alone than in the company of the arse-lickers who seem drawn to the theatre like hogs to a watering hole. Yet somehow, she still believed it would be the life for her.

Now, looking around, she began to doubt it all. When it was her turn to audition, her hands shook, and the audition paper began to rustle noticeably. She was intensely aware of the line of girls just five metres away from her. She could hear the hum of their hushed chatter and the occasional line from the script, muttered aloud, in their cut-glass English. She could hear her voice: high-pitched, unconvincing, out of her depth. She could see the director and the producer rolling their eyes. Afterwards they didn't say anything apart from 'Thank you' and 'You should find out in the next few days'.

After her audition, on her way out of Gonville and Caius, she saw Claudia chatting to a few of the other girls who had auditioned. She decided to go over and congratulate her on her audition, not because she was particularly impressed but because she wanted to know a little more about the girl who had most likely clinched the part.

The theatre is like one big trembling, pulsating ego; all it needs is a soft hand to massage it, thought Clementine. She hovered at the edge of the group before the blonde invited her into the huddle with the words 'Great audition by the way'. The words had a veil of positivity that rang hollow and insincere.

'Thanks,' Clementine replied, in her best, polished, happy actress face. 'Yours was so great, I bet you've got the part!'

The blonde shrugged. 'Really, I'm not sure I could

manage it even if I had. I'm in plays in fifth and sixth week already.'

Bitch, thought Clementine.

'I'm Claudia.' She offered her hand, but as Clementine took it, the hand was so limp that Clementine was unsure if she wanted a handshake or a hand kiss. Who does she think she is? she thought.

'Want to grab some lunch with us?' asked Claudia. Even though Clementine's inner voice was screaming no, she accepted the invitation with great enthusiasm and they made their way to Fools to eat whatever variety of tepid pasta with Bolognese sauce was on offer that day.

Clementine kept sneaking glances at Claudia as they ate. Her features were so perfect, it was hard not to stare. From the narrow, beautifully formed nose, to the perfectly spaced, ice-blue eyes, she was a work of art. All the other girls that had latched onto her clearly thought some of her brilliance would rub off. They say having beautiful friends makes one appear more beautiful, thought Clementine. Perhaps there is something in that. Hanging around Claudia meant that all males in the vicinity would have their attention diverted from whatever else they were doing at the time.

When Claudia smelt a rival she tried her hardest to get the measure of that person. Mostly, she came to the conclusion that she had nothing to fear: the other girl was less pretty, less talented, less clever, less sparkly. But during their brief lunch Claudia had decided that Clementine was one to watch, especially if they were to inhabit the same theatrical sphere at the university. She critiqued Clementine's looks without the other girl noticing. She emerged satisfied that she was the better looking of the two but that Clementine had attributes that many would find appealing. One of the directors of *Streetcar* had slipped Claudia his number after the audition. Claudia decided, then and there, to take control of the situation and try to sway things in her favour. After all, given the success of her audition, it seemed likely that she would be offered the star part.

★★★

Clementine received the news that she had been given a role in *Streetcar* via email. Before opening the email, she read the first line, which appeared in her inbox, the usual thanks for auditioning, and so on, but she had a feeling that the following message did not contain an outright rejection – and for a moment, her spirits rose.

Then all was shattered, 'They loved her performance' and 'really wanted her to be part of the production' so they had given her the role of the Mexican flower seller, who has a grand total of one line. The email continued positively – you may be given another small role if the director decides to include the part of Negro woman. Clementine punched her pillow, cried, broke a pencil. But the email was what it was. If she refused the 'small' part, she would be blacklisted in future. She had to accept, but acceptance felt like such a blow to her ego that it was almost unbearable.

After writing the humble and very grateful acceptance email for the part, Clementine slipped into bed and cried for an hour. She found out a few days later that Claudia would play Blanche, and one of the other girls she had had lunch with would play Stella. Clementine's chest constricted when she heard the news. She imagined the long weeks having to watch Claudia rehearse, having to be there ready with her one line. It seemed like such a tremendous waste of time and effort. Still, Clementine bullied herself to turn up to the first rehearsal.

At the rehearsal Claudia pulled out all the stops: her cleavage was on full display, her jeans looked torturously tight.

Clementine found out she might also be helping with sourcing costumes and props, as, the director said, she didn't have a whole lot to do. She saw the rehearsal period drawn out like a long road with no interesting scenery, and all the while she would have to watch Claudia enjoying herself. She wished she could just view her current predicament as a minor blip, an anecdote that she would be able to retell when she was as famous as Meryl Streep. Unfortunately, for Clementine, it was too difficult – it required the eating of too much humble pie for her liking.

Clementine stopped turning up to rehearsals, stopped replying to the increasingly demanding emails from the director and producers. This of course meant that every time she stepped out of her front door, she was doing her best to avoid a long list of people who she would have to explain herself to. This list included the detestable Claudia, who continued to email her, asking if Clementine was ok, and if she wanted to go for a coffee and chat. No thank you, thought Clementine. I would rather pull out my own fingernails then have to sit at a table with that creature, so that she can gloat about how fabulous she is.

Clementine decided to keep a low profile after this. She went to her lectures, supervisions, the library, incognito, with a thick pair of spectacles instead of her usual contact lenses. Her dream of becoming an actress now seemed like one of those childhood dreams of becoming an astronaut. She had to find something else to occupy her time. Clementine began to look around for some new object of fascination, something to pour her energy into, something that was truly marvellous and out of the ordinary.

Hong Kong

Jojo arrived on time. It was seven o'clock. The exact time Lucian had told her to arrive. She was a good girl. The coke had made him anxious. Had she told anyone where she was going? No. Did anyone expect her back tonight? No.

'Where's the party?' she asked innocently. She had her white cape on and the witch's hat, as well as white stiletto heels, but thankfully, thought Lucian, no Halloween face paint, apart from two dark flicks in the corners of her eyes, which made them look feline.

'Oh, they're all coming soon,' said Lucian. 'What, are you afraid to be alone with me at Halloween?'

Jojo raised her thumb and index finger to indicate that, yes, she was a little afraid.

'Let me get you a drink,' he said, moving over towards the drinks cabinet, where he took out two Riedel Veritas coupe glasses. He had the bottle of Dom Pérignon ready in an eighteenth-century brass champagne cooler stationed on top of his drinks cabinet. He could see she was on edge, as she had been fully prepared to attend a bustling Halloween party. But she was a street hooker, thought Lucian. It couldn't be the first time a client had told her a little fib.

Lucian took the champagne from the cooler and dried the neck with a white linen napkin. He removed the foil and then unscrewed the wire. He could feel Jojo's eyes on him. He looked at her and smiled. Then he took the napkin and placed it over the top, held the bottle at an angle and eased out the cork. It did not make so much as a whisper. Lucian hated the exuberant popping of champagne corks – he thought it was perfectly vulgar. He secured the linen cloth around the neck of the bottle and poured the champagne into the two coupe glasses. Lucian knew that champagne tasted better in flutes but he loved the shape of the coupe glass, which he had once been told was modelled on the left breast of Marie Antoinette. He knew the story wasn't true, but liked to pretend it was.

Lucian looked down at Jojo, trying to judge just how much alcohol would be needed. He wanted her to lose some of her inhibitions, but he did not want her inebriated. No, that would spoil all the fun he had planned.

'I propose a toast,' he said. 'To beauty.'

Jojo made eye contact with Lucian and they clinked glasses.

'Now,' he said, 'before anyone else gets here, show me something to make me really happy.'

She cast her eyes downwards with a coquettish expression on her lips as she rotated the stem of her coupe glass between her fingers.

'Come on now, are you wearing what I told you to wear?'

She nodded.

'Then show me.'

Jojo put down her glass on the low coffee table.

Lucian's hands were shaking with excitement. He clasped them behind his back as she stepped out of her dress and showed him her lingerie. It was just what he liked, all red with lots of straps and buckles. The fishnets clung to her thighs and backside, reminding him of the string on the roast pork at Sunday dinner back home. He could not resist pulling the bra strap and letting it thwack against the skin on her shoulder blade.

She said, 'Oooh,' as if she liked it, but he wanted to know.

'Now, Jojo, did you like that?' he said softly.

'Yea,' she whispered and giggled like a little girl. Though she was not that young, Lucian thought. Her hips were quite wide, an indication that she had given birth at some point. Her features were regular and symmetrical but her skin had small imperfections which she had tried to conceal with thick make-up, but this had somehow rendered them even more noticeable. Her eyelashes were clumped together with black mascara, and on the lower lid she had used a white eyeliner, to give herself a younger, wide-eyed look. Asian girls try to give themselves wide Caucasian eyes, and God knows why, he thought; he loved the way their eyes tapered.

There were fine lines between her strong eyebrows, which were even more visible because of the powder she had used to control her naturally greasy skin. It was strange, she had looked so much younger when he had met her on Lockhart Road the previous evening. He dimmed the lights to make her imperfections less obvious. But he was annoyed that she wasn't the beauty he had thought. So he decided to ask her directly.

'How old are you, Jojo?' The coke had taken away any sense of decorum that he might once have possessed.

She flicked her hair nervously. 'I carnt remember, sah.'

'Now don't lie to me, Jojo, I'd say you were pushing thirty, is that right?'

She said nothing, but the expression on her face changed, as if she could smell the menace in the room and her usual buoyancy *had suddenly disappeared. She lowered her gaze and dug the exposed toe of her right foot into the carpet.*

'Ima lady, sir, we dun say our age, it not nice, not po-lite.'

His voice was low and calm but there was something icy in the way he clipped his words short. 'Ok, never mind, we'll say you're a mature twenty-eight.'

The instruments were covered, but they seemed to pulsate across the room. Lucian could hear them calling to him beneath their covering.

He moved to the drinks cabinet and took out a Paşabahçe diamond martini glass and a bottle of Belvedere vodka. He poured himself a glass but didn't offer Jojo any. Women shouldn't drink vodka, he thought; it made them drunk too quickly. Also, it dimmed the senses, and he wanted her alert, in the moment, feeling to the full extent of her capacities. He sat down in his armchair, took a sip of the vodka and looked hard at her. He had begun to salivate as if in expectation of a delicious meal. He swallowed and continued to stare. Then he motioned for her to do a spin with his right index finger.

'Wha yu wan me tu do, mista?' She had a slight quiver in her voice.

'Tonight, Jojo, you are not going to be called Jojo; let us call you Cindy instead.'

She nodded in obeisance.

'Please sit down on the sofa, Cindy, and let me pour you another glass of champagne – a suitable drink for a lady, I think you'll find.'

He got up from the armchair and took the bottle from the ice bucket and topped up her glass.

Then, he took a remote and aimed it at the sound system. Suddenly, Pink Floyd's "Dark Side of the Moon" started to play. He sat down in the armchair once more.

'You know I had my first sexual encounter to this music; it's so mysterious and yet erotic. She was a beautiful girl, and we were only fifteen.'

'Tha's nice, mista. We can do now if yu like.'

'Um, no, I just wanted to tell you that this piece of music is significant to me.' Lucian paused for effect. 'I think I loved that girl.'

'Wher she now, why yu not married?'

'Well, you see, she died.'

'Ver sad.'

'No, no, not at all,' he said, filling his martini glass up with the cold vodka and knocking it to the back of his throat, where it burned. 'It was her time, you see.'

Lucian got up from his chair and moved towards the table with the instruments. He knew she was watching him intently, trying to figure out what was going on. He ran his fingers over the pocket square, feeling the hard appliances below his fingers. He had stored the blowtorch in the bedroom. He had rehearsed everything in his head so many times before, but now it was finally time for the performance, the epilogue, the denouement, and he hardly knew where to begin. Lucian took a deep breath. *It will come*, he told himself and closed his eyes, trying to sense which implement was calling to him to most.

CHAPTER 3

Falling asleep under a tree is not romantic, and I am not the serene type, thought Clementine. I am not the girl in Arthur Hughes' eighteen ninety-nine painting *Asleep in the Woods*. And yet, she thought, every time I attempt to slumber under a tree, 'she' (the unknown model in the painting) is the person I wish to emulate. I want a white apron and bonnet. I want to look comfortable sitting on the roots of a tree among moss-coated rocks with my backside sodden and the sensation that something with six legs is scurrying around inside my underwear. I would very much like a red squirrel to observe my peaceful slumber like a guardian angel. And when observed, I should very much like a studious young man to gasp, 'Ah, there is a Pre-Raphaelite beauty!' I am attempting to sleep under this tree to draw attention to myself. And yes, no doubt, this is not what it should be, it is the very opposite of emancipation. And what is the antonym of emancipation?

Clementine mulled it over, frustrated that the antonym was not immediately obvious; imprisonment or incarceration just did not feel right. It was a form of self-flagellation. She was chilled to the bone; it was 2 am, mid-November, on The Backs at St John's College. Nobody was around, no porters, or tourists, studious young men or squirrels. Nobody knew or cared that she was there, freezing to death in an aesthetic manner. I am damaged goods, she thought. It was not the first time she had thought that. There had been too much sherry before formal hall, too much wine and too much port. The food had been plentiful too, especially the cheese. Clementine's stomach churned as she thought of the veiny Danish blue on charcoal biscuits. She was willing herself to get up but somehow once she had fallen onto this damp, mossy root it became quite impossible to right herself. She fell into her thoughts, deeper and deeper, and suddenly she was thinking about Bea. Good old boring Beatrice, who was her only friend (though not confidant) at this university. Beatrice was such an odd little thing. Clementine began to think about a conversation she had had with Bea the other day.

'It's all about the male gaze,' said Bea, 'Scopophilia – the pleasure of looking.' Yes, yes, yawn. God, Bea went on and on, lipstick looking feathery, with only a blood-red rim left around the lip-line. Bea had been conscientiously sipping a pint of Bombardier in a forgotten corner of The Eagle. Clementine had been gazing at what she supposed was a pneumatic blonde at the bar. I wish I liked women, Clementine wanted to say, but could not in present company. Bea would have recoiled like a snail poked in the eyes. Bea loved women, felt sorry for women, did a dozen things pro bono for the betterment of women. It was almost glorious to spend so much time with a suffragette and to secretly loathe women. But all women loathe one another, and that is why nothing really improves. When one country seems to be getting to the end of a long and bitter tunnel, another country is still putting women in isolation when they get their periods or practising FGM. And anyway, if there really is a corporate ladder, thought Clementine, with a glass ceiling, you can bet your bottom dollar that a dozen well-manicured hands will be pulling you off the first rung before you've even begun climbing. 'Women are bitches,' muttered Clementine into her pint of Bombardier.

'What?' asked Bea.

'Oh, I said she must need stitches.'

As Bea had just been talking about the girl who had impaled herself on a broken punt pole when she dived into the River Cam at Trinity May Ball, she simply nodded and said, 'Yes, three hundred in total!'

'God, that's disgusting,' said Clementine. Ha! Clementine laughed to herself, suddenly feeling the cold and the hard, knotty roots beneath her. She looked at the shadows playing about the lamp posts and the trees that were spinning around her head. It was time to get out of this rut and start living – she had spent too long licking her wounds, feeling sorry for herself. She remembered a random quote and wondered why she could not access a decent quote when other people found it so easy.

Ninety-five percent of the time I want to die from embarrassment. The other five percent of the time I'm looking for an attractive man to fuck. Clementine read and re-read that line, written in the margin of Swift's *A Modest Proposal*. For marginalia, it was quite a wordy piece. Sometimes it was like the urge to defecate, thought

Clementine. One could not hold on forever, and then there it goes; not the most eloquent statement or witty, but someone just had a metaphorical shit in this book.

Just a week ago, Clementine had been sitting under the cloisters of Trinity College library looking out at the river. It was muted grey and Fenland fog was rolling over the lawns. She smoked her Djarum Black right up to the filter and stubbed it out on the flagstone. There was no point wasting time with soft-bodied, wispy bearded boys reading English. Clementine was on the prowl. Not in a dull, conventional way and not even with the desire to consummate. She wanted to create a tableau of everything she considered beautiful and in it there would be a man. She told herself that, once she had seen this man, he would be hers forever. Most likely he would never know this. Clementine had many men in this way. Fuck unrequited love. She anatomically reconstructed them in her mind, gave them personalities and scripts. They would do as she pleased and live in glass cases that she had designed. If only Bea knew, she would be so fucking proud.

And then, as if by magic or design, the specimen arrived. He had walked by where she was sitting, filling the air with a dangerous masculine scent. Clementine treated this development with the caution of a lab technician handling a pregnant woman's urine in a plastic container labelled biohazard. The specimen went by the name of Lucian – a third year, reading History. He was a rower in the mornings, a History undergraduate by day and semi-lad by night. Clementine believed he was a semi-lad because of his passion for staying in his room most evenings, apart from Fridays and Saturdays, where he joined the usual mediocrities on the streets of Cambridge for their routine debaucheries.

Although Lucian types were two-a-penny at Cambridge, Clementine believed that there was something a little more out of the ordinary about Lucian. No doubt public-school educated, no doubt one who excelled at everything he tried, he had a touch of fastidiousness about him, he looked at the world with barely disguised distaste. Tall, good-looking with slightly hooded eyes (short-sighted but he mostly wore contacts, she thought). Outwardly calm, almost robotic, maybe it was only Clementine who could see how thin his skin was, how he was merely dormant and waiting for the right moment to emerge. Angel or devil, mused Clementine, it is strange to be so certain that a human is only one or the other, most people are a diabolical shade of moral apathy. Clementine observed him, first by sitting opposite his boathouse in the mornings, where he rowed out with his eight, and then by following him to his college, Peterhouse, and then on to his lectures. Gradually, she was building up a picture of Lucian in her mind. She toyed with it, revelled in the secrecy of being a stalker and in what nobody ever talks about – the female gaze.

As she fell in and out of sleep, lying uncomfortably on the tree roots, Clementine had an epiphany: that Lucian would be hers. She believed it was fate. A few hours later, she awoke with the dawn, frozen stiff, her clothes sodden with dew. Enough of this behaviour, she told herself, you've got to get a grip. She promised herself that her life from now on would be devoted to her new-found hobby: the acquisition of Lucian Dorsey.

★★★

Evensong at King's College Chapel was Clementine's time to muse and refrain from the necessity of speaking to people. Looking up at the fan-vaulted ceiling, she imagined the master masons overseeing the chapel's construction. It was Henry VIII's vision and here it still was, dimly lit at night, with Rubens' *Adoration of the Magi* above the altar. Clementine was there, partly because Lucian was there. She had followed him one evening from Peterhouse, down King's Parade and through the porters' lodge at King's. She had kept her distance and marvelled at the grace and dignity of his walk, the undoubted confidence in it.

Lucian liked to sit alone on a pew at evensong or close his eyes, as if listening intently to the music. Once, she followed him in, and then decided to show up every week and surreptitiously attend the service. He was a creature of habit; he always departed his rooms at the same time – 5.30 pm on the dot – and walked out of his college, where Clementine positioned herself on the opposite side of the road. He never noticed her, but then again Clementine only snatched sideways glances at him; she never allowed herself the pleasure of just gawping at him – something she would have dearly liked to do. Maybe he observed her when her eyes were lowered; maybe he was just as curious about her as she was about him. No, that was too much – that was in the realm of her wildest fantasies.

Here, in the ancient nave, Lucian was always alone; he

left a little distance between himself and the other members of the congregation. It was a Thursday, and for the Introit it was Allegri, *Miserere mei, Deus*. Forbidden to be transcribed because of its beauty, the Renaissance polyphony soared up, taking the soul on a journey to the heavens. Only a fourteen-year-old Mozart was not afraid to commit its hallowed notes to memory on a visit to the Sistine Chapel. And thus, Mozart gave this piece of perfection to the world. The chapel at King's is a fitting place for it, thought Clementine; it shows how genius can illuminate the darkest corner of our world, the most beautiful corners of the soul. And that beauty has its ways of being seen and heard, no matter how incarcerated it might be.

Lucian could not open his eyes during the piece. He had well and truly left his body behind. Clementine believed she could see him floating by up in the fanned vault. It was wonderful to behold a person so affected by music. A person who was otherwise indifferent, hostile even. This piece could turn even the most hardened heart to putty. Clementine never wanted to forget the way his face looked at this moment. He was the most angelic youth one could imagine, curly light-brown hair, tanned skin, with the soft peaches and cream of youth. His body hard, muscled under his shirt, used to the strain of daily morning rows. It is a wonder that men think the female body is so delicious, for a young man of perfect proportion is truly made in the image of God, thought Clementine.

The reading was from Job 1:13–22, 'Naked I came from my mother's womb, and naked I will depart. The

Lord gave, and the Lord has taken away.' Poor old Job, Clementine heard the man next to her whisper as he leant towards her, wiping a tear with his pocket handkerchief but not forgetting to eye her up. Never mind the nudity, it's all that dressing up in between that's the real issue, thought Clementine, as she pondered what she was going to wear under her gown to her formal hall that evening.

When the last organ notes had been played, the sound still lingered, reverberating around the chapel, like the low growl of a large animal. Lucian straightened up, and without lingering to say goodbye to his fellow congregation members, he pushed his way out to the exit. She had been careful not to catch his eye, knowing that her own gaze would betray her, and therefore no connection had been made between them. Had he noticed her? Looked her way? Clementine thought not. He had been far too absorbed in the beauty of the music. She thought he was a true aesthete.

Clementine could breathe more freely once he had departed, but with that came the great longing to see him again. The texture of the air changed when he was near her; everything became more intense and poignant. Clementine both loved and hated being so governed by her feelings for someone she barely knew. She kept reminding herself that she was in charge, she was the hunter here, but however hard she tried she could not help feeling like the prey.

Hong Kong

He didn't stop to think how unflattering the camera angle was. He was in the bathroom; the camera skimmed over the white tiles and then stopped close to his nostrils until he adjusted the phone and it stared up into his eyes, floating above the rim of his stubble.

He was a little breathless.

'I've had her in here for two days. I've hurt her really badly, I've raped and beaten her, I've made her do terrible things. I think I'm a real psycho now; I think I might just be the devil.' He laughed a soft, breathy laugh that rumbled in his throat. His pupils were overly dilated, there were drops of sweat on his forehead and the hair on his receding hairline was damp.

The camera swivelled down and left to a crumpled, half-naked form lying on the tiles. There was a lot of blood, but she was still breathing. Her dark hair covered her face, which was pressed to the floor. There were welts on her back and small open wounds. The camera shifted to the toilet bowl, where a stool was floating in the murky water.

'I just got her to lick this dirty bowl,' he said. 'Hey honey, did that taste good?'

As there was no reply, he poked her with his index finger and she groaned.

'Still hanging in there; good to see. I said, did it taste good, you little bitch? When daddy asks you something, it's only polite to reply.'

'Yea,' she replied but didn't raise her head.

'Good, good. Glad to hear it.'

He sat back on his haunches and trained the camera back on his face.

'The time is 2.15 am, Monday. And God, I'm pumped!' He ran his hand over his unshaven chin, his eyes darting from left to right and back again. 'Stuff has been happening, and it's been truly life-changing. I don't think I've ever felt this good before.'

He trained the camera back on Jojo. 'I think I just want to give you a hug and say thank you!' Lucian's phone lunged forward as he embraced her. All that could be seen for a few seconds were his bare feet with black hairs on the toes, and then he stood up again.

'She's still got her eyes.'

He sniggered, holding the back of his hand to his face and wiping away a rivulet of sweat. 'I just can't decide what to do with them.'

He laughed again. 'Maybe it's time to ask the audience. Should I, A, gouge them out. Or B, light a cigar (as you can tell I'm not a cigarette man). Handmade Cubans are the obvious choice, an H. Upmann. I've got one left in the humidor. I wonder what a roasted human cornea tastes like.'

He was really amused by this suggestion, and it took him a good few minutes to stop laughing enough to offer option C.

'Option C, now let me see.' More laughter exploded, the phone shifted around crazily, and it took him a few moments to contain himself and for the camera to be trained back on his face.

'Option C, bleach. Yes, I'd like to watch that, I think it would be remarkably interesting. And you know what, I've got a very good idea, I think I'll let my friend Byron decide; he loves that fucking stupid game show.'

Lucian's teeth were chattering now, with cold (he had set the AC to five degrees and was wearing nothing but his boxer shorts), or maybe it was the sheer exhilaration of the experience.

He propped up the phone on the mirror and left the bathroom for a few minutes. He returned to the bathroom holding his iPad.

'Hey girl, you should listen to this. I'm going to Skype my friend Byron. You might know him, stupid fellow with tight trousers, comes to The Old Junk to get fawned over by women. I know his big secret though, because I've seen him looking at porn in the office, and let's just say it's not the fairer sex he's looking at.'

He tapped the screen and the familiar Skype call tone began. He put it on speaker phone. It rang, once, twice, three times.

'Come on, you bastard, pick up.'

Then the click came, and Byron was suddenly on screen, topless and rubbing his eyes.

'Lucian, man, what the fuck, why are you calling now?'

'Hey, just wanted to phone a friend. I'm playing Who Wants to be a Millionaire and I just wanted you to help me.'

'God, it's a bit late, but hey fine, just read me the question and the answers.'

'Uh no, this one's a bit different,' said Lucian, trying to pull himself together. 'There's A, B or C and you don't get to know the question or the answers.'

'What the fuck! I really don't understand, but if I pick one will you stop phoning me?'

'Yep, that's all you have to do,' said Lucian gleefully.

'Fuck it, B then, and stop ringing me at 2 am, you twat. And get your arse back in the office; you're clearly not sick.'

The call ended.

'Ha, he loves me really,' said Lucian. 'That bullshit was just banter. That cocksucker is my best friend; he's just pissed off with me at the moment. It will all blow over, you'll see. In a few weeks we'll be back in The Junk checking out the laydeees, hooah!'

'Please let me go,' came the small, scared voice from the floor.

'Oh darling!' Lucian was squatting on the floor beside her. 'But aren't we having so much fun.' He pointed the camera phone in her direction. 'And besides, now it's time for whisky and cigars.'

Jojo moaned on the floor.

'I have a rather excellent single malt, which will pair perfectly with a fine Cuban cigar. I will just go and get the cigar from my humidor. It's been waiting in there for six months ready for a special occasion. I think that occasion is right now.'

Before he left the bathroom Lucian checked Jojo's wrists, which were secured with zip ties and fixed to a bathroom rail. He skipped through to his living room and unlocked the large, glass-panelled humidor in the corner. He breathed in the lovely scent of Spanish cedar and hand-picked tobacco. He selected a Montecristo No. 2, with its lovely torpedo shape, so beautiful and phallic. It was exactly the right one, not too expensive or ostentatious but always satisfying, with a nutty flavour and a great draw. He removed the wrapper and band and took his cigar cutter from the drawer. Then he neatly cut off the tip. It flew onto the floor with the speed of a guillotined head. He then took a long Cohiba cigar match and lit it, putting the cut side of the cigar between his lips and lighting the foot of the cigar with the match. He drew the smoke into his mouth, savouring the delicious flavours. He took a couple more draws, never inhaling into his lungs but letting the smoke swirl around inside his mouth.

Then he walked back to the bathroom, humming, "Oh, what a Beautiful Mornin!"

He stepped inside the bathroom, took the electrical tape and wound it round Jojo's head. She squirmed and wriggled, and the cigar fell onto the tiles. He slapped her round the jaw for that. 'This is a Montecristo, you basic bitch!'

He got her into a semi-seated position and put the cigar back between his teeth. Then he took her head in his hands and looked deep into her eyes. Her irises were very deep brown and in the very centres her pupils were huge, dilated with terror. He held her chin very hard while she shut her eyes tight.

'It won't help, my love,' he said, chuckling and making a little clicking sound with his tongue.

CHAPTER 4

Kimberley played the tin whistle outside The Gardenia, or Gardies, as it was known to Cambridge locals and students alike. It was a kebab shop – an institution on Rose Crescent. Its windows were always crammed with hungry students waiting for souvlaki and cheesy chips. On the walls hundreds of polaroids were tacked: pictures of students in mad, unguarded poses. The staff would always ask if they could photograph the students when they were dressed up in white tie, Halloween costumes or fancy ball gowns. These pictures gave the place a warm familiarity and the students would return on a nightly basis after the nightclubs and bars had closed to staunch their looming hangovers with hot Greek food, dripping hummus and tzatziki all over their expensive clothes. Afterwards, they would spill into the streets with Gardies' lollipops stuck in their mouths, looking no older than schoolchildren.

Sometimes Kimberley sat next to Tony and his scrawny dog. Tony and the mongrel huddled beneath an Edinburgh Woollen Mill picnic blanket, which had been donated by a passing student a few days ago. It was customary for students to offer the homeless food from their takeaways. There were many homeless people in Cambridge; some said they congregated in university towns like Oxford and Cambridge because of the generosity of the students.

They had been instructed during their induction talks at their colleges never to give the homeless money, in case it went towards fuelling a drug habit. Kimberley enjoyed asking for fivers just to see the uncomfortable look pass over the young faces, each feeling somehow awkward that they should not resolve this problem of the beggars by throwing money at them. Mostly, Kimberley saw that they would like nothing better than to throw some coins in a cup and be done with their day's altruism. But though they squirmed, most went the extra mile and returned with food of some description.

Kimberley was from Yorkshire; she had a piercing in her nose and one in her tongue, in addition to the numerous metal loops and studs that decorated her earlobe, from the antihelical fold to the scapha. She looked like her blood contained no vitamins at all; she was yellowish, with eczema on the backs of her hands, which she itched constantly when she wasn't playing her tin whistle. Kimberley was extremely slim, her wrist bones protruding from her skin, and when she pressed her back she could feel every single vertebra under the slightest pressure of her fingers. Likewise, her ribcage jutted. A previous boyfriend had likened it to a cheese grater.

She was nineteen years old and all alone in the world. There were no friends or relatives who she could contact to help her out of her situation. She had run away from home at the age of sixteen because of her mother's abusive boyfriend and had been on the streets since then – more recently as a *Big Issue* seller. She had made up her mind that she would only contact her mother when she was off the streets for good – when she could finally offer her a better life and get her away from her boyfriend.

Kimberley loved to play Irish jigs and had taught herself all the famous ones by listening to a cassette tape called 'The Irish Heart' in a Walkman she had been given by a passer-by. The tape had been left in the Walkman and she began by listening to the tunes over and over again. Then one day she saw a busker playing Irish jigs on a tin whistle in the streets. She had watched him for hours, mesmerised by his nimble fingers. Afterwards, she plucked up the courage to ask him about his playing and how he had learned. He was a nice old man, and he took her for a pint at The Mitre. He told her that the tin whistle was easy to pick up and cheap to buy and then he put his hand on her thigh and gave it a squeeze. He was about fifty, with greasy long, grey hair but his eyes were very dark and kind. Even though she was not attracted to him she liked the attention and being taken out for a pint, so she had gone off down a side alley with him and given him a hand job. He must have been surprised and quite pleased because he made a show of giving her his spare whistle – a glittery silver thing – and then he said he had to get back to his wife. She still thought about that man, from time to time, and wished they could play a few tunes together. She had gotten good and could play continuously for hours on end.

Tony, the homeless man beside her, was slightly delirious, and had a large leg ulcer. The ulcer was uncovered, even though the temperature was close to freezing, and had begun to stink. Kimberley kept shifting her cardboard patch away from him, a few inches at a time so as not to insult him. Tony was very sensitive and perceived everything as a slight. He had recently discharged himself from hospital, as his ward did not have a TV and he had grown bored. Because of the ulcer, which made him hallucinate, he tended to ramble on and on, his mongrel gazing at him with black, mournful eyes. He talked about his 'mate' who'd gone and hanged himself in a garden shed.

'Dropping like flies, mate,' he said to the clean-shaven student with curly black hair, who was offering him a kebab. 'Can I have something fresh?' he asked.

'Like fruit?' the student offered.

'Nah,' he bit his lip, 'like Irn Bru or Appletize.'

Kimberley felt sorry for the students, who were just trying their best to be good people. Tony would talk on and on at them about nothing – a circular monologue that the students felt they had to look interested in. She mostly took whatever food they offered. Sometimes she got a bed for a night at the shelter, but often it was full up. Also, she hated being kicked out of a warm, cosy bed at 7 am, which was the usual procedure when one slept at a shelter.

Nights on the streets were always unpleasant but in late autumn they were starting to get really bad. First, because of the cold, which crept into the marrow of your bones, and, second, because as a girl she didn't want to go anywhere too secluded, because someone might try to take advantage. It was safer to be sat in a doorway of a busy street like Rose Crescent, but this meant that she hardly got any real sleep. She started taking micro-sleeps, her head nodding forward, every time she got to the end of a jig. Tony was starting to get on her nerves. He was dying from the infection, but still he would not readmit himself to hospital. Their time together was almost over. There are enough heavy burdens on the streets weighing you down without having a millstone around your neck too, thought Kimberley.

At 2 am she told Tony she was going for a wee. Urination and bodily functions become even more problematic when one is on the streets, especially at night when all the public facilities are locked up. Kimberley had been taking the pill without a break for a year as she never wanted to experience a homeless period again – she had a doctor who she visited every few months for a prescription. For calls of nature most of the homeless people she knew favoured an alley just off King's Parade. The alley had a permanent stench of piss; she wondered if the students ever wondered why. Then again, she thought, the students have a piss down there from time to time too.

After all the McDonald's coke and coffee she'd drunk, she was quite desperate. She picked up her sleeping bag, her small holdall and a piece of cardboard. Tony didn't even register that she was taking her stuff and he mumbled a 'See you later'.

No, you won't mate, she thought.

She made her way through the Market Square and onto King's Parade. There were girls sitting on the wall outside King's in their expensive winter coats – cream-coloured or smart black ones that cinched at the waist. Kimberley was wearing an old hoodie on top of every item of clothing she possessed, a long tie-dye skirt, stockings and two pairs of woollen socks in her battered Nike trainers. She was glad most of her clothing was dark, as it didn't show up the grime and dust as much. Kimberley wanted to avoid everyone and just disappear into the night; she felt so grubby and dishevelled compared to the pristine students everywhere. She made a point of walking over the slab that read 'High Maintenance Life'. She scuffed her holey shoes on that idea. For some, she sighed, for some.

She got to the alley and looked down it as far as she could. Sometimes some old drunk ended up sleeping down there – you would have to be drunk to ignore the smell. She walked down there, pleased no one was about, hitched up her long skirt and started to piss, trying not to get her shoes wet in the process. The relief was overwhelming, it almost made her cry. Then she heard footsteps coming from the opposite direction, from the Queen's College entrance to the lane. She got her things together quickly and ran back to King's Parade. She decided to sit in the doorway of the old Copper Kettle, play a couple more tunes, hopefully get a bit more cash and then bed down for the night. The piece of cardboard went down flat – she was always amazed at how the bare pavement could suck the warmth out of the human body if there were no barrier between. The cardboard made a good insulator. She unrolled her sleeping bag and put her legs inside. It was getting colder and colder by the moment, and she knew as soon as she stopped moving that the cold would wriggle into her sleeping bag and make drifting off an impossible task.

She took out her whistle and played old Morrison's jig, which kept her fingers warm and busy; it also kept her mind off the cold, which felt like a solid thing. It would only be a few hours until dawn, she told herself. At 3 am she had curled into a ball and was flitting in and out of a fitful sleep. Footsteps grew louder and then softer as they passed her doorway. There was a lot of male laughter and some girls cackling, then silence.

She was vaguely aware of someone stepping close at one point. Something touched her but she was too tired to pay much attention, so she pressed herself tighter into the doorway, her back facing the street, and fell asleep. It was so common for her to be disturbed by passers-by at night that she barely paid any attention now.

Later, she did not know what time it was; there was the sound of a lighter flicking, which woke her up again, then the smell of smoke from a lit cigarette. In the past she would have launched a tirade against the people who constantly and deliberately interrupted her sleep; now after a broken nose and a few chipped teeth, she knew better.

Suddenly, she had the sensation that someone was very close by; she could smell the smoke as it was breathed all over her sleeping bag.

'Are you awake?' The voice was soft but definitely male, most likely a gown (a student), not a townie (a Cambridge local).

She didn't answer. She would often get verbal hassle on the street, but most of the time that was where it stopped.

'Look, if you are awake, I just wanted to tell you that

someone might have just taken your bag.'

'Wha?' She was now very much awake.

'Yes, a black holdall. Was that yours?'

'Yea.' She was thinking, fuck this, fucking life – her last few remaining possessions were in that bag. Slowly she got into a seated position. 'Fuuuck,' she moaned, her head in her hands.

'I didn't get a good look at him; he just walked away really quickly. I'm so sorry, no one else was around at the time; have you got any idea who would want to take your stuff?'

'No, well, maybe,' she whispered.

'Look, I feel really bad leaving you here after this,' he said. 'Do you want to make a call? I don't own a mobile but I have a landline at college.'

She looked up at his face for the first time. Slim, handsome, tanned. She was suddenly a bit ashamed of her dishevelled appearance. She used to think she could read people, by the look of their face. His eyes were greenish-blue with very dark lashes, piercingly dark. She was too tired to read his personality; he said he was from a college, he looked college age, he sounded educated and all the students that she'd encountered who were studying at the university, and not at APU, had been decent to her so far. Because of all these things she decided to trust him. It would soon be dawn and then she could head off, but she should report this to the police, and she did not fancy traipsing all the way over to the police station at this time.

She got up groggily and began to pack away her sleeping bag.

The student stood there smoking, looking off into the

distance. He turned round to introduce himself briefly. 'Lucian, by the way.'

She took his hand, noticing the hard calluses that brushed against her own dry hands.

They walked together to Peterhouse and then through the porters' lodge, where no one stopped them or questioned them, as Lucian confidently waved them through with a smile and a word of greeting to the porters. It was strange for Kimberley, entering this tranquil, unseen part of the city, where everything seemed ancient and orderly. No wonder the students here swan around the city without a care in the world, she thought.

She was wary about going to his room, but everything seemed so safe in the college; there were so many people so close by.

He unlocked his door and ushered Kimberley into a big room with a bed at one side, a large desk with books carefully piled in stacks of no more than five.

'You must be tired,' he said with concern.

'Yes,' she yawned.

'A bath perhaps?' he suggested.

'I should probably just report the bag stolen?'

'Oh, was there something valuable in it?'

'No.' She paused. 'I mean yes,' she stuttered, 'just sentimental value, a few photographs that I'd like to keep.'

'You know what the statistical probability of the police retrieving your bag is?'

'No,' she replied, confused.

'Well, let's just say it's pretty poor odds.' He smirked, though not unkindly. 'Look, things come and go, I can buy you whatever you need tomorrow, but for this evening take the weight off your mind, have a shower or a bath, sleep in my bed. I'll sleep on the sofa. I'm sorry I didn't catch your name before,' he said, offering his hand again.

She took his hand and shook it, feeling the strength of the tanned fingers close around hers. Kimberley was so mesmerised by the marine-blue eyes and the perfect smile that she faltered for a moment. 'I'm sorry, wha?'

'Your name?' His smile did not falter.

'Oh, it's Kim, Kimberley,' she replied, throwing the name from her lips like it was a cheap disposable thing.

'So, shall we see about that bath?' he said, smiling all the more.

Kimberley did not have the will to say no; she was so tired, and the bed looked so comfortable and inviting. He gave her a white, fluffy towel, which smelt of meadows and lavender, a fresh bar of Pears soap and a toothbrush with a travel toothpaste. When she closed the bathroom door behind her she saw there was no lock. She hesitated for a moment, scrunching her bare feet into the bathroom mat. I'm in a college, she thought, he's not going to try anything funny; besides, he's too posh and well-mannered.

The bathroom was sparkling clean. She had expected to see a bit of grime; it was after all the bathroom of a young male college student. But Lucian's bathroom was pristine. There was also no gungy toothbrush left by the sink or waterlogged soap left to dissolve in the soap holder. The basin was completely free of shaving foam or facial hair. Although it was nice to use a clean bathroom for once, Kimberley felt a little unnerved by the cleanliness of the place. Perhaps it's not him that does the cleaning, she thought; he's sure to have a cleaner to keep things so neat.

She turned the taps on the bath and soon a warm gush of water came out. She poured in a cap-full of bath oil that she found in the cabinet and closed her eyes as the bathroom filled with the scent of vetiver and rose. She peeled off her clothes, which were stained and greasy, and let them fall around her like the discarded shell of a hermit crab.

The warmth of the water as it touched her feet and toes made her shiver with pleasure. Lowering her body into the deep, enamel bath felt like a return to the womb. She pricked up her ears to try to hear what Lucian was doing. She could hear the beat of some music. She looked again anxiously at the door, wondering if Lucian were a pervert who would enter the bathroom and make a pass at her. At least he's not ugly or stinky, she thought, like all the men she encountered on the street.

But Lucian did not seek to enter the bathroom. He was busy in the bedroom, changing the sheets on his bed, fluffing the pillows. He felt triumphant. It had been so easy to get her to come back to his place. And she was a nobody, unconnected, not part of his world. That was the way he wanted it. He hated everyone knowing his business, and girls at Cambridge whom he had initially flirted with all knew each other. They were terrible gossips and so proud; they strutted around like peacocks with all their daddy's money and the accolades they had won at school still gleaming in their smiles like abalone shells.

This girl would be all his, he thought, this girl would need him and be grateful.

Hong Kong

What does one do after a murder? That was the question Lucian asked himself after he had cleaned up his bathroom and hidden Jojo in his largest Bottega Veneta alligator-skin suitcase, which he deposited on his balcony. Somehow, he couldn't face the world, even after the comedown from his drug-induced frenzy. For the past two days he had called in sick to work, but now he started to compose a new email: his letter of resignation.

A few weeks ago, it would have seemed impossible to Lucian that he could ever contemplate leaving his job, no matter how much he loathed it. He kept thinking about Clementine – it was her fault all this had happened. She had made him so angry. But he had gone too far – even he acknowledged that now. If he could get his hands on Clementine, he would wring her neck.

He began to fear being found out; he knew that in the warm temperatures outside, the body would quickly begin to decompose. He thought about dismembering the body, stuffing it into bin bags and throwing it into the garbage chute, but he didn't have the stomach for it. So, he remained semi-paralysed in his flat, until the sobering effect of not taking his medication or drinking took its toll, and he popped a few pills and began to feel the old confidence coming back.

He began writing the email to work. 'I have left, gone for good. If you feel the need to contact me, please don't, or else find someone who is not a deranged psychopath. If unsuccessful, please try God, but I fear evil will have claimed all.' In the valediction he wrote: 'Diabolus fecit ut id facerem.'

It felt satisfying, adding that last little flourish. He had already made enough money to live a good life until retirement. He began to contemplate the possibility of just disappearing somewhere. He could book a flight right now to Panama or Mexico City. He could leave everything behind.

But with his system revving up again because of the drugs, the old arrogance returned. He felt untouchable. Why should he run? Nobody would miss an ageing drug-addict hooker. He filled a tumbler with Laphroaig and downed it; refilled his glass and drained it again. The warmth spread down his throat into his stomach and his limbs felt lighter. He took his phone and scrolled through all the pictures and videos he had taken of the past forty-eight hours. He began to touch himself – he loved the way Jojo had seemed so scared, had done anything he wanted her to. Lucian half-wished he had managed to keep her alive as a slave for longer. Jojo's death had been an unexpected anti-climax. He zoomed in on her face, into the dark hollows of her eyes, and all he could see was a reflection of his own face.

It was then that he heard a soft tapping at the front door. It was very faint, and he was confused as to who or what might be causing it. Because the drugs had once more mellowed him out, he didn't feel at all panicky. He made his way to his front door and looked through the spyhole. He had to look down quite far, as the person who was at his door was so short. A small, oval face looked up and then a hand tapped once more. It was a masseuse called Sue-Lin who came round every fortnight on a Wednesday morning before work to give him a Thai massage and a pedicure – which really set him up for the day. They were semi-seeing each other but it wasn't an official thing. Sue-Lin never put pressure on him to make promises – which Lucian appreciated.

Although it wasn't great timing, Lucian really felt a massage would do him good. So, even though there was a tiny nagging voice at the back of his mind saying that this was not a good idea, he ignored it. His back was full of knots and his toenails needed to be trimmed. He didn't think about the crime that had taken place a few days before, or the fact that there were still small blood spatters on his bathroom tiles (he had cleaned most of it), or that his bloodied clothes were draped over a chair in his bedroom. He didn't even think of the body on his balcony. Like so many things, he felt he deserved a massage, and he wasn't about to deny himself the pleasure of Sue-Lin's small but firm hands pummelling his back.

She entered, smelling of the sandalwood incense they burned at the massage parlour where she worked. She took off her small red pumps by the door without making eye contact with him. For a moment she seemed to hesitate on the threshold, just before Lucian closed the door behind her, as if, somehow, she had a sixth sense that something wasn't right.

Lucian led her through to the living room with its views of the early-morning city – he lay right down on the floor, and noiselessly Sue-Lin opened her bag and prepared the massage oils and cloths. She asked him which area he wanted her to concentrate on. He told her that he felt he had knots in his upper back and neck area. She took the first of the beautifully scented oils and poured it onto her hands, warming it up before she began massaging Lucian's back. Lucian groaned with the pleasure of it, and after a while he dozed off, into a deep, peaceful sleep where there was no worry or stress.

When he woke up, he was still lying on the floor and Sue-Lin was still by his side, massaging his arms, hands and fingers. He rolled onto his back. His bowels had started to protest at all the abuse of the past few days. When the stabbing pains in his lower intestine began, he had to make a speedy dash for the nearest lavatory. He grabbed one of the fresh towels that Sue-Lin had brought, quickly wiped off the excess oils and hurried to the bathroom. Once he sat down on the seat, he knew that he would be there for a while. The shit streamed out as if he'd had a bout of food poisoning. But Lucian knew that, for him, this was normal – his doctor had said he might be suffering from IBS, but Lucian had been careful not to tell him how much of an addict he was, and how purging his system always helped him to get a better high. Lucian put his head between his hands and gave into the stabbing pains, the nausea, the light-headedness.

After he had been sitting on the lavatory for five minutes, his mind flew back to Sue-Lin. It was then that his gut twisted in horror. He could smell the smoke of a lit cigarette. Sue-Lin never smoked in his apartment; she always, out of a type of courtesy, smoked on the balcony. He hurried to wipe himself and pull up his boxers. As he ran down the hallway, he felt everything moving into slow motion.

He understood what had happened before he saw what had happened. He charged through the dingy living room and saw that the balcony door was open. Sue-Lin was crouching down looking at something. Because of the noise of the city she did not hear Lucian approach. He wanted to see what she was doing before he decided what to do next. Sue-Lin, with a lit cigarette in one hand, was undoing the buckle of the suitcase on his balcony.

She must have noticed the smell. Now that the balcony door was open, and the temperature outside was warm, the stench was becoming nauseating. He saw she had not got to the body, but he had left Jojo's blood-stained white stiletto heels outside and she must have noticed. Although he didn't rate Sue-Lin's intelligence, he knew you wouldn't have to be a genius to have some suspicions.

With a macabre interest, Lucian watched Sue-Lin's tiny fingers lift the lid an inch and saw her peek into the suitcase. At once she jerked backwards, recoiling in horror, and almost losing her balance from her crouching position. The lid of the suitcase slammed shut.

Sue-Lin stood up quickly, spun around as if by instinct, and at once they were standing facing each other. She was panicking.

Sue-Lin looked into his eyes for a split second and then her gaze dropped to the floor. He could see a hundred fears pass through her head. She was going to scream, try to save herself, but then she was clearly scared she might get thrown off the balcony. She thought he was insane.

Stupid, meddling whore, thought Lucian. It's her fault. I'll have to kill her. She backed away a couple of steps, closer to the railing on the balcony. Lucian shook his head. The tears started to fall down her powdered cheeks.

'I'm not a bad person,' Lucian heard himself say. 'If you keep quiet, I'm going to let you go. You can keep quiet, can't you?'

Sue-Lin nodded but looked unconvinced.

'Please can you just step back inside. I'll let you go. You didn't see anything here, did you?'

Sue-Lin shook her head.

'Well, there you are then,' said Lucian. 'There's nothing to be afraid of. For either of us.'

Sue-Lin was beginning to come around. She had been very scared that Lucian might hurl her off the balcony. Even though his words were calm and reassuring, she could smell the malice in him. She was clutching her phone in her right hand. She wanted to ring someone, anyone, and scream for help. But Lucian was looking right at her.

'Give me the phone,' he ordered.

'No,' Sue-Lin pleaded. She was looking across at the next balcony. It was visible but about fifteen metres away. There were also balconies above and below, but they all seemed extremely far away. The apartments in Lucian's building were huge with lofty ceilings.

'How can I trust you if you don't give me your phone?' said Lucian, his eyes darkening.

Slowly, with tears streaming down her cheeks, she gave him the phone.

Lucian was glad that he lived in such an empty building with neighbours who really didn't give a fuck. Also, the sound of traffic and building work in the city completely drowned out any balcony conversations. Even if someone screamed you would be very unlikely to hear them. *The cold-blooded murderer finds his paradise in the anonymity and loneliness of the city,* thought Lucian.

Once he had hold of the phone, Sue-Lin knew she had given away her lifeline. But it had not felt like a choice.

He stood to one side of the balcony door and allowed her to pass through. Once Sue-Lin was inside, he closed the door and locked it. Then he told her to sit on the couch.

'I think we both need a drink,' he said. But Sue-Lin didn't stay put. She began to sprint for the front door, haring across his living room and down the hallway. Lucian picked up the heaviest and largest object he could lay his hands on, which happened to be a trophy from his schooldays. It was a bronze laurel wreath, mounted on a marble base, bestowed for the Winchester history prize. On a small bronze plaque set into the marble were the school's crest and mottos, 'honi soit qui mal y pense', the motto from the order of the garter, and the personal motto of the school's founder, William of Wykeham, 'Manners mayketh man'.

As Lucian caught up with Sue-Lin, he hit her on the back of the head once as she was running. When he landed a second blow, she was knocked to the floor.

She didn't have time to scream. But Lucian could see that, although she was unconscious, she was still alive. Her chest still rose and fell in a steady rhythm. The blood from Sue-Lin's head started to pool around her long, black hair. There was a spatter of blood down her left cheek and a string of blood wound down from her mouth to her neck.

She was unlikely to gain consciousness again. But Lucian needed to make sure. He couldn't have a crazy half-dead woman running around his flat creating mayhem. So, he went to his spartan, unused kitchen and made his way to the knife rack. He selected his eight-inch Japanese chef's knife with the non-slip handle. He had never chopped anything with any of his knives. They had stood there, pristine in their gleaming rack since he first bought them on a whim. He had intended to start cooking delicious, healthy food. But his chaotic lifestyle had got in the way. Looking up, he saw the faded fridge magnet for pizza orders. The colour had all but disappeared from its blue and white pizza box design. *I should have taken better care of myself, then all this might not have happened,* he thought.

Lucian kept thinking how greasy blood was, how it had made his hands unable to grip anything. He didn't like all the mess in his home. If only this had happened somewhere else. Don't take a shit in your own bed — that was the advice from Piers that he kept hearing in his head. But it was too late for the giving or receiving of advice.

He took the knife with its sharp blade and made his way back to the living room, where Sue-Lin lay making a god-awful mess of his expensive pile. He paused for a few moments, looking down at her face, trying to decide if he felt anything. Lucian knew he ought to feel something — pain, regret, guilt — but there was nothing. No human response at all. He pressed the tip of the blade to Sue-Lin's jugular vein and pressed harder, watching a hot geyser of blood spew into his face and up his nostrils. He was disgusted by the strong metallic odour.

He didn't enjoy killing Sue-Lin because her death was not as he would have liked. It hadn't happened on his terms. After it was over Lucian brooded as he sat on the sofa. He could do things to her dead body. The thought popped into his mind more than once — but necrophilia really didn't appeal to him. He liked his bodies alive, capable of feeling pain and reacting. There was no pleasure to be derived from an unresponsive corpse. Even so, he undressed Sue-Lin and took some pictures as a memento.

Lucian kept imagining that the two women were not really dead. He felt like a child who had got to the end of a packet of sweets. His senses were ready for more pleasure — but there was none. He cut another line of coke and snorted it from the surface of the coffee table. Even the hit was dull. He sat back on the recliner with his oak-aged whisky and swigged from the bottle. He knew he should clean up the body and clear up the mess, but his hands were weak and useless. He decided he would give it a few hours and then begin. Both bodies would have to be stored on the balcony until he could think about what to do with them. *This was the ugly part, he thought — the part he had not planned.*

The day stretched ahead of him, and he knew he could not go back. The deed was done. He started thinking about the trail he had left. Everything was still vague and fragmented in his mind. The body of Sue-Lin still lay where she had fallen. He didn't have the energy to pull himself together, to start to conceal his actions. Then a wave of misery overcame him, and he cried — big heaving sobs that wracked his body. He was sorry for himself: sorry that all his early potential had been so comprehensively pissed up against a wall. There were so many who had been responsible for this — not least his parents. With shaking, unsteady hands he took his phone, which was slimy with blood, and dialled emergency.

The woman who answered spoke Cantonese.

'Please,' he said, wiping away his tears and feeling some of the old mania return. 'You must come right now. Something bad has happened. I have killed her. Yes, there's blood everywhere.'

He gave them the address and told them he would stay put. He sat on the living-room carpet next to the body and took a gulp of vodka. Then he took the last remaining stash of cocaine (wound up in a little clear plastic bag) and emptied it on the table. He stuck his nose in it and snorted. He didn't want to be fully aware when the carnival arrived. And this was, no doubt, the last time he would get high as a free man.

He lay beside Sue-Lin and stroked her lovely, soft dark hair, avoiding the patch that was matted with drying blood. He vaguely wondered about the future, but not with the usual sense of fear and panic. He thought about his father and how he'd have a heart attack when he heard the news. This made him chuckle — he couldn't help it. Then he thought about his acquaintances *from school, his rowing teammates from Cambridge, the wolf pack he had left behind in London. His was the kind of crime that would make him infamous around the world – a decadent westerner preying on marginalised women from poor countries. Women who were just trying to earn a wage out on the streets of Hong Kong. He would be compared to Jack the Ripper, Fred West. This gave Lucian a sudden thrill. The idea that he was some potent, powerful killer would win him legions of adoring female fans. He examined his conscience again for a sense of remorse or guilt but discovered that there was none.*

I must be the devil, he said to himself, and this gave him a buoyant feeling, as if something diabolical had touched him.

★★★

And that is what the world saw, thought Clementine. *Lucian Dorsey, bunched into his seat in an armoured vehicle, his guilt undeniable, his fate sealed.*

He had made a full confession of his crimes while high on cocaine and rambling to a lacklustre audience on an Internet chatroom. He revealed that 'Heavy shit had been going down' at his apartment, and he was asking for advice on how to get 'blood off a cream carpet'. He even went as far as to ask if human bones could be dissolved as easily as they could in films. It was like a cattle prod in a soft orifice: the chat room exploded, and the police received over a hundred calls. But Lucian had already alerted the police himself.

Detective Xin Xiao from the Hong Kong Police Department was first on the scene. The apartment was in one of the new high-rises in the financial district. It boasted two indoor swimming pools, a gym and a squash court. The moment she saw the news, Clementine knew that the papers would go into a feeding frenzy. Everyone wanted the inside scoop.

Lucian's apartment was decked out in playboy fashion, from the ergonomic chairs to the king-size waterbed. He had even had an expert in to feng shui his study. The apartment was home to some of the city's most successful businessmen – it was one of the most sought-after pieces of real estate on the island.

The wiry, bird-faced detective was due to retire in a few months' time. He shook his head in disbelief.

'Now murderers don't even bother to try to conceal their crimes,' he muttered to the officer next to him with a tone of disbelief as forensics commandeered the scene and a puffy, cocaine-high Lucian was led away from the scene. They were later to discover that Lucian had filmed over forty hours of torture, leading up to the eventual murder of two women.

Jojo, female, Indonesian, mother of one, was found wrapped in plastic and bath towels and stuffed into a suitcase on the balcony. Her petite forty-seven-kilogram body bore dozens of lacerations. Her breasts had been mutilated, as had her genitals. Cigars had been stubbed out in both eyes before death. The footage showed her bound on the floor of Lucian's bedroom. Lucian had urinated into an ashtray and told her she must lap it up like a dog. She had refused so Lucian flicked open a small blowtorch lighter and branded her with an 'L' on her left buttock, after which Jojo drank whatever he gave her.

His second victim, Sue-Lin, also Indonesian, was considered to be Lucian's on–off girlfriend. An article from The South China Morning Post published photographs of Sue-Lin sitting on Lucian's lap in a Hong Kong bar. The article revealed that Lucian had, for the past few years, liked to surround himself with women during his 'down' time. He was a generous lover, giving Sue-Lin thousands of pounds' worth of jewellery over the course of their ten-month romance. If romance was what it could be called. Sue-Lin had frequently complained to her girlfriends that Lucian's tastes in the bedroom were perverse. She had suffered numerous cuts and bruises, as well as a concussion, which led to her being admitted to hospital. After that episode friends reported that she had broken off the relationship for a couple of weeks. However, the lure of gifts and a good time had won her over, and she was seen with him in public twice more before her death. Sue-Lin had confided to one friend that she felt sorry for the lonely hedge fund manager. According to her, he was uncomfortable with his way of life but unable to stop, given his various addictions.

The statement given by the police was brief and to the point. They did not go further than the hard facts of the case. Everyone knew the press would fill in the sordid details. Already, Lucian's deeds were front-page news. His life was laid open, but what no one could find were the answers to why he had needed to take two lives in such a diabolical and protracted way. The families of the victims were interviewed, speaking from their small, shanty homes, where they cried through their grief.

But Lucian, the Cambridge boy, was the bigger story. He was allegedly sorry about it now (a few days after being charged with first-degree murder). He sat in court, as a man who closely resembled his former self but was really a shell of nothingness. But still he refused to cooperate. He had pleaded 'not guilty', claiming the charge should be reduced to manslaughter because of diminished responsibility.

He wanted to be transferred to the UK. Being incarcerated in Hong Kong was not to his liking. During his first few days in prison, he went through a terrible withdrawal process. It was *like the worst case of flu he had ever had, and he had to go through this in front of other people. There was no privacy in his five-by-five-metre cell, as the fourth wall was reinforced glass. Some might say a well-deserved torture, thought Clementine. He moaned and cursed and beat his head against the concrete. Prison warders had to go in and restrain him. He was given medication and put in a straitjacket. He soon discovered that human rights were a little different in Hong Kong. There were nights that seemed to last years, and as he was on suicide watch the lights in his cell were never turned off.*

After a week his head cleared and he was able to think straight. Though with this new clarity came the realisation of what had taken place, which was dream-like up until that point. The awful truth attacked him in stages, one terrible deed after another, until he felt like one of the sinners in Bosch's hell being devoured alive by a demon with a bird's head.

PART II

CHAPTER 1

Lucian was on bow, although he was a natural stroke. He was annoyed. It was a biting November morning on the river, where feet and fingertips were frozen well before the boat left the boathouse. Only rapid exertion would restore warmth to them. The cattle stood coldly together, and all the blades of grass were white at the edges. The water by the banks was dark and slushy. The boats heaved up and down the river leaving lines in the black seam of the river. Catz First Women's Boat glided past – each girl's hair tied up in high ponytails: brunette, blonde, redhead. One searched for the most beautiful face in each boat. It was always easy to spot the man or woman who had the most superior features. Lucian liked to think of himself as a connoisseur of beauty. He could see the most beautiful face in a line-up of women in just a few seconds. He was never wrong on these matters.

The coach of the Peterhouse Men's First Boat set off on his bicycle, ahead of them on the towpath, as the coxswain began to shout instructions. They left the boathouse and sliced through the water, like scissors through grey sugar paper. Faster and faster, blades feathering in unison. There is nothing more elegant than the silence of eight blades hovering above the water for an instant and then cutting the water neatly again, thought Lucian. Rowing gets into your blood; it is a difficult habit to give up. Lucian pulled as hard as any of them, but his face was glazed over – as if his mind were elsewhere. The coxswain put the crew through an intense warm-up, which lasted all the way to Baits Bite Lock. First, they practised quarter slides to half slides, to three quarter slides, to full slides, trying to get the blades all in unison. Then they practised square blades, went through their pause drills, first pausing at the catch, then pausing at the finish.

Lucian tried to extract some pleasure from the experience, but on that morning it was difficult for him to muster any enthusiasm. He usually appreciated the way rowing forced him to focus and forget about all the other pressures in his life, but on this occasion his mind kept wandering to the essay he had to hand in later that day, to thinking about how he could make sure he made a good impression at the Goldman Sachs social and then about Kimberley and what to do about that development in his life. He knew he should keep things simple, stay single, keep his head down, study hard, but there were urges in him that would not be silenced and without indulging them from time to time. He wondered how he would manage to stay sane.

Lucian had bought Kimberley new clothes and cooked for her sometimes. He didn't want her there during the day as he told her that he had stuff to do, but he expected her to come round twice a week. She was to sneak in at around 9 pm and if there were anyone hanging around in the gyp or on the staircase she was to wait and phone him. He had bought her a little pink Nokia and told her she was only to use it while communicating with him. 'And don't use my name in your phone,' he told her. 'Put something like Brian or Chris, and if anybody asks you your name, just make something up.'

She never understood why he was so strict in these matters. He demanded obedience from her and in return he was sweet to her. She was now in a halfway house, so things were a bit easier; she was clean and well-rested. He acted like he was her boyfriend, but he didn't want anyone to know who she was. He invented a story about her being a waitress.

The arrangement involved sex, but she didn't mind. He was very gentle, though he seemed so young and inexperienced. Often, they watched porn together and then he wanted to act out some fantasy. Nothing too weird. He liked to be dominant, but they had a safe word and he respected it. She often asked why he had chosen her, and he said it was because there was no one like her at his university. He said the other girls were all entitled bitches who want to use men as puppets. He was old-fashioned, liked to spoil a girl but also demanded respect. He had a very neat and tidy life, which he did not share very much with her. She was allowed to be in his life at the specified times, but if she showed up on a spontaneous visit, he was cold and abrupt.

It suited her quite well, and he bought her lovely things. He said, 'I like how grateful you are for this gift; I can see it in your eyes.' It was like the other girls he had been with had not been grateful to receive things from him. He said she must not be upset, as he had to go to events with a Cambridge girl for appearances. Kimberley was too worn down by the world to entertain notions of jealousy. She simply nodded and got on with the life she had been served. But she retained her dignity, and it was that dignity that sometimes winced at the more perverse of Lucian's sexual fantasies. Kimberley knew she could only go so far, and to go beyond would be a degradation she would not be able to endure.

★★★

The coach was yelling at Lucian to pull his head out of his arse. It was true, he was not pulling hard enough, he was letting the whole eight down. He felt angry with himself, and then on the way back to the boathouse he caught a crab that badly winded him and managed to lose his oar – it was more of a spectacle than he would have liked. To hear the other rowers laughing at him was more than he could bear.

That morning part of the river (from the Quayside to Jesus Green Lock) was being dredged. A female undergraduate had gone missing from Magdalene College four days ago and finally the town council had agreed to trawl the riverbed. News crews were stationed by the Lock-Keeper's Cottage on Jesus Green. They were there day and night – hovering like vultures, waiting for a body to be discovered.

Just the night before, a drunken man had decided to throw himself into the river from the footbridge opposite the Lock-Keeper's Cottage. He jumped in feet first while sticking two fingers up at the news crews and shouting,

'Mother fuckers!' Just before he jumped, he had been complaining to passers-by that the news presence was bollocks and that they should rubberneck somewhere else – it being so disrespectful to the missing girl's family. The moment he hit the icy water his breath must have been knocked out of him, as he went limp and passed out from the shock. Luckily for him, search and rescue teams were already there on standby to resuscitate him.

The student's picture was in all the local papers – a slim-faced girl with big blue eyes and fair hair. The papers had picked up the story because she was beautiful, and young, and at Cambridge. It was an instantaneous story. Everyone hoped she would turn up safe and sound. The papers threw up mystery after mystery. The student had allegedly given her purse with all her cash and cards to a friend before she disappeared.

★★★

Clementine had been watching Lucian, following him, as much as possible. Lucian's life continued to be regular as clockwork. Rowing every morning, at the History Faculty by 9 am for lectures, back to the library with his head in his books until 1 pm, a quick lunch (always BLT on brown bread and a banana) and coffee. He smiled when someone (one of the other History students) came over for a chat but never looked keen to talk.

She felt he had been looking at her the other day, across the coffee shop at The Sidgwick Site. She just managed to catch his eye before he looked back down at his plate. He must have noticed her constant presence everywhere he went. Was he annoyed, amused, intrigued? He was too polite to say anything, thought Clementine. Or maybe not, perhaps she was not his type? Clementine didn't like him as much as she wanted to be him. She wanted to crawl into his body, through the side of his mouth, to occupy that temple of strong limbs and nonchalant movement. How other girls looked at him. This made Clementine feel slightly sick. Clementine watched as a brunette with a bob and porcelain skin asked if she could share his table. He smiled, showing his neat top row of teeth, his eyes narrowing mischievously. Clementine reminded herself that this would happen, and she burrowed deeper into her voyeurism, trying to learn more about him through his interactions with the 'bob' girl. The girl was really trying to strike up a conversation. All his responses were seemingly polite but he was clearly not interested. He hurried to finish his lunch, put his book back in his rucksack, bade the girl goodbye and headed off back to the faculty.

Nothing would get in the way of his success, Clementine noted; he did not like distractions. He had demarcated his time into rigid routines. He probably factors in some sort of downtime too; people like him who are wound up so tight (overachievers) often go pretty wild when they allow themselves 'rest' periods. She wondered what he did to unwind. He liked women and could have his pick, but somehow he seemed uninterested in the cream of the crop at Cambridge. Why? Perhaps he liked submissives, or women he had intellectual or cultural power over. This would explain his dislike of the alpha females that hurled themselves at him on a daily basis.

They were all at Cambridge, and he would never be 'in charge' of them or distinctly superior to them.

Clementine wanted to have a look inside Lucian's room. Specifically, she wanted to have a look at his bookshelves and see what he read for pleasure. She wanted to know the music he listened to and find out any other dirty little secrets that he kept hidden from the outside world. She knew he was at Peterhouse. She followed him home every day as far as the gates but could not bring herself to follow him inside. That was too stalker-ish even for Clementine. But how she wanted to walk with him to his rooms, for him to open the door and let her inside.

CHAPTER 2

Clementine overheard a conversation between Lucian and his friends about the Varsity Trip. She had followed Lucian to a coffee shop where he sometimes met his rowing teammates. At first, she had hung about outside, getting colder and more curious about what was going on. She felt so conspicuous shadowing him everywhere, but she fancied that she was good at blending in and not being noticed. When she finally plucked up the courage to enter, she pulled her scarf up and her hat down so that only a small section of her face was visible. The shop wasn't particularly busy, so she ordered a skinny latte and surreptitiously looked for a place to sit down. Once she was handed the coffee, she meandered her way to a table opposite Lucian and his friends. She kept her eyes lowered and sat down on a chair with her back towards them. Jack Johnson was playing on the speakers, but the volume was quite low. The milk frother made a low whir and cups and plates clattered, but other than that the cafe was not particularly noisy. Lucian's friends spoke loudly and confidently about their courses, about women, about people she had never heard of. They didn't seem to care how they came across – Cambridge was theirs by right of conquest. They seemed utterly at ease.

At some point the talk turned to skiing and where they would be going during the season. Various resorts were mentioned, and someone talked about bombing down a couloir (a word Clementine later had to look up), and something about a daffy. She got bits and pieces of skiing terminology, which meant very little to her, but then the conversation switched to what she swiftly realised was a conversation about the Varsity Trip. They spoke so fast and with the use of so many in-jokes and alien terminology that Clementine only just managed to piece together the plan to be at the event that was being held at Val Thorens in the French Alps. Lucian seemed to be involved with these plans, and the four of them reminisced about their time on the ski trip the previous year when someone had face-planted and someone had snotsicles.

Clementine had seen the posters for the trip displayed in her faculty building and by the pigeonholes at college. She didn't know how to ski but she was possessed with the idea of going along just so that she could be close to Lucian. She knew she would look ridiculous on the slopes, but she thought she could hang about around the chalets and at the bars and go to the parties that were held every night. It was expensive but Clementine's grandfather had recently died and left her two thousand pounds. She told her parents that she really wanted to use the money for the trip. Since they knew Clementine couldn't really ski, they were a little confused as to why she wanted to go. The trip was scheduled for the first week in December, and once Clementine had reserved her place and paid, a little shudder of a thrill ran through her body every time she thought about it. Clementine imagined Lucian gliding down the piste – she was sure he was a very accomplished skier. It was Lucian's world that Clementine wanted to be a part of. If she couldn't understand the life he lived, how would she ever truly know him.

It was a Friday afternoon at the end of term when all the students who were on a budget gathered with all their luggage to board the coach. Much to her disappointment, Lucian and his friends had decided to fly – their trip to the slopes being only an hour and a half as opposed to twenty-four hours. This would happen to be the first in a series of disappointments for Clementine.

Clementine took a window seat and quickly stuffed earphones in her ears. She had her MP3 player full of tracks by Cat Power, Simon and Garfunkel, Devendra Banhart, David Bowie – an eclectic mix with tracks that she could listen to time and again. Clementine tried to reserve the seat next to her by putting her rucksack on it. But the coach was packed, and the seat ended up being occupied by a skinny, pretty girl wearing a pink and black ski jacket. She wanted to chat about how excited she was, but all Clementine wanted to do was stare out of the window. It was wonderful to observe the wintery scenes as they travelled to Dover.

The ferry crossing was a little rough and several students were ill. Luckily, Clementine didn't suffer from seasickness. The dark grey waves rolled and frothed. Clementine was mesmerised by the scene. She drank a sugary hot chocolate and watched the other students interacting. It was on the ferry that Clementine decided she would try to make an effort with the girl she was sitting next to on the coach. If nothing else, having one connection might be an effective camouflage for watching Lucian. Once she had boarded the coach again, Clementine had become someone else.

Clementine apologised for being quiet. She blamed it on motion sickness. The girl introduced herself as Tilda (short for Mathilda). She was a second-year CompSci at Newnham. Clementine asked her how she liked being at a female-only college. She said it was great because the girls just did whatever they liked and were far less self-conscious than they would have been if there were men around. Mathilda didn't say that she preferred women but the way she spoke seemed to imply it. Either that or she's a lug (lesbian until graduation); apparently that was a thing too at Cambridge. Clementine had already met a few girls who seemed to alternate the sex of their partner on a weekly basis. Others' sexual preferences were not something that interested Clementine. She was focused on what and who she was pursuing. Everything else was a dull background drone.

When they finally arrived at the ski resort, stiff and sore from sitting for such a long time, the coach struggled up to the ski chalets, as the road was on a steep gradient. Everything was covered in a thick pall of snow, making the scene look like a winter fairy tale. Clementine and Tilda decided to share and two of Tilda's Newnham friends joined them.

The first day out on the slopes was disappointing for Clementine. She had on her ill-fitting hired skis and equipment. It was bright red and Christmas tree green.

Next to the others, who had all been skiing since the age of three and were wearing the very latest designer gear, she looked comical. In addition to this, while Tilda and the other girls took the ski lifts up to the black runs, Clementine was left with two or three other stragglers on the nursery slopes. Tilda had said that she looked like she'd make a good skier. The reverse turned out to be true. Clementine's thighs, unused to the squat ski position, began to shake and burn with the build-up of lactic acid.

That first day Clementine kept an ever-vigilant eye out for Lucian. The whole morning, she did not see him. No doubt he was on the black run with his Wykehamist friends. When everyone came down for lunch Clementine got her first glimpse of him. She saw a figure glide effortlessly down the slopes and then come to an abrupt stop. The snow flew up in the air like it would in a ski holiday commercial. She recognised the mouth below the ski goggles. Then three other men joined him, and they stood together for a couple of minutes laughing and joking. Then he took off his ski mask and she saw the beauty of his face. Her heart was hammering in her chest again and she thought, even if I make a fool of myself every day, even if I never learn to ski, and I must survive on eight pence noodles and tinned beans for the rest of the year, it would have been worth it to see that perfect face here in his natural habitat – the playground of the rich.

The other girls came back from the slopes, exhilarated, their cheeks glowing with health. They ate a hot lunch outside under the glare of snow on Pointe du Bouchet. Clementine tried to listen and stay interested in what they had to say but it was too difficult with Lucian around. She could not take her eyes off him, and Tilda had noticed her distraction.

'It's that one, right?' Tilda pointed to Lucian in an offhand manner.

Clementine reddened; she had not expected to be found out. She always thought that most people noticed absolutely nothing.

'That one, right, the one in the blue Canada goose jacket?' Tilda had the look that says I know.

Clementine nodded and looked at her plate.

'He's fit,' said Tilda, 'for a guy.'

The other girls laughed.

'But I have to tell you he looks like a tosser. I wouldn't go near him if I were you.'

Clementine resented this. She didn't need Tilda's advice and, what was more, she would never approach him.

'Oh,' said Clementine airily, 'I just like window shopping.'

'Good girl,' said Tilda and lifted her glass of glühwein to clink with Clementine's.

★★★

The late afternoon into evening was the time for après ski. Clementine was struggling to walk but the others were ready for dancing. It was an outdoor party at La Folie Douce. The snow was still falling, and the temperature was freezing. It was strange to party with ski jackets, hats and thermals but the music was good. Lucian was there with his friends. He stood around drinking and laughing, showing off his perfect smile. A gaggle of girls that Clementine did not recognise from the coach were around him. They were the ones that had flown across a day earlier. They were still wearing their expensive ski goggles and earmuffs. Most of them had long peroxide blonde hair, and neat, straight teeth. They spoke with cut-glass accents and came across as very self-assured.

Claudia from *Streetcar* was there of course. As usual, she stood out as the most confident of the group. She seemed to have singled out Lucian as her choice. She danced provocatively around him (or as provocatively as one can dance in a ski suit) and all the other men seemed to be enjoying it. As for Lucian, Clementine was not so sure. He was flattered by the attention perhaps but remained aloof and separate. He did not give much commitment to anything, least of all the advances of drunk girls. Of course, it drove them wild. Before long, Claudia was circling her arms round his neck, trying to push her body onto him. Lucian smiled awkwardly at the others, who were taking pictures and laughing. His friends liked the fact that he was such a chick magnet. But Lucian did not seem to be having the time of his life. He was there in the flesh but somehow absent. No wonder the girl was trying her hardest to get him interested, but it all seemed a little futile. I wonder why he is acting that way, thought Clementine. Is it a game to make women hornier, or does he just hate all the attention that he gets?

Clementine's interest was more than a little piqued after this observation. Tilda and the other girls were already pretty drunk and dancing with each other and with a group of Etonians. These Etonians were not King's

Scholars; they were, without doubt, trust-fund babies. They were handsome, sporty and self-assured. They were the types that just seemed to glide through life on a gilded surfboard. Clementine was a little wary of them because they stuck together like a wolf pack, and she always had the feeling that they talked about girls behind their backs. She had heard that they scored girls on looks and then ribbed each other if any of them had got with a girl below an eight. It was only a story but looking at them it seemed perfectly possible. One of the boys kept dancing close to her. He had dark eyes and sandy hair. He was uncomfortably good-looking, but Clementine felt relaxed in his presence. The party was still going strong when she made her excuses and left.

She returned to the chalet and ran a warm bath. It was good to be alone after being pressed so close together with so many bodies hour after hour. Clementine was never energised by a crowd. If anything, crowds drained and made her feel small and insignificant. She needed to be alone, to feed her ego. She removed her clothes and sank back in a bath of lavender and patchouli. Her body felt sore, and she had no idea how she was going to get back out on the slopes the next day. She thought about Lucian's face, the beautiful smile at once arrogant and shy. I admire him so much that I do not just want to be with him: I want to be him. It was a strange type of jealousy, as much as an attraction. In her stomach there was an ache of loss, and she mourned what she would never have, just as if she had been given something and it had been taken away.

The next day Clementine ate her breakfast croissants

and drank her thick hot chocolate with Tilda and the girls at the cafe overlooking the slopes. Claudia was with Lucian today, but they seemed to be more friends than anything else. Claudia came over to her to say hello. Clementine felt awkward wearing her sagging ski gear, looking like such a beginner. Claudia stood next to her.

'Hi, babe,' she said flicking her ponytail.

'Hello, Claudia.'

'So, what happened to you? I didn't see you all term.'

'Yes, I was busy.'

'So you say,' Claudia laughed, showing her teeth. 'You heading up?' She knew the answer of course.

Clementine smiled. 'I think I'll stay around here.'

'Shame, it's going to be awesome today.'

Clementine just nodded.

'Catch you later then.' And she was off on the chair lift with her friends.

Clementine breathed a sigh of relief. She wondered what it was like to be Claudia. She tried to think of at least one negative aspect of being that perfect, but she just couldn't. It wasn't worth wasting energy on.

Then it was back to the slopes for the morning. Again, Clementine tried to get some control over her snow plow, but her thigh muscles were unused to it. She caught a glimpse now and then of a blue ski jacket flying down the black run. At this distance it could be anyone but to Clementine it was always Lucian. She could not concentrate on her own progress when she felt that Lucian could be close by. Once she managed to pull herself together for half an hour, so that her instructor began to praise her for her progress. Then she managed to lose her balance and somehow ended up on her back, her skis in the air. It was then that she heard the laughter. A group had formed at the bottom of the nursery slope; their intention: to laugh at others' limitations. This time it was Clementine who was the butt of their jokes. To her horror, Lucian was with them. But he was not laughing. He was barely paying attention to the slopes. Instead, he was looking up into the clear blue sky. There was a golden eagle circling, its huge wingspan dark against the sun's blaze, setting it apart from the smaller birds. It must be looking for carrion, thought Clementine.

That afternoon it was the Varsity Blues ski competition. All the students lined up with food and hot drinks at the finish line. Lucian was there too, standing on the opposite side. Clementine could see that he was enjoying this competition more than he had enjoyed himself at La Folie Douce the previous evening. Claudia was competing. Clementine hadn't realised she was so good. Everything felt worse again. Clementine felt a wave of jealousy overcome her. She beat down the feeling. It was better to watch and wait. The sponsorship had brought huge speakers and they listened to 1990s and early 2000s acid music: "Underwater Love" by Smoke City, "Sandstorm" by Darude and "Hey Boy Hey Girl" by The Chemical Brothers. It was Cambridge who won, and they all celebrated on piste. Of course Claudia placed first in the giant slalom so she got the Blue. Of course she did. But did it matter to Lucian? He competed as well and managed to get a Half-Blue.

That evening Clementine got into the spirit a bit more. The Etonians were there again, and again they were hovering around Tilda and the girls, who weren't exactly discouraging them. Other girls were completely off their heads. Boys were picking up girls and carrying them around on their shoulders and everyone was having to scream to be heard. Again, Lucian was with his friends and the gaggle of girls around them had only increased. At some point in the evening Lucian's reserve slipped and he started kissing one of the girls. It seemed that the indefatigable Claudia had already moved on with one of Lucian's handsome friends. One of Tilda's friends kept urging Clementine to go over and talk to Lucian. God, thought Clementine, I'm not about to do that when he's clearly busy ramming his tongue down another girl's throat.

So, Clementine danced and drank and danced some more. The snowy scene started revolving but she didn't stop. Then she was dancing close to someone. The only part of their skin that touched was their lips. The kiss seemed to last an eternity and then Clementine lost the function in her legs. They gave way beneath her. There was a lot of laughter, and Clementine herself was laughing too. She was too drunk to think about Lucian and this gave her some small comfort. Then she was being carried through the snow with her face turned up to all the constellations spinning in the night's sky. She could have watched that night sky until dawn. It was at this point that she must have passed out. She had a vague sense that she was inside and someone was undressing her and she was being kissed. Her body was completely numb from the alcohol, but her stomach felt worse and worse. Then she vomited everywhere, and her last memory was a man's voice saying, 'Oh god, oh god.'

She awoke the next morning in a soggy bed that stank of vomit. It was strange to look out of her window at the cold, perfect mountains while covered in the contents of her stomach. She vaguely noticed that her knickers were around her knees and her bra had been unhooked. None of it seemed to matter. She needed to have a shower. It was 6 am and none of the other girls were up. She bunched the bedclothes together and went to put them in the washer. Then she locked herself in the bathroom and stared at herself in the mirror as she ran the shower waiting for the water to warm up. Her face was pale beneath the ski tan. Her body looked thin and girlish. She tried to remember the face of the boy she had been with that night. She had snapshots of his eyes and lips, but they didn't add up to a whole face.

She washed away the vomit and when she got out of the shower she was just as she remembered. She hated the thought of being someone's sexual conquest when drunk. That wasn't the way she liked to play the game. Clementine brushed her hair and dried it. She put on fresh clothes, downed a large glass of salty water and popped a 400mg ibuprofen. She still felt like shit. She hoped Lucian had not noticed her last night. She didn't want to be known as that girl who got trashed.

That day on the slopes Clementine fell badly, and managed to fracture her wrist. She wound up in a nearby hospital with Tilda keeping her company. Three days in and it looked like Clementine's skiing adventure was over. It didn't matter so much. Clementine was content to watch the others from the comfort of the chalet or the cafe. There was the guy who she had slept with, or almost slept with (she didn't know which) looking sheepish and keeping his distance from her.

Tilda kept relaying his messages of sympathy and saying, 'I think he really likes you.' Clementine shrugged. She wasn't interested at all in that guy. It had just been a drunken fumble, nothing more. Tilda kept saying that he was very nice and everything – but it didn't matter. All she wanted to do was to get back to the slopes and sit there all day waiting for a glimpse of Lucian.

Tilda and the others helped her get back to the accommodation. They were nice to her, and Clementine was beginning to feel a genuine affection for them. She had been determined to watch coldly and detachedly from the sidelines and yet she had found some real friendship. The only problem was that friends might get in the way of her real goal of observing Lucian and all he did. Clementine sometimes reflected on her predilections. At night she scrutinised herself and wondered what was wrong with her. A few years ago her mother had suggested that it was autism and wanted her to get a diagnosis. Clementine had been outraged. Even if she were autistic, the last thing she wanted was to be labelled autistic – so that she could be the token autist in any group of people. She preferred the word 'strange'. So I'm strange. Aren't we allowed to be that anymore – must we all be normalised into acceptable categories to make our idiosyncrasies more acceptable to others, more acceptable to ourselves? Her mother had been shocked at the vehemence of her refusal. But things had carried on and at school Clementine had excelled in everything she put her mind to.

She could not make a lasting friendship happen – but that was not something that Clementine ever felt she needed. If you've never experienced something, thought Clementine, it is very hard to miss it. In addition to this, Clementine was pretty. This meant that people gave her attention and wanted to know her. Men complimented her, and women thought she was quirky and cool, so she was never alone. She enjoyed the fleetingness of sudden acquaintances who would soon fade completely from her memory. She woke every morning ready for the new day with new experiences. She stuck to no one and no one stuck to her. If someone did hang around she would quickly shed them as easily as trees lose leaves in autumn. She was free, or thought herself to be free. But she was never truly free of her fixations. And now more than chess, or stamp collecting, or fossil hunting, or mouse breeding, or memorising Shakespeare, it was Lucian that occupied her mind, her waking hours and her dreams.

The weather was clear and perfect for the next few days, and everything continued as it had before. Except that Clementine was enjoying herself rather more now that she had an excuse not to be out on the slopes. She took her coffee and cake at late morning, all the while watching for Lucian out on the slopes. Most days she saw him skiing down the mountain just before lunch. He looked tanned and radiant – bursting with health and vitality. His white teeth looked even whiter and his grey eyes shone. Then she would watch him eat his lunch with his friends, amused at the way he seemed a little reticent around the girls who flocked to be near him. Then he would disappear for a couple of hours, but he would always return for the night's revelries.

Clementine was still able to party as much as she liked. Lucian seemed to be nominally involved with one of the girls from Oxford. Tilda told her she was the daughter of a famous singer. Clementine had never heard of the singer. The girl was tall, lean and perfect-looking. Just what Clementine would have picked out for Lucian had she been given the chance. Tilda was laughing at her reticence to go over and talk to Lucian. The fact that there was another girl wouldn't have deterred Tilda — if she were straight. Clementine didn't try to explain what she was doing. It really wasn't about Lucian — she didn't particularly want to know him personally. Clementine had created his life and personality for herself — as viewed from a distance. To meet him or touch him, or talk to him, would no doubt destroy her fantasy. Clementine was old enough to realise that fantasy always trumps reality.

On their last evening in Val Thorens, one of Lucian's crowd came over to Clementine and asked her why she was always staring at him. Clementine laughed. He seemed interested and hopeful in some way, like he had been hoping she would explain. Clementine could see that he had felt chosen by her. She did not want to tell him that it was not him but Lucian that was the object of her attention.

She decided to play the femme fatale and deny all knowledge. He looked crestfallen and confused. It pleased her greatly to have this power over someone. He had got his hopes up, and she had dashed those hopes upon the snow. It felt good to reject someone, thought Clementine, to not care about someone's feelings. The girls seemed shocked that she would behave in this way. They seemed to think she should be grateful for any attention she got. Clementine wondered if it was because the boy was one of the rich kids and she was clearly not. Clementine shot down their questions with a withering glance.

Claudia came over to her that evening, with a pint for Clementine. Clementine felt it was Claudia's way of cornering her. They sat side by side.

'Sorry about your wrist. That must suck,' said Claudia.

'It's ok,' said Clementine.

'You know if it hadn't happened, we'd have invited you to Courchevel. We're off there tomorrow.'

Of course, Clementine thought. For some the party never ends.

'We'll be there for a week or so. It should be epic.'

'Next year perhaps,' said Clementine.

'Sure,' said Claudia. 'Next year you'll be off the nursery slopes.'

On the coach going back, with her arm still in a sling, Clementine reflected that the trip had very much been worthwhile. It had been amazing to see a snapshot of Lucian's life – to live vicariously through the experiences of others. What was more, Lucian still didn't appear to realise her infatuation with him. He had not yet even registered her existence, and this gave Clementine more confidence to simply carry on and see where this new experience would lead her. Again, she had the old feeling of yearning for something she would never possess and then the stranger feeling of jealousy. She was jealous of Lucian's life, the way he belonged in a sphere that was so different to her own. The way others sought out his company. Being close to him would be an unbearable thing, because she would always be reminded of how deficient she was. Clementine put her earphones in her ears, pressed play on her discman, shut her eyes and imagined a hundred scenarios that would never happen. On the plus side, her wrist was feeling better. She listened to "Jagged Little Pill" by Alanis Morissette. It was an adolescent album but sometimes she liked to regress. The mountains passed as the coach took to the narrow roads that wound round them. The rest of the coach was quiet, exhausted from the week of exertion. They would sleep most of the journey back.

CHAPTER 3

It was the beginning of Lent term. Lucian had gone to Courchevel with his friends, plus Claudia and her lot, and then spent the rest of the Christmas holiday at home swatting up on his course. He had met up with a few members of his rowing team at Dorney Lake after Christmas for practice so that he didn't get rusty over the vac. When he returned to Cambridge, he felt glad to be back living on his own. He hated having to be involved in family activities at home; as an only child he felt the pressure weigh down upon him, though neither of his parents had any definite expectations for him. Lucian's father had damaged his back in a car crash ten years before and was now confined to a wheelchair. Lucian hated having to accompany his father to the Sunday church services in their village. He loathed having a disabled parent whom people pitied. Why couldn't his father have gone and died instead of living this half-life as a cripple, thought Lucian. Lucian never mentioned that his father was wheelchair-bound to anyone – to him, it was a great source of shame.

Lucian was relieved to be back in Cambridge at the start of the new term and surrounded by youth and vitality. Before leaving for Christmas, he had cooled his relationship with Kimberley. He had given her cash of course but had told her he would be away for six weeks. Now he was hungry to see her and others, if he could fit it into his schedule.

The morning started off in the usual way: with a flurry of activity along the staircases and corridors of the college. The student's rooms were receiving their daily clean from a team of women mostly imported from abroad.

The bedders were a mixture of Polish and Ukrainian women. Lucian's bedder was Polish, dark-haired, slim. He was out most of the day, so he had only noticed her by chance the previous term when he'd caught a bad cold and was in bed at the time she arrived to clean. She looked shy, moving the chairs about so she could vacuum, using a sparing amount of polish on the old furniture, running a duster over the spines of his books.

Today he was pretending to read a book in bed, which added to the awkward atmosphere. It's not right to fraternize with staff, he thought, but what the hell? He asked her what her name was. She didn't hear him, as she was over in the opposite corner of the room with the hoover on. He asked again, a fraction louder.

This time she heard: her name was Magda.

'Do you want a drink, Magda?' As it was only 11 am she looked at him quizzically.

'Don't laugh,' he said with a grin. 'I'm not an alcoholic, I just like a drink on occasion. And I have a headache; brandy is good for headaches?'

He got out of bed. He was wearing only his boxers, so Magda looked down at the carpet.

'I don't drink,' she said, looking nervous.

'What?' he roared. 'Where are you from?'

'Poland,' she replied.

'I thought they all drank like fish in Poland.'

'The men drink a lot,' she said, looking embarrassed, 'sometimes too much.'

'Come on', he said, putting a shirt on but not doing up the buttons. 'Have a drink with me. My room's already tidy. Take a break, cheer me up.'

'I'm not allowed,' she said quietly.

'Ok, well tell me what you like to eat?'

'What?' she stammered.

'Do you like cake?'

'I don't understand,' she said.

'Tomorrow you will come and clean my room at 11 am, right?'

'Yes,' she replied.

'Well, when you come tomorrow, we will eat cake from Fitzbillies. Ok?'

'Ok,' she said and quickly left the room in a haze of confusion.

Lucian reclined on the bed with a smile on his face. He thought about cakes: chocolate éclairs, sponges, red velvet cupcakes.

The next day Lucian did not forget his promise.

He had bought dozens of cakes. There was cake on his desk, cake on the windowsills, cake in boxes on the floor and on his bed. Magda knocked on the door of Lucian's room at 11 am, as usual, and he bellowed, 'Enter'.

She shuffled through the doorway with her mop and hoover. Once the door was closed her eyes alighted on all the marvellous confectionery that he had bought for her delectation. Chelsea buns, macaroons, Florentines, fairy cakes like a rainbow. She let out a little gasp.

He sat on the bed, dressed in his beige chinos and a white shirt. He stretched out. 'The room looks tidy?'

She nodded.

'I did it myself, comes from being at public school, one always has to be so spik and span.'

She stood in the middle of the room, not sure what to do.

'Please sit down,' he said. Lucian made a space for her on the bed.

She shook her head and remained in the centre of the room. He had just noticed the cross on a thin, silver chain worn about her slim, white neck. It was hidden last time, under her clothes, but today perhaps she had made sure that it was visible. Catholic, he sighed internally. Not that it's much of a problem; plenty of Catholics seem to be able to square the most appalling behaviour with their God. He stood up and moved an armchair to the centre of the room. Suddenly, there was a terrible awkwardness between them, and he worried that he had got it all wrong, that perhaps he was no Casanova, and not every woman would fall at his feet just because he was Lucian, reading History at Cambridge, a rower and a handsome chap.

'You want something to eat?' he asked, feeling foolish and small, and grandiose at the same time.

She still didn't sit down. She raised her eyes to meet his. Their colour was ice blue; he hadn't noticed the strength of them before. 'I come to clean your room,' she said, looking him in the eyes. 'The room is clean.'

He half-laughed.

'Ok, so I go.'

'No, you stay and eat cake,' Lucian insisted. She shook her head. Maybe she's a lesbian, thought Lucian. Not the butch type but the feminine one, the type that drives men crazy.

Magda got her things together, the plastic handle of her mop and bucket in one hand, the hoover in the other.

'Please,' he entreated, 'just stay for five minutes.' He hated not having the upper hand in any situation. This was not how it was supposed to play out. She was supposed to be grateful, to sit and eat her cake like a good little girl. She was supposed to blush at his attention and try to please him.

'I have boyfriend,' she blurted out suddenly, 'and I'm not a prostitute.'

He went to the door and swung around, blocking her exit. 'You can go,' he said, his eyes narrowed, 'but take a cake first, and one for your boyfriend.'

'I don't want any cake.' Her blue eyes looked hurt and tired.

'Then I just can't move from this door,' said Lucian.

She shrugged and picked up a box of cakes. 'Will this be enough?' she asked resentfully.

'Yes,' he said, imagining shoving the colourful macaroons into that beautiful mouth. 'That will do.' He stepped aside from the door and allowed her to pass by.

Such a bitch, he thought. No doubt she will complain about me, and I did nothing to her. Lucian mulled over what had gone wrong; obviously she wasn't quite as poor and desperate as he had thought she would be, desperate for attention, for a rich man to spoil her. Weren't all poor women like that? He supposed he wouldn't know. He had only thought this was the case because prostitutes were invariably poor and desperate for money. He hadn't reckoned on the faith thing, which obviously meant she was a 'good' girl. He needed to get Kimberley back. She knew her place.

That evening Lucian had an unexpected visit from Claudia, who knocked on his door and invited herself in. She had been messaging him through the Christmas vac after their trip to Courchevel. She laughed until she ached at the boxes of cakes he had piled up by the window. She helped herself to more than a few and lay on his bed in her seductively short skirt. He wanted her and she knew it. Another bitch, but this time the worst kind, a rich bitch. She was the type to keep him on a leash like a dog. If he got into something with her she'd be parading him round to endless things she wanted to do; there was no getting the public school out of the girl. It would always be there, like the coterie of semi-starved bitches who hung around her like her looks would rub off.

So he played hard to get. It usually either puts them off or drives them wild. He said he was very tired and needed to get up early the next morning for rowing. That did not go down well with Claudia, who was used to getting her own way. Yet, the more she wanted her own way, the more Lucian was determined that he would call the shots. He told her she must go now like a good little girl but that he wanted to invite her to a Pitt Club dinner. She knew that only the prettiest girls got invited to these dinners, so it seemed to satisfy her vanity and shut her up. When she left the room Lucian smirked thinking about how Claudia would most likely boast about the invitation to her pals. She would be talking about it non-stop. She would probably get her little gang to help her shop for a dress, all the while driving them mad with jealousy because they would not have received invitations. How amusing, he thought, to have such an effect on the female of the species.

CHAPTER 4

Lucian paid his subs every term so that he could go and eat pizza in a leather-backed armchair in the Pitt Club's illustrious upper room. Downstairs was now rented to Pizza Express but that was in many ways a good thing in terms of readily available hot food. Yes, there were parties, when you would bring along fit girls only; leggy blondes or brunettes, the type that the patrons liked so much. For the club's Lent event Lucian decided to make good on his promise to invite Claudia. Who cared that she was as attractive to him as a piece of cardboard. He had the feeling that the other chaps would be envious and that was all that really counted. They hadn't yet done the deed together. He loved to keep her waiting.

Lucian told her to wear something 'sensational' and Claudia didn't disappoint. She wore a turquoise dress, deeply plunging at the back; her flaxen hair was worn up and there was a small diamond pendant at her neck and diamonds in her ears, which matched the hollow sparkle of her smile, thought Lucian. He offered her his arm to ascend the steps. The music was deafening. There were always a couple of nerds at the door, salivating over the girls who got invited to the Pitt Club dinners. They had their cameras, which they tried to hide because they knew if one of the Hawks got sight of one, they would have their head on the pavement quicker than you could say perve.

For a moment Lucian felt proud as a peacock, but one look at Claudia and the dead feeling returned again. She would never be his; her eyes darted around, looking for brighter futures, new opportunities. It was utterly soulless socialising with this type of girl, thought Lucian. One day she might settle, but she had everything, and she knew it. She was in no hurry. She would probably make him feel like this evening was a great favour. Claudia would bestow her glorious rays on him and the others for a few tragic hours. 'Be a happy little puppy,' her smile said. 'Be grateful because this body, this hair, this face, this mind, is something you will never fully possess.'

This was the natural pattern of Lucian's thoughts when he took out a girl that was equal to or greater than himself. He wanted to fuck her, then throw acid in her face and tell her to be grateful for it. As he pulled the chair out for her to sit down, he imagined gouging his initials into the skin on her back. Claudia did not sit down; she was too busy working the room.

A chap called Simon Featherstonehaugh came over and slapped him on the shoulder. He was the kind of person nobody really wanted to be around, but everyone licked his arse because he was well connected.

'Hey man, great plus one.' He took a sharp intake of breath as he looked over Claudia's behind as she chatted to another girl. 'I'm going to change the table setting so you two can sit next to Sherry and me.' Sherry, or Scheherazade, was the daughter of a famous director. This essentially meant that she had all the directors and casting teams at the ADC Theatre begging her to be in their Michaelmas plays. It was during this time that it was discovered that Sherry couldn't act. This, however, didn't seem to affect her chances in the Lent term, where the same scramble took place for her presence in their plays (albeit slightly smaller roles). People whispered that she could get 'a good friend', an internship with her father, or a role in one of his new projects.

Simon was an embryo thesp with big ambitions. He rather fancied himself on the big screen – hence his new girlfriend, Scheherazade. Although Scheherazade may have had all the stars aligned in terms of her fortunes of birth, she was not in any way an exceptional-looking girl: a little heavy around the hips and thighs, with chunky calves and big, wild hair, which she always wore swept up into a bun. She had an expensive smile, but one could not help thinking that it was not the smile she was born with. The large white teeth did not fit terribly well in her rather petite mouth. She laughed a lot, throwing her head back and making other couples turn round and stare. They all knew who she was; in fact, everyone had known within a few days of her arrival at Cambridge. Some freshers have that effect. There were one or two at Peterhouse, the son of so and so world-famous painter, the daughter of an eighties pop legend. The Etonians, whose parents run such and such bank in Hong Kong; the list went on. Cambridge could make a somebody into a nobody quite quickly.

It was easy to see why Simon wanted Lucian and

Claudia sitting at his table. He had been missing real totty. It was not as if Scheherazade ticked all his boxes – not even close. He sat next to Claudia, and Scheherazade and Lucian sat opposite. From this position Lucian had a full view of Claudia and Simon hitting it off. He kept leaning towards her. He even whispered in her ear a few times. Lucian felt his blood boil. Claudia would have done her homework and would know about Simon. In fact, they had already figured out that they had friends in common who dated for a time – they both agreed it was strange that this was the first time they had bumped into each other.

Claudia hardly took a bite of her first course, but this was because she was seafood-intolerant (she swore that she had told Lucian!) and the starter was crayfish, mussels and periwinkles on a bed of lettuce. She did not eat much of the second course either. The duck, she called 'rubber ducky' with a little smile, like she knew how duck should be prepared, and this was not it. The creamy potatoes she scraped to the side with her fork, saying that she was on a low-carb diet because her personal trainer recommended it. The one thing she did eat were the roasted vegetables, which she speared seductively, bringing each small piece of courgette, fennel or carrot to her lips slowly and then taking them into her mouth as she looked deep into Simon's eyes.

Scheherazade had already decided that the brooding Lucian was too much like hard work and had started up a loud and lively conversation with the girl who looked like a *Vogue* cover model and was the date of Sebastian, the Count from Austria. Scheherazade was knocking back margaritas; little crystals of salt were stuck to the corners of her mouth. On the other side of Lucian there was a Rugby Blue called Tarquin, and opposite him, his date for the night, a child actress who had decided to leave acting for a few years and have a normal life at university. These two were hardly talking to each other because Tarquin was seated next to another Rugby Blue called Edmond and they were discussing the Six Nations. The child actress was talking on her phone, discussing a part she might be interested in (even though she swore in the papers that she would be having a hiatus from acting during her time at Cambridge).

Lucian sat there feeling his skin prickle with the unfairness of the evening. Yes, women thought he was attractive, but really, he could not compete in these circles, with these men and women, who were all standing in their ivory towers kicking the ladders away from anyone who dared to climb up. Claudia, that bitch, was now sampling some of Simon's crème brûlée from his spoon. Well, no matter, Lucian always knew that this evening soirée might go south, so he had prepared a little packet of MDMA in his pocket, which he would imbibe to make it all much better. He did not even bother to go somewhere private. He just started to do a few lines right there on the table after the waiters had cleared the pudding.

Simon, who had been unreachable for at least an hour, jumped out of his seat and shouted at his friend Silas to 'Shut the fucking doors!'

'Look man, do you want to get us shut down? Someone had a bad trip last year and it almost got into the papers. A girl nearly died!'

At this point Scheherazade and the *Vogue* cover model were engaged in a long kiss, which no one noticed, until they all did, and, taking advantage of the shift in attention, Lucian snorted his first line.

The evening went from bad to worse. Claudia was still talking to Simon; Scheherazade seemed to have switched sexual preferences, or maybe she was bi-curious. Most girls at Cambridge now claimed to be, thought Lucian. Lucian was slumped in a chair with the world seeming very far away. His ego felt enormous. He had a fantasy that he was the king of all he surveyed. He floated above his minions as they did his bidding. In reality nobody was really paying any attention to him at all. The doors had been locked and there was only one trusted servant administering drinks to the group. This meant that Lucian's drink had run dry a while ago and had not been replaced. He looked at the three olives, from what had been his dirty martini, and imagined that they too were commending him on his brilliance.

It was soon time to leave, and Claudia returned to him to tell him about an after-party.

'You've been such a misery guts all night, Lucian. Why didn't you just join in? So silly of you to take those things; it does nothing for the quality of your conversation!' She looked at him with that clever, pretty face, which was so full of itself. Her pouty arrogance, her bright blue eyes, sharp as glass. He felt powerless to deny her anything. He shrugged and shuffled around on his chair, trying to remember what he needed to get back to college. She was wrapping a turquoise cape about her shoulders and standing in a huddle of Pitt members and their dates. She was sparkling as usual, and the whole group had their faces and attention turned towards her. At one point everyone started speaking fluent French and then they all switched to Greek. Lucian's ego slowly deflated, making him feel like a barrel of lead. He pulled himself together, put his jacket back on, shuffled over to the throng and pretended to muster some enthusiasm. His eyes flashed darkly with a simmering jealousy, when he supposed nobody was watching.

The after-party was being held in a grimy, damp, moss-clad building called the Lock House on Jesus Green. A friend of a friend's place. Something had already been happening there; the place was full of odd people (not all Cambridge students). Some were from APU (Anglia Polytechnic) and some were definitely homeless. "Chan Chan" by Buena Vista Social Club boomed out from speakers in the kitchen, which also served as a living room. Each of the five bedrooms in the house was open to visitors. People often chose to end the night here, at the Lock House, as it was in the middle of the green, next to the weir, and one could make as much noise as one liked and never receive complaints. Open door meant open to all the weirdos who might be passing along the towpath that night.

The fridge-freezer was still relatively full of beer and there was a table laden with bottles of spirits. Lucian nabbed a bottle of whisky and sat on a bed in one of the downstairs bedrooms. Claudia had already gone upstairs. Lucian was sitting next to a Chinese girl who was playing the guitar and singing a Communist party song rather loudly. At least that's what she said it was when he asked her. There was a couple sucking each other's faces off in an armchair by the door, an older man (possibly in his sixties) sleeping on the floor and a red-headed American girl who kept popping in and out of the room telling everybody that she wanted to 'fuck them up'. She had two men with her and as she swayed in and out of the doorway they took it in turns to snog her, although she slapped them hard in the face every time they did. However, this did not seem to put them off attempting to do it again.

Another girl offered Lucian a line of ketamine and he snorted it with her; then she started kissing him hard on the mouth. He was too tired to care who or what she was. She looked vaguely female so he reckoned that was enough for now. Later in the evening, when he was half-asleep on the bed with the girl gone off somewhere else, he was woken by what sounded like a gunshot. His back spasmed and he found himself on the floor next to the sixty-year-old man, who rolled over with a smile on his face. The man was no longer wearing his clothes and appeared to have stripped down to his white y-fronts. Clearly, he thought that Lucian had just made a pass at him. Lucian leapt up and stumbled off into the hallway looking for someone to save him from the situation.

Where the hell was Claudia? The Lock House had emptied somewhat, but there were still bodies all over the floor, some sitting, others dreaming and drooling, lost in their own private k-holes. Lucian pulled himself upstairs, leaning heavily on the banister. The upstairs had three rooms and a separate bathroom. Lucian lurched towards the bathroom door. It was half-open and the interior was in darkness. His bladder was beyond full after all the drinking and being passed out for so long. As he entered the bathroom, he groped around for a light switch or a pull switch. His hand brushed against a cord but missed it. Just as he did that he heard a sound coming from the corner of the bathroom in the shower cubicle. Without thinking he pulled back the shower curtain to find a naked man in a shower cap with a sponge and a back scrubber.

'Join me,' said the man. 'I'm conserving water and electricity.'

Lucian fell backwards from the shock. It seemed that the house had a resident lunatic in every corner. There was another pop again as if a gun had been fired. The sound echoed around the upstairs landing. Lucian peered through the doorway of the middle room to see the red-haired American girl lying on a desk by the open window with a gun aimed out over the river.

'Now I'm gunna shoot me some joggers!' she yelled at the top of her lungs.

Lucian turned and retreated down the stairs, trying not to make a sound. He bolted through the back door, past a group of hooded youths loitering in the light of a lamppost. Then he dove into the bushes by the side of Jesus Green Lido. There he unzipped his trousers and urinated over the damp, early morning grass.

'Oi, paedo!' one of the group of youths shouted at him. This one was no doubt a member of the traveller community.

Lucian wanted to avoid an altercation, so he zipped up his flies and sprinted across Jesus Green in the direction of St Mary's. Someone gave chase but gave it up once he had reached Portugal Place.

Claudia, was all Lucian kept thinking. Claudia, that bitch. He wanted to ring her neck, while fucking her of course. As he ran he had a vague memory that she had come into the bedroom in the Lock House while he was lying in his k-hole. He remembered her face hovering above his. She had kissed him and then gently undone his belt and slipped her small, cool hand into his underwear. He remembered the movement of her hand and the way it felt so distant and disembodied, and then she said something like, 'Oh Lucian, how very disappointing'. Her face faded away, and he could no longer see her, even though he was still grasping for her small throat with his two hands.

CHAPTER 5

The body of the female undergraduate had been found in the first week of Lent term. Somehow it had got attached to a canal boat's rudder. It was even dragged through a lock unbeknown to the boatie, so that when the river was drained up to Jesus Green Lock it had mysteriously disappeared. She wasn't easy to identify, as she had been in the water for weeks, but she was still wearing the remnants of a red dress and a gown. Clementine was by the river when she noticed the throng of reporters, police and rescue divers. She had just seen Lucian's boat glide off in the direction of Baits Bite Lock.

The morning was the usual mix of weak sun and mist. The grass on Midsummer Common was stiff, frosted with rime. A small herd of amber-coloured cows huddled by the nettles, their nostrils wet with mucus, breath steaming in warm hoops. The towpath was busy at this time in the morning, filled with joggers, cyclists and all the crazy early-morning sports enthusiasts. On a bench near The Fort St George lay a drunk, zipped up in his grubby sleeping bag, his face golden in the morning light, eyes shut tight, mouth part open. A beautiful young homeless man, reddish stubble beneath his child's mouth. She took out her camera and photographed his face, so innocent and at odds with the beer bottle and cigarette stub detritus around him. She took five pounds from her purse and left it by the side of his sleeping bag. She felt stupid as she walked away and hoped that no one had seen her pointless act of charity.

She walked closer to the scene, thinking about a piece on homelessness in the city that she might write for *Varsity*. The divers were untangling the woman and her head bobbed up. There was not much hair on it; it looked like the skin had dissolved almost to the bone. It was as if she had been exposed to acid and her flesh had just melted away. Her hands were no longer hands, more like branches onto which a few leaves of skin still clung. The body was quickly put on a stretcher and covered up with a plastic tarp. The reporters buzzed around asking questions, making notes, and a TV crew appeared. A woman in a beige coat buckled tight and a red scarf stood in front of the cameras; her blonde hair looked like it had hurriedly been scraped back in a ponytail. Her make-up couldn't disguise the bags under her eyes or the red tip of her nose, pinched by the cold. Clementine stood and watched the reporters with their big reusable coffee cups, their breath billowing in a caffeinated haze. The police were there, gathered in a fluorescent huddle, trying to act as if they had some respect for the dead.

Clementine wondered if they thought it was suspicious. Deaths on the River Cam are more common than one would think, especially when freezing temperatures and alcohol consumption are mixed. She imagined the poor young student slipping in and having a heart attack from the shock. Or maybe she had jumped after a supervision went wrong, or split up with her boyfriend, or she had an eating disorder – the list of reasons one might do away with oneself at Cambridge were endless. For the perpetually miserable there is always enough perpetual misery.

Clementine ate a packet of half-frozen cashews as she paced along the towpath, filled with excitement at the thought of seeing Lucian's return to the boathouse. She loved the way his hard face gleamed with exertion after the two hours on the river. Some of his teammates had noticed her loyal vigil each morning. They shouted at her across the river, asked her who she was after. Clementine never replied. The coach who cycled down the towpath alongside the boat passed her each morning. He greeted her cheerily but did not pry into her reason for watching the early-morning session. Lucian seemed to make a point of not looking at her. Though once she caught him sneaking a glance at her, getting the measure of her, no doubt finding her wanting in some respect. Once Lucian had returned to the boathouse, Clementine wandered away quickly. She didn't want to stay and get more attention from the rowers.

Later that day Clementine sat on the wall outside King's College and smoked a pink Sobranie Cocktail (the brand she had observed Lucian smoking) just to try and get a quick glance of Lucian going to and from Peterhouse. It was spitting rain as usual. Rain was a constant thing in this part of England; hardly a day passed without the heavens opening, and the pavements reflected a world within a world beneath the feet of passers-by. There was a girl playing a tin whistle outside what used to be the Copper Kettle. She was covered in a blanket and wearing a tie-dye top. Her hair was pulled into a scruffy ponytail. She closed her eyes while she played. A group of girls cycled past, their long hair streaming out behind them, causing a group of boys on the other side of the road to collide with pedestrians walking the other way. Such is youth, thought Clementine. It was an irresistible expression of life's raw energy. Even the fat, acne-covered girls were delightful in their own youthful ways. Everyone was dressed like a bohemian or a Sloane, having spent a small fortune on the 'look'. As they walked along King's Parade each of them passed over a stone slab, much like all the other paving slabs; yet this one bore the words 'High Maintenance Life'. On enquiry, Clementine had discovered that, during repairs to the pavement in 1998, a sculptor named Ekkehard Altenburger had illicitly laid the paving slab, under cover of darkness, as part of his 'disruptive' guerrilla art campaign. It was a strange, though somewhat fitting, addition to life in this panoply, thought Clementine.

Every night, Clementine collated all that she knew about Lucian as she lay in bed with the lights off, eyes resting on the dark bulb in the centre of the ceiling. She knew Lucian was fastidious and competitive. In the boat he always pulled hard. Rowing was not a pleasant pastime for him; rather, it was a way to assert his physical dominance. It was a way to impress the other rowers and be in a team that won. Winning was top of his list of priorities, and it also seemed to influence the type of people he wished to be seen with. Clementine had seen him take

Claudia to the Pitt Club. She had followed them all the way to Jesus Lane, almost weeping with jealousy. Clementine would always remember that moment – seeing them together: her fantasy lover and her rival – as one of the worst moments in her young life. It was an image that was seared onto her soul.

He chased the real princesses, the type of girls who weren't just going to settle for a guy in their first term. Most of them probably have an IQ of a hundred and fifty or over. Beauty and brains come together at Cambridge, to create some of the most nauseating individuals, thought Clementine. She pictured Lucian's face from different angles. She saw the soft down on the skin of his cheek. The cheekbones that could be seen from the back, just in front of his ears, which were tidy and perfectly formed. The lips were red and soft but could turn into something menacing in a split second. His eyes were grey-blue, like a mix of the sky and sea. They looked into a person. They allowed no hiding places. For Clementine, this could be both terrifying and marvellous. She knew, if he ever looked at her, that she could not look him in the eye for long. Her own dark irises might melt under the intensity of his gaze. She wanted to be with him, but she also wanted to be him. To inhabit his mind and body. She was insanely jealous of his life and his abilities. She wanted to be as silently domineering as him, to have an aura of mystery.

Still, she felt that she could not see the whole of him. She had found a couple of puzzle pieces but there was no solid being in front of her yet, no fully rendered man that owned the name Lucian. He was beginning to take on a life force inside her mind and her body. She half-believed that she knew what the touch of his hand was like: the calloused grip of a rower. She almost thought he had already whispered something in her ear about a rendezvous; she could smell his breath on her cheek, which smelled like cold water and moss. When Clementine went about town in a vain effort to keep her own life ticking over – shopping for food, or visiting the library to avoid academic ruin – she always felt as if he were a hair's breadth away. That his would be the next face she would see. She was conscious of trying harder with her appearance in the morning. She styled herself in accordance with what she believed he found attractive, and she hated that she did it. Because most of the women he had displayed an interest in were blonde, she had decided to buy blonde hair dye. Clementine kept it in its box on her shelf for two weeks before taking the plunge and slathering her head with its peroxide fumes. She was no longer herself, and slowly she was also giving up on maintaining her academic endeavours. She was slipping into a relationship without being in a relationship at all. All the while a little whining voice at the back of her mind kept telling her to pull herself together.

And what did Lucian want? Perhaps he didn't have the slightest interest in being serious about any woman. The women he was with performed some function, whether it was eye candy for a university function or sexual gratification without strings attached when he was in private. Perhaps everyone left him feeling cold, and he was just putting on a display of normality. Sometimes, thought Clementine, he looked like he was wound up so tight that one day the elastic band might snap.

Clementine had finally broken her own rule. She had followed him all the way to his rooms one evening after formal hall, so she knew now where he lurked. There was a kitchen opposite his set, so she had decided to ingratiate herself with the girl next door (a hopelessly antisocial girl called Samantha). Clementine would go over to the kitchen with cappuccinos and biscuits from Nadia's bakery and knock on Sam's door. They would sit together for half an hour in the kitchen while Clementine played music on her laptop. Mostly Lucian's door never opened but, as fate would have it, Clementine did see Magda the bedder going in once or twice. Clementine noticed she was pretty and wondered if something might be going on when she happened to see Magda exit the room looking unhappy with a box from Fitzbillies. Lucian had taken to giving Magda a box of cakes every time she cleaned his room – after being rejected by her it seemed like an amusing punishment.

Clementine wanted to know more, so she made up a story, to tell the porters, about having left a squash racket outside her friend Sam's room. She went down to the store cupboard, which was where the bedders congregated at noon, to pack away the cleaning products and chat in Polish. Magda answered her questions abruptly as if she thought Clementine were trying to imply that she had stolen the squash racket. Clementine tried to steer the conversation onto Magda's encounter with Lucian.

'So that student in 6a, is he trying to seduce you with Fitzbillies cake?' she joked.

Magda didn't laugh; she started to pack away the Henry hoover she was carrying.

'God, I'm only kidding,' said Clementine. 'It's just that guy's got quite the reputation.'

Magda was giving nothing away.

'I'm just going to tell you that one girl got rusticated because of him.' This little piece of fantasy that Clementine had just dreamed up seemed to produce a little interest on the part of Magda.

'Rusticated?' Magda asked, looking confused.

'Yes,' replied Clementine, now eager. 'Y'know, sent down, asked to leave,' (wilfully simplifying the Statues and Ordinances to the point of inaccuracy – she had no intention of wasting further time).

'Why?' asked Magda.

God, thought Clementine, this girl is queen of the monosyllable.

'He made her crazy,' whispered Clementine, 'promised her this and that, then lost interest; she ended up attacking another girl he was seeing with a broken bottle.'

'Yeah I know, these things happen at Cambridge,' Magda responded, looking somewhat concerned.

No they don't happen at Cambridge, thought Clementine, but Magda seemed to have bought the story.

But even after this, having warded off a potential love rival, Clementine was not content. Watching Lucian had become a full-time occupation. Her academic studies were falling by the wayside. She was extremely annoyed with herself. She had thought that the quiet observation of a love interest was enough to satisfy her and now she realised in the case of Lucian it was not. She had to get him out of her system, to experience an interaction with him that was real and physical. She shuddered at the thought but was also aroused by it. She was beset by doubt. What if she offered herself to him on a platter and he flat out refused? She would burst like a popped balloon. He had noticed her watching him and probably thought her strange, bordering on stalker-ish. But he was so wrapped up in his own life. How could Clementine find a time when Lucian was unoccupied? How could she make it clear that all she wanted was no-strings-attached sex? That it would be a kind of therapy.

After Clementine had said goodbye to Sam and left the kitchen, she noticed a girl standing before Lucian's door waiting to be let in. The first thing that struck her were the girl's ears, which were covered in piercings. She was dressed like a student, with a Corpus Christi scarf, but the scarf looked incongruous with the piercings and her messy ponytail. Clementine quickly turned and walked down the stairs, not waiting to see if Lucian opened the door. Her mind was racing. Where had she seen the girl before? Then she remembered: it was the homeless girl who played the tin whistle outside Sainsbury's. Clementine could hardly believe what she had seen. Lucian had girls like Claudia offering themselves up to him and yet he chose to spend time with an ugly homeless girl. Something did not add up. Maybe she had misunderstood the girl's reason for being there.

Clementine went through several days of procrastination. If anything, seeing the girl at his door had undermined some of her assumptions about Lucian. Maybe he did not have a particular type. Maybe he would be up for anything that was offered to him. If he could be with a homeless girl, then why not Clementine herself?

Clementine convinced herself that she could go through with it and close the chapter on Lucian. If she simply collected one more 'real' memory that she could gnaw on forever, that would be enough. She knew he was bad. There was something that bordered on the insane with him and that was perhaps what drew her to him in the first place. That and his extraordinary good looks, which seemed to her to get more attractive as each day passed. She must have him, and once that was done, she must forget him. She was not stupid enough to think a relationship with Lucian was possible; it would be like a dream come true turned into a nightmare.

She imagined he tasted of durian fruit: sweet at first, with the flavour becoming more complex and disgusting with each bite. She fixed the day in her mind. As she knew his movements down to the hour this was not too difficult, but planning for the unexpected was a little more difficult. Clementine came up with stories to tell should he be occupied with his other girls when she paid the call. He would not believe her but at least she would have something to say.

And then one sunny afternoon, as she was walking back from the Sidgwick Site through Trinity Backs, she spotted him sitting on a bench reading a book. She hesitated, wondering if fate had thrown them this unexpected moment with no one but the two of them about (apart from the punts, with their loud tour guides forever going up and down the river). The sound of her feet on the gravel suddenly seemed unbearably loud. Any second he would look up and fix her with those grey-green eyes and she would blush crimson. He would know by the hue of her face that he had her in his thrall, that she was his for the taking.

This made her furious. She stopped and fumbled with her bag, groping down to its depths for a cigarette. She needed to collect herself. She found the carton and took out one of her last two Lucky Strikes. 'It's toasted,' read the label, which she always thought was hilarious. She turned her back to him, to light the cigarette, took a big draw on the filter and filled her lungs with the toxic smoke, filled with carcinogenic particles and formaldehyde. There was a cough from behind her, from Lucian's direction. She turned around, mortified, hoping that he wasn't going to begin a lecture on quitting smoking. He sat in the same place on the bench, but he looked straight at her, into her, and waved her over to him as one might summon a child or a small dog. She walked over to him slowly as if she were an acrobat on a tight-rope strung over a waterfall. He offered his right hand in a greeting.

'Hello, I'm Lucian. I believe we've met before.'

She awkwardly switched her cigarette to her left hand and shook his hand. She felt the roughness of his fingertips worn hard from rowing. She was aware of her dyed blonde hair and how he was staring at it. Does he think it looks absurd, she wondered?

As if in answer to this thought he remarked, 'I like the colour, but you suit brunette better.' Now she was blushing and wanting to run away and scream. He was going to toy with her and there was nothing she could do now.

She offered him her last Lucky Strike and they sat together looking out over the river. The crocus heads were just coming up through the grass; it was almost the end of the Lent term. She would soon be going home for the holidays. Home to nothing.

He told her about his love of music. He mentioned Talking Heads, Whitney Houston and Phil Collins. She had only heard of Whitney Houston. It sounded like pretentious claptrap. She could tell he was not that into music; he was just speaking.

'I want you,' she said all of a sudden. His eyes turned to hers with a look of mirth.

'Not forever,' she stammered, 'not a relationship or anything, in fact nothing more than a one-night stand.'

'Don't try to explain,' he said. 'It just spoils the fun.' He got up to leave, throwing his cigarette stub onto the gravel. He walked two paces away, turned around in his nonchalant manner and said, 'Come and see me tonight at 8 pm.'

Clementine's mouth fell open and then she remembered to close it. 'Uh, ok,' she managed to say.

'I'm guessing you know where I reside?'

She nodded and blushed. She felt like such a desperado. She went away with shame and jubilation in her heart. It felt like a summons, a forbidden assignation. How could she not obey, but there was an aura of dread about the time he had stipulated. She would not dream of being late.

Clementine couldn't get his face or expressions out of her mind. Ten times she decided that she would not go, and ten times she realised she could not help but go. She had to see him again, and, after all, what had all the waiting and watching been about, if not this final consummation of her feelings? She wondered what he would expect from her. She took three hours getting ready: bathing, shaving her legs, plucking her eyebrows. There was no doubt that he didn't feel the same way about her. But somehow she still hoped to win him. When she thought that, she told herself she was crazy, deluded, naïve. She decided to wear her black cocktail dress (it was the only one she owned, and it was her go-to formal hall dress). It looked good on her – was tight around the waist and bust. She kept her legs bare, though it was still stocking weather, and fastened her black high heels. She wore a simple silver necklace and small studs with lapis lazuli in her ears. She felt like a sacrificial offering, about to be gutted at the altar of some cult religion. The truth was she needed to know, finally, who this man Lucian Dorsey was. She had had enough of her own dreams and fantasies. Tonight, she would find out, whether for good or ill. It was a terrifying prospect. She went to the bar at The Eagle beforehand and had a double whisky. She waited five minutes for the drink to take effect – and then she felt it, a wave of pseudo-confidence.

She was ready.

CHAPTER 6

Clementine arrived at Lucian's door at the appointed hour. Her fingers touched the white lacquer on the wood, softly as one would touch the hand of a dying relative. She rapped on the door with her knuckles bunched into a fist. There was no answer, no sound at all. But then there was a rustling, and a note was pushed under the door. She unfolded the yellow paper, which read: 'You are early.' She looked at her watch, which was always set five minutes fast so that she always remained punctual. In fact, she was ten minutes early. She had thought to remember her earliness and refrain from knocking on the door until the appointed hour, but her excitement had got the better of her. She took the note and descended the stairs like a schoolchild reprimanded by her headmaster. Her new obedience to Lucian was a strange facet of their relationship, and one that she was trying to get used to. If she didn't think about it, it seemed a perfectly natural thing, and she could wander around in a dream-state without the feminism that she so loathed rearing up in her mind and making her question her purpose. I am trying this out, she told herself, and there is no shame in either staying or going. I am an autonomous being, she told herself, I can do either. She decided to smoke while she waited.

The sky was overcast and the first drops of a thunderstorm that had been brewing all day started to fall. The smoke smelt good, mixed with the heavy, earthy smell of imminent rain. She saw a group of freshers, larking about on the other side of the court. Three boys and three girls. It took her only a few moments to see who led that particular pack. A tall boy with a mop of curly-brown hair who was simultaneously joking around and flattering people, keeping all eyes on himself. Each of the girls wanted him. One showed her interest brazenly, but this did not stop his eyes wandering for the approval of the other two. The other young men followed and laughed at his jokes. At some point in the future these other boys would feed on the lead boy's scraps. The girls might settle for them, marry them even. And the boy with the beautiful hair would smile at them from their dreams, ghostly as the morning mist on the fens. Then he too would age and perhaps realise his age too late. Then he would be the one to laugh and caper and feel rejection too.

Clementine felt heartbroken for every boy and girl who must mingle love's ecstasy with its pain. Mostly she just felt sorry for herself.

Her feet felt heavy as she ascended the stairs ten minutes later. She knocked once and Lucian opened the door immediately. He acted like she had just turned up. He didn't mention the note, or keeping her waiting; he certainly did not apologise.

He poured her a scotch from a crystal decanter. The glass was delicate, with a gilded rim and a diamond-cut pattern around the sides – Bohemian crystal. He had a window that overlooked the backs. The treetops were flailing and even through the glass they could both hear the hissing of leaves and branches in the wind, like waves breaking on a shore. He gripped his glass and looked down at his bare feet. He has long toes, with beautifully manicured nails, thought Clementine. It seemed absurd that Lucian would fuss over his feet but they certainly appeared very well tended.

Then there was a knock at the door. Clementine watched Lucian as he walked to the door and opened it. It was Kimberley. She appeared a lot cleaner and neater than she had been the night he had met her five months ago. However, this change in circumstances did not seem to have made her any more outgoing. Rather, she hung her head as she leant against the side of the door. Lucian took her firmly by the shoulder and led her into the room. Clementine felt a stab of jealousy, which caused her actual visceral pain. She recognised Kimberley as the girl she had seen at Lucian's door, the girl who sat on the streets busking.

'Clementine, meet Kimberley,' he said. Clementine stared with her mouth half-open. Kimberley had brushed her peroxide blonde hair and straightened it; she had bright-red lips and a Cambridge undergraduate gown on. She had removed the piercings from her ears and her face looked clean, if still a bit worn. On her feet were five-inch heels. They were Jimmy Choos. She tottered past Clementine without greeting her and made straight for the couch. She sat down without saying a word. Clementine was angry that Lucian hadn't told her they would have company. She decided not to say anything; after all she was only there for the sex. And as long as she got that, she thought, she would be satisfied. Now Clementine wondered what she would have to do to get Lucian to have sex with her. He seemed to be laughing at her behind his eyes, at the centre of the small dark pupils in his apple-green irises. It was as if he were saying that she was not enough to satisfy him. Not even close. Lucian mixed a drink for Kimberley without asking her what she would like. She took the drink without saying a word.

Kimberley had become accustomed to these nighttime visits. He paid her well, but she was sometimes unhappy with the way things were going – the things that Lucian expected her to do. Lucian knew that busking and her job selling the *Big Issue* would never be enough to cover all her expenses or keep a roof over her head. He told her she should make the most of this opportunity. She had been making secret plans to move away; London perhaps, where she had an aunt who lived in Tower Hamlets and would let her stay on the couch. Kimberley knew that she couldn't afford to have a huge amount of pride, but somehow what Lucian had encouraged her to become jarred with her sense of self. There were other girls on the streets who would call her crazy for looking a gift horse in the mouth. Yet though she had been poor as a child, she had been brought up to have a strict moral code, which as an adult she found harder and harder to escape.

Kimberley twirled the toe of the tricolour Jimmy Choos about on the carpet, suddenly loathing how its soft, expensive leather still managed to pinch her foot and give her blisters.

Lucian turned on the music – Phil Collins' "Invisible Touch" again; Kimberley knew she could sing every track on the album. Lucian had got his copy of *American Psycho* down from the shelf. He began to thumb through the pages.

'So, Kimberley, tonight you will be called Christy, and you will be called Sabrina.' Clementine had read the book even if Kimberley hadn't. Of course, Clementine thought, this is who he really wanted to be: a Patrick Bateman impersonator.

He closed the blinds on the large windows looking out onto the backs. Clementine watched as the sodden green of the trees and the rain-lashed window disappeared under the office-style blinds. Now they could not see or hear the spring storm rumbling outside or see the tourists bunching together under umbrellas in the court.

He sat in his armchair, his perfect face cupped in his tanned hands, his legs spread wide.

'Christy, take off your gown.' Lucian held the book, but he knew the words by heart. He liked to think he was leaving his own little mark by changing the word 'robe' to gown. Kimberley was used to this routine now, she was used to being called Christy, she now almost felt like she inhabited the body of a fictional character. She opened the gown to reveal black lacy lingerie.

Christy looked over at 'Sabrina'. Kimberley had seen this girl around Cambridge, passing her on the streets when she sold the *Big Issue*. Kimberley never forgot a face, though the girl's hair had changed; she was now blonde with dark roots beginning to show through. It was tough to maintain the illusion of being a true blonde, thought Kimberley, who was in fact a natural blonde. This 'Sabrina' was a Cambridge student for Christ's sake, thought Kimberley. What was she doing acting like a hooker, Kimberley wondered? Maybe the girl was insane and got her kicks through being Lucian's plaything.

'Sabrina, take off your dress.' Again, Lucian read the line from the book, stirring the ice in his gin martini with his finger. Clementine flushed pink all over her face and neck. The humiliation dug into her flesh. It would be bearable if Lucian were the only person there to witness her nudity, but this other girl, who looked sullen and life-hardened, looked at her like she was out of her depth. Clementine didn't want to touch this 'Christy'. She looked used up, done in and Clementine only ever considered touching people she thought were 'clean'. This girl had been around the block, with Lucian no doubt, and others. The horror of venereal disease swam in front of Clementine's eyes: genital warts, gonorrhoea, syphilis, lice. Clementine did not consider herself to be a lesbian, and she had never had a sexual fantasy about another woman. When another woman wished to hug her or show physical affection she would often squirm inside. The idea that sexual desire was fluid was anathema to Clementine. She had only ever liked men, and only certain, very specific types of men at that. Clementine hated the softness of women's bodies, their floppy breasts and curves. To her a woman's body looked strange, unfinished and weak. 'Christy' was very thin, her hip bones jutted out from her pelvis, her elbows made sharp angles when she placed her hands about her waist. Her ribcage could be clearly seen; it was deeply defined like lines in a ploughed field undulating between her breasts. Her lower legs and ankles were thin as a baby fawn's.

Clementine had removed her dress. She stood there with her toes turned in, excruciatingly self-conscious. She felt as if she were in the spotlight, even in the dimness of Lucian's room. To make her more uncomfortable, Lucian turned the head of his office lamp on her so that he could better scrutinise her body from his armchair. His eyes narrowed, as if he were taking in the view. Then he sighed, as if he had found her body lacking somehow.

'Do you work out, Sabrina?'

She squirmed under his gaze but managed somehow to look into his eyes as she replied 'No'.

'You should think about it,' Lucian said nonchalantly. Clementine thought, how dare he, and then her glance fell to her belly and the slight protrusion of fat. Yes, maybe he had a point; she was unused to standing naked even when she was alone and contemplating her imperfections. The Cambridge weather made her want to wrap up and protect her frailty against the winter-long damp and cold, although Clementine half-knew that Lucian was just being spiteful and trying to prey upon his perception of her vulnerabilities. She frequently received unsolicited comments from men about her appearance, and they were always positive. She was complimented on her eyes, her alabaster skin, her small nose and high cheekbones. She was definitely a pretty girl, and some had even gone so far as to call her beautiful. So, Clementine tried to ignore Lucian's remark and focus on being in the 'moment'. She didn't need every man she met to think she was a knock-out. Although she would have liked to impress Lucian.

'Sabrina, why don't you dance.' It was not a question. He looked at Clementine expectantly.

As if it weren't the most humiliating situation already, thought Clementine. Now she had to be as awkward dancing sexily as Jamie Lee Curtis' character in *True Lies*. Clementine's hips started to move as if attached to a string pulled by the hand of an invisible puppeteer. Her arms moved limply by her sides.

'Come on, Sabrina,' Lucian taunted, 'aren't you enjoying yourself?' He went over to the sound system and cranked up the volume. 'Christy, get on the bed; show Sabrina your asshole.' Now that he had fully entered the fantasy, the book slipped from his grasp. Kimberley hesitated, got up onto the bed. She was not happy with where this was going. She had been here before and she knew how the evening would end. In a moment of defiance, she sat on the bed, knees together, still looking down at the floor but resolute in her determination that Lucian would not have his way. Lucian jumped out of his armchair and walked over to Kimberley.

'Remember what we agreed, Christy, you won't get anything if you don't do this. I'll cut you off. I can be generous if you do the right things and behave.' Clementine did not hear this conversation, as Lucian was whispering in Kimberley's ear. He was holding Kimberley's chin in one hand and stroking her hair with the other. When he stopped talking to her he released her, and Clementine could see a red mark on Kimberley's face from the pressure of his fingers.

Kimberley let her head drop. She was unsure if she

could leave, if she had it in her to break off this agreement with Lucian and be on her own in the world again. In some ways her life had been better since she had met him. He was a generous lover, even if he was strange and demanding. Kimberley looked at her expensive shoes and thought, I do not need them. She knew she was not a 'high maintenance girl' and never had been. The allure of nice things was never as appealing as being treated with respect. Lucian did not respect her. He used her and paid for it with money he didn't earn, from the generous trust fund set up by his grandparents. He had learnt that he could buy most things he wanted over the years – even affection – up to a point. But Kimberley could not go on with this.

She slipped her feet out of the shoes and left them pressed against one another by the bed. She took off the expensive bracelet on her wrist and the diamond necklace, and the two rings that Lucian had bestowed upon her. All she took was the gown, which she wrapped about her body. Clementine watched Kimberley walk proudly to the door. Barefoot, she walked out into the evening rain, never to be seen again by either of them. Perhaps her destination was happy, perhaps not, but this girl from the streets was able to choose it herself. Clementine could see that Lucian was in a terrible rage about Kimberley. She really surprised him with that move. He thought he would have her as a sex toy for good, or at least for as long as he wanted her around. Clementine was secretly satisfied by this turn of events, but she was still annoyed that he had tried to involve another person in their hook-up.

The music continued playing; it gave the room a

strange atmosphere, like a party that everyone had left early. Lucian sat in his armchair, deflated and seething. Clementine could tell that having her to himself was not his idea of fun. She was not enough for him, or maybe she was too much, too demanding, too sure of herself and her position in this world. For a second, she wished she was nothing, a woman with no future, no prospects, no cultural or economic capital. That would excite him, that would turn him on. She could not be Lucian's fantasy as she was, and nor would she give up those things that made her 'high maintenance' to please him. It was stalemate and the electricity Lucian felt with Kimberley in the room had dissipated, in a flurry of Jimmy Choos and cheap perfume; there was no longer the scent of the street, or the hungry, in his rooms. All that was left were two privileged individuals looking at each other, unable to stir any desire in their opportunity-fattened hearts.

Without speaking, Clementine reached for her dress, tugged it quickly over her head, pulling her hands through the short sleeves. She drank the rest of her whisky, acutely aware of the ring of moisture left on his expensive desk. Clementine hesitated before she left. She wondered if she should say something? Lucian's depression had descended like a fog around him. There was no penetrating that cloud. Legs feeling like lead, sinking feeling in her stomach, Clementine made it to the door. She ran down the spiral staircase into the rain in the court. She had no umbrella, and the rain pelted her face, washing away her make-up, her mascara, and leaving only dirty streaks down her face. Clementine walked back to her room feeling hungry and unsatisfied. She bought a kebab from Gardies that night and sat on the floor to devour it, swigging from a bottle of cold white wine that her gyp-mate had left in the communal fridge. She would be annoyed when she found it gone. She could go to hell, thought Clementine.

CHAPTER 7

The Easter term began easily for Lucian, with the warm weather, the girls in their short, floral dresses, the endless rounds of pints in the beer garden at The Anchor or a couple of bottles of Bollinger beneath the willows on Lammas Land. The students took whole days off from study, to punt along the backs, or all the way to Grantchester, mooring by the side of the river under the shade of the weeping-willows, to eat strawberries and drink. It was pure *Brideshead*, and Lucian was not immune to its charms. Lucian had almost forgotten Kimberley, and her dramatic exit from his life, and he certainly had no desire to give her much thought. It was the final term. Lucian knew he should be in the library, but the fine weather was like monosodium glutamate; the sun, once felt, warm on the back, and nape of the neck, and the warm grass, once breathed, were irresistible, and put him in an urgent mood to be outside.

Lucian lay on the banks of the Cam at Paradise, amid the yellowing grasses, waiting for the punt to come by and collect him. The sky was tear-drop blue. He was reading a book and switching from his back to his stomach every fifteen minutes. He timed these regular turns on his watch. It would be foolish to get burnt. He prided himself on his perfect summer tan. The sun made the soil smell like clay fresh from a potter's kiln. It was almost the end of the academic year. He was alone and satisfied with his solitude. People were irksome to him; of course he needed them, women, in particular, to satisfy his more craven urges, and he needed them, men and women, to be in awe of him. But he did not care for them much at all, and this made life a little bitter. It made him feel hollow and lonely as if right in the centre of his being there existed a yawning chasm, an oubliette where happiness went to die. Sometimes it was necessary to express an emotion towards one's fellow human beings, and Lucian could only think along the lines of what was required of him and what was the done thing. These expressions of emotion, even the subtler ones, were for him a source of irritation and failure. Yes, he got what he wanted, mostly, but when he didn't, or when he was unable to hold onto a sense of power and control, he found himself all at sea. It was at these times that he truly doubted himself. After a moment like this he would have to prove himself in some way, by winning on the ergs, acing an exam or fucking a girl who might be out of his league or already taken. These were the only ways to pacify his greed.

Lucian, as he was on that perfect Cambridge summer day, was almost as complete a being as anyone, to all outward appearances. He swigged water from his flask and contemplated two swans gracefully meandering down the Cam.

There is a feeling one gets in youth, thought Lucian, where things are almost perfect; all the ingredients are there. Youth, for one, time, beauty, sunshine, cool flowing water, Cambridge, being considered brilliant, being slim and sporty, being admired, your life altered forever and only twenty-one years old, Cambridge would be with you no matter what happened. Over the years, people will ask where you studied and when you reply they will raise their eyebrows or breathe in like the word is a sweet scent or a shard. You will have impressed them with the utterance, you will have gone up in their esteem, or you will have made them feel small and unworthy. It will colour your life and all the interactions you have forthwith. Any country you visit, the world over, will have heard its hallowed name; it is difficult to go on without feeling like a cushion has been placed beneath your feet. That you will forever walk on your own slice of golden ground, head and shoulders above the rest. A tall poppy, an object of admiration, and jealousy. It is folly to pretend otherwise, thought Lucian.

But Lucian was not the type to be so easily satisfied. Now, he thought, I must square my shoulders to the next thing, the next rung that I must climb. Lucian thought about where he stood in relation to his peers. Sometimes this type of thought was painful. He saw things in his peers that he would rather not see, talents and abilities that made his own pale in comparison. No matter, he would say, I'm running on a different fuel: unstoppable ambition.

There are, broadly speaking, two types who receive a place at Cambridge, thought Lucian: the outrageously gifted – those who are Newton's or Wittgenstein's already; and those who have the terrible and burning ambition to be there. The first types are interesting, no doubt, and works will be written about them, but they are brilliant without effort. So what about the rest? Cambridge is possibly more full of people from the second category, for whom no other institution would be good enough. They have seen their Durhams and their Bristols and they know nothing else comes close. So let us talk of blind ambition.

No other university would have done for Lucian. He had aced every exam at Winchester. He was a sportsman: rowing and rugby primarily. He excelled at history and debating, he played the violin and piano to grade eight but considered music to be only a small embellishment on his academic record. From the age of fourteen he had Cambridge well within his sights and nothing, no person or turn of events, would get in his way. He even had his life planned after Cambridge. He would be picked up by a top investment bank, he would earn millions in bonuses, he would have a Victoria's Secret model girlfriend. He was cold in his determination even then. Anyone who he perceived to be an obstacle between him and his goal would be ruthlessly cut out of his life.

He did not speak to his mother for an entire year. She had set her sights on him attending Durham as she had done. He could not understand why his mother would set her sights so low. He could sleepwalk his way into a place at Durham. To make a point he never put it on his UCAS application form; he only applied to Cambridge. Never would he go to any of those so-called 'universities' even though he was positive all of them would offer him a place. Cambridge was the real prize because it was so exclusive and difficult to get into. Not only did you need the right grades (well, that's a given), but you also needed to ace an interview; in fact, you needed to persuade people who were at the forefront of their field that they would enjoy teaching you. Then, you needed to sit an exam, to prove on paper that you weren't just some spoon-fed automaton from the private-school system. And nowadays private schools were on a type of quota system, so you had to really stand out at school. Lucian stood out. He always had and always would.

So, as he lay on the grass, he felt content for a moment. A moment was all he allowed himself, because his sights were now set on the next prize – lining up a job in investment banking. He would take a First in his part two exams; nothing but a First would do. He was more than capable of achieving a First according to his DOS and tutors.

Sometimes, he had the urge to take time out. Perhaps because he was wound up so tight most of the time, these moments of relaxation sometimes became reckless or debauched. He would plan for these debacles, these three-day benders, scheduling them into his jam-packed schedule, making sure he had one every three months (usually during the holidays). It was strange to step off the treadmill. He would begin by looking up some old school acquaintances (people he was unlikely to need in the future); somehow one can be more oneself around people you do not esteem. Being around them was light and fluffy and safe. He could be a dickhead.

It was then he heard a familiar voice calling from the river, the sound dragging him away from his thoughts.

It was his coxswain, Reuven, in a punt with a bunch of other rowers. Although Lucian had vowed that he would chain himself to his desk rather than waste this golden opportunity to revise for his final exams, he had somehow been persuaded to go on an afternoon punt by his fellow rowers, to drink and stare at girls out on the river.

Lucian packed up his leather satchel and blanket and walked, topless, to the edge of the river. One of the boys shouted, 'You sexy motherfucker!'

Lucian jumped into the punt, which almost sent the boy who had shouted into the water. Lucian laughed and settled himself on one of the cushions. Reuven passed him a cold Leffe. They watched as three teenage girls swam in the river alongside a big hay bale, which someone had thrown in for a lark. The girls took it in turn to try and sit atop the bale. As they passed them, one of his fellow rowers wolf-whistled, causing the girls to giggle and swim away; they were too young to know what they should do when they received attention from men.

They continued up the river, each taking turns to stand on the till and punt – at the Cambridge end. They drank Pol Roger cooled in a large ice box they had taken with them. Turquoise-bellied dragonflies danced around the boat and water skaters flitted over the brown-green surface. Halfway down the river, towards Grantchester, there was an immaculately kept strip of lawn with two sets of wooden steps down to the river. Behind the lawn was a thick laurel hedge, behind which emanated the sound of men and women's voices and laughter. It was called the Newnham Riverbank Club, and it comprised various members of the university and their families. Many of its members liked to sun themselves and take swims without the formality of swimming costumes. A sixty-year-old woman swam by the lawns in her floral swimming cap. She waved to the boys as they passed on the boat and asked for the time. One shouted back the time, remarking to his fellows, 'Isn't she a bit old for that? Not the kind of thing I want to see on a Saturday afternoon!' They all laughed, and the conversation turned to the latest girls that the squad were fixated on. They always rated them with marks out of ten and discussed how far they thought each would go. Lucian was bored; he lolled in the boat. He did not care to discuss women with other men. He liked to hold tight to his sexual experiences, guarding them like a hungry dog. He never wanted them to know who he was hunting for fear they might upset the chase.

There was a party on Grantchester Meadow. Long-haired, pale, goth types lay on the grass, high as kites, having snorted vast quantities of MDMA. Others were smoking weed from yacht pipes bought from Frederick Tranters. Lucian liked Tranters; the chap behind the till looked with surly exasperation as students went in trying to appear knowledgeable about tobacco. It was his dominion and he appeared to prefer all his days to be customer-free, even if that meant he would go bankrupt in two years. Cambridge used to be consistent and predictable, and now horrific modern arcades had sprung up like mushrooms, encouraging the shopping classes into the city's historic heart. Lucian never wanted to see the modern; he avoided it where he could, sticking to the well-worn streets between the colleges, trying not to venture more than a mile from St Mary's. He believed that he would one day live in a beautiful European city like Riga, Venice or Prague.

They moored the punt by the soft soil of the bank with the rope wrapped around a protruding root. Lucian walked with the others towards the disposable barbecue, where a smell of overcooked burgers and sausages lingered in the air. The girls all had daisies and dandelions in their hair and buttercup bracelets on their wrists. Some were sitting topless in the high grasses by the river. A floppy-haired second year sat in their midst with his guitar, singing requests. A gaggle of young girls were around him, looking up like he was some deity. The sun was going down, but it had been hot enough to burn a few of the fairer-skinned students, who were beginning to look very uncomfortable as they examined the white marks left by the straps of their tops and the raw skin either side.

Lucian took off his jacket, seated himself on a patch of grass, within viewing distance of the group. Close enough to feel the warmth of the fire when it was lit. Some of the girls occasionally threw him sideways glances, but as he had separated himself slightly from the pack, they were unsure what to make of him, so they did not approach.

He sat alone and watched the sun set over the fields of sugar beet and yellow rapeseed. There were still a couple of swimmers in the river; he listened to the steady splash of their strokes. The cicadas started their evening chorus. The other rowers tried to beckon him over but he maintained his supercilious repose. Socialising was sometimes a necessary evil. Eventually, he got up and joined the throng by the fire. His teammates slapped him on the back; he was a real mensch, a dude, one of them again. The touch of their fingers upon his skin, even through the cotton of his shirt, was repulsive to him. He did not need physical contact with acquaintances; he didn't understand the informality of hugging as a demonstration of feeling. Men should be men: aloof and unreachable, always strong. Even if a woman he was sleeping with were to hug him he would shake her off and get rid of her quickly for not getting the measure of him fast enough. That type of affection was anathema to Lucian. The firelight lit up the young faces with their clear eyes and white teeth.

Someone suggested a game of strip poker around the fire. As the clothes came off, the group became tighter, more intimate; those who had already coupled off lay down next to each other, their faces in the shadows.

Lucian didn't want to play; he was quite tempted to just grab the hand of the girl nearest to him, as that was always a good excuse. Luckily, he was good at the game and only had to remove his shirt. Once he had revealed how ripped he was, two girls shifted over to his side of the fire, one on his right, the other on his left. They seemed to be competing for his attention, but he remained cold, causing them to compete harder; he loved that feeling best of all. One had a hand on his thigh and the other tried to lean her head against his shoulder while circling his bicep with her arm. One, he guessed, was a Cambridge girl. It was the preppy look that was the giveaway, the brown brogues at the end of her long, tanned legs, the white cricket jumper slung around her shoulders and the small diamond studs in her ears, the hair half-up and half-down, a messy look, painstakingly crafted.

The girl on his left looked like an art student from APU. The giveaways were: she was white but had her blonde hair braided into tight squares on her head, which, to be honest, looked a little straggly given the fineness of the hair and nothing like Bo Derek. She had inkings on her inner arms and some sort of insect on her neck; it could be an artistic impression of a grasshopper. She had big blue eyes as pale as the sky and she used them to her advantage, to look up into his face when she spoke to him. As she paused between comments she bit her lip seductively, which Lucian found extremely distracting and irritating at the same time. He could not take his eyes off her. He couldn't decide which one he would have; maybe they would be amenable to the idea of a threesome, but he didn't want to have to work that hard. He decided to choose the one who probably thought she would not be chosen. The preppy girl was better-looking objectively, so he decided to go for the APU one. He'd like to keep the private-school girl's ego in check, so he discarded her like a toffee paper and led the other girl off into the taller grass. He wondered how the Cambridge girl felt; it was great when women gave him power like that. Why do they do it, he thought, debasing themselves all the time, looking desperate. She would probably go home and stick her fingers down her throat, wondering why she wasn't pretty enough.

CHAPTER 8

A line of girls in ball dresses wound down King's Parade, every colour of the spectrum, like a swarm of hothouse butterflies; the men in their white bow ties and tuxes looked like awkward penguins. It was a warm, balmy evening and the festivities would be in full swing within the hour. They were already swigging Pol Roger from the bottle. Girls lifting the bottle with their bony arms, and laughing at how puny they were, their lipstick smudged on the cheeks of their favourites.

Lucian hadn't bought a ticket for the Peterhouse ball. He had won a bet, with a fellow rower called Johann – a Danish guy – who had forfeited his ticket to Trinity May Ball. Johann was supposed to be turning up to his room any moment now to deliver the ticket. Lucian couldn't wait to see his fair, honest face with that look of disappointment hiding under a cheerful veneer. If Lucian hadn't won the bet, he would've squirmed out of the deal like a well-oiled rat. There was no way he'd miss this ball if he had a ticket.

He licked his lips thinking of the girl in the Novice Boat that he'd given his number to yesterday. She'd been texting him, checking that he was going to be there. It somehow felt much better that he'd acquired the ticket by this means rather than forking out three hundred quid (although it wasn't like money was ever an issue for Lucian). Money probably was tight for this fucking Danish guy who the girls swooned over (more than they swooned over Lucian – which was a fair amount). Anyway, this guy was a good rower, but not as experienced as Lucian, who had rowed all through school and immediately made First Boat at college, to become stroke and get his blades. This Johann sat in seven seat, directly behind Lucian, who lost no time in correcting his every slip. Lucian was known as the 'beast'. He liked 'beasting' his crew on the ergs. He shouted like an angry sergeant major with a hernia during their erg sessions when the coach wasn't present, and then afterwards he would go back to being taciturn and monosyllabic. And Johann accepted all of this calmly.

The bet had been about a fresher who was trying to make the First Boat. The new guy was six five and built like a tank, but Lucian had whispered to Johann that he could make this guy vomit from a beasting in under twenty minutes. Looking at the guy, you wouldn't think it were possible for him to even break a sweat, so Johann's incredulity was understandable. However, Johann made the mistake of betting with Lucian – and betting something that was rather valuable to him, namely, his Trinity May Ball ticket. The new guy put on a good show, but Lucian knew the underhand tricks, got the guy to down a litre of water before the beasting under the pretence that it would do him good to hydrate. The guy called him a cocksucker afterwards, but he made the squad, so everyone was laughing apart from Johann, who looked bemused.

'But you cheated,' he said in his matter-of-fact Danish way.

'No,' said Lucian, 'I won.'

Lucian had hung up his white tie from Henry Poole. It looked like a headless spectre hanging up on the cupboard door. He was in his boxers, smoking a pink Sobranie Cocktail, drinking gin, just to get him in the party mood.

At eight o'clock there was a knock at the door. It was Johann, but he was not alone. He appeared to have two bodyguards: Claudia and a brunette. Lucian smirked to hide the fact that he was annoyed at the surprise of seeing this little throng. He had hoped that the ticket would be transferred to his person without any complications, but now he smelt a trap.

'Lucian, man,' said Johann in his earnest English, 'I'm sorry, I was going to come alone.' That was as far as he got.

Claudia quickly butted in. 'He's not giving you his ticket,' she said saucily, her off-the-shoulder baby-pink Alexander McQueen dress quivering over the edges of her décolletage.

'Ladies, ladies,' said Lucian in his most disparagingly paternal tones, though he was raging inside, 'Please, why don't we start the party in my room, no one wants to arrive early at this ball – it looks desperate.'

All he could think was fuck this blonde Danish Johann with his two stuck-up bitches. Why the hell does he have two, the greedy motherfucker?! I'm not letting this get in the way of the evening.

'Are you going to offer me a drink?' Claudia asked

sourly.

'My dear, I have a drinks cabinet in here and a range of other recreational pharmaceuticals, as you well know.'

Her neat light-coloured eyebrows raised, and she barged in.

Lucian still hadn't forgiven Claudia for her behaviour at the Pitt Club. Lucian felt she had embarrassed him. That was not something he could easily forgive or forget. He made up his mind to get her wasted – see if he could humiliate her just a teeny bit.

It was true that he had weed and a little MDMA; his dealer had been less than forthcoming recently, as he was buying on credit. He would only offer MDMA, as it gets girls in the mood – and why not, even the brunette wasn't bad-looking.

The brunette came in more cautiously, looking around the place, sniffing it out. Claudia sat down on his bed while the brunette perused his bookcase. Johann didn't know where to put himself; he had the look of a Chelsea ratdog who's taken a shit in a Prada handbag.

'Johann, sit down, take the goddam chaise longue.'

'God, what's that for, Dr Freud?' The brunette clearly thought of herself as a bit of a wit.

Lucian ignored her and turned his attention to Claudia. 'So, gin and tonic or perhaps something stronger?'

Claudia smiled, showing a neat white row of teeth, all the whiter because of her cardinal red lipstick. Lucian was still in his boxers but this seemed to be having a profound effect on Claudia. She kept checking out his abs, with little shy sideways glances as if she had caught him in flagrante delicto. Yum, thought Lucian, it almost made him forget his desire to punish her. One of the great things about clever people with clever people is that you don't have to spend the evening trying to outsmart each other, you simply get down to the task of getting your enormous brains entirely wasted, Lucian thought. That brunette, thought Lucian, is probably a Com-Sci. Claudia was reading English. Female English undergrads are all nymphos, probably because the male English undergrads are all gay, thought Lucian. It makes them horny, that lack of testosterone in their tutorials.

Lucian went to the cabinet and slid out a small, concealed inner drawer. MDMA is the perfect party aperitif: it makes your ego inflate to the size of a helium balloon and the night just gets better and better until it pops in an entirely mellow way. Lucian prepared the powder, cut it on a small mirror, divided it into four neat parallel lines. He rolled up a five-pound note, carefully selecting the least grubby one in his wallet. Normally, he would use something a good deal more sanitary, but he was trying to appear reckless and wild. He handed it to Claudia. He still didn't know the brunette's name, but who cares, he thought. She snorted up the line and rubbed the remainder on her gums. The others took their turns while he passed around the bottle of gin. After he had his line, Johann had another moment of earnestness.

'Yo, man, I'm sorry. Claudia doesn't take no for an answer. I told her you won the ticket fair and square. I mean, she doesn't give up.'

Good Lord, sighed Lucian internally, a guy like that, built like Achilles and he just follows that little bitch like she's goddam Helen of Troy. Well, this isn't the face that sunk a thousand ships; it's just a barely passable little girl face with blonde hair and straight teeth. Sometimes, thought Lucian, he'd like to make a girl eat shards of glass, just for fun. It would be great if he could do that one day.

Claudia was looking at him, her pupils dilated, spilling out of her blue eyes. The brunette was now sitting on the bed too. The brunette had a pointy, weasel-like face; she thinks she is very superior, thought Lucian. She took a cigarette out of his case and lit it up without asking his permission. Johann had by now relaxed a little, reclined in Lucian's ergonomic desk chair. Claudia was rummaging in her little silver Gucci handbag; she pulled out a ticket.

'So, I have this as a spare,' she said nonchalantly.

'Of course you do,' laughed Lucian.

'I was waiting to see how much of a dickhead you were going to be.'

'Lucky me,' said Lucian.

Johann looked embarrassed.

'He wasn't wrong,' she teased.

'I'm not sure I care to go now,' Lucian said with mock hurt.

'You'll come,' she smirked.

'Claudia, you didn't tell me you had another ticket,' wailed Johann. 'God, I feel like such an idiot. Lucian, I'm sorry.'

'Don't worry, Jan, shit happens.'

'To happy endings!' Claudia lifted the bottle and glugged too freely, and the expensive nectar ran down her chin.

'Shit, my fucking make-up,' she said, scrambling to pull out a small compact from her bag.

Lucian reached over to her chin and the little droplet and scooped it up with his index finger. 'Exquisite,' he said as he licked it from his finger with his tongue. And with that one little half-compliment he knew he had her hooked again somehow. There was an almost imperceptible flush on her honeyed cheeks, eyes a little wider, lips moving slower, more seductively. Lucian felt the catch in his stomach, the blood beat in his chest, saliva filling his mouth. It tasted like winning.

They all did another line and had a few more swigs of gin before making their way out to the court and the mayhem that abounded. Buena Vista Social Club was playing "Chan Chan". You'd have thought they'd pick something a little less nineties chic. A man dressed as a Turk was slicing off champagne corks with a scimitar. The theme was Empire. The college was divided into Greek, Roman, Egyptian, Ottoman and British.

Lucian put all his effort into getting pretty little Claudia drunk. He ordered glass after glass of champagne and tried to get her to shake off Johann and the brunette. Unfortunately, drinking only seemed to make Claudia more gregarious and sociable. No, she would not retreat to the lawns by the river. No, she was not interested in leaving the bright lights of the party to go and be alone with Lucian. She twirled round and round and would not be satisfied until all the boys around her had hard-ons. Lucian looked on, hating her, hating himself.

Eventually, Lucian had had enough and snuck off. He had spotted someone else, a girl looking pretty and drunk by Imhotep's tomb. She sat on a sarcophagus and sipped her aviation cocktail. Her legs were coiled together; she looked cold. Her companion had fallen asleep, propped up against a sphinx.

She was Asian, with thick dark hair cut into a bob. Lucian introduced himself and found out that she was from Hong Kong. She was slurring quite badly and had lost one of her shoes. Lucian took this to be a good omen. She had wonderful skin, he thought. They played a drunken game of spot the public-school boy. It was not hard, as most of them were congregating around a piano singing made-up drinking songs. Whoever failed to come up with a line had to down a shot. Lucian secretly despised the rowing drinking game called pennying. He took part so as not to stand out too much but he always secretly hoped that someone would choke on the penny and die. It would do wonders for camaraderie and morale – a team united in mourning, emerging stronger and better afterwards – Champions of the Cam.

'Oh shit,' Lucian almost said out loud. Claudia was back. She was meandering towards him with mascara smudged around her eyes, a top hat (that she must have nabbed from some admirer) and her dress falling off her shoulders. This looked promising. Claudia was the type of girl who got overdramatic when she was drunk.

She came over to him and draped her arms around his neck. She said she'd been abandoned by Johann and chastised Lucian for leaving her alone by the chocolate fountain.

'You naughty thing,' she said, wagging her ringed finger at him seductively. Her mouth was close to his neck; he could feel her breath and smell the alcohol on it. It took all his self-restraint not to fling her down on the lawns and do what she wanted him to do to her. The other girl raised her eyebrows sleepily, smiled like she was unimpressed with this turn of events, but she was too drunk to be greatly dismayed.

'Claudia, meet Susie. Susie, meet Claudia,' he said politely. The girls nodded to each other and Claudia crossed her slim arms over her chest in a defensive pose.

'So, what are you reading?' she asked Susie, utterly uninterested in her answer.

'Nat-Sci,' replied Susie.

'Oh nice.'

'You?' asked Susie.

'English. Which college are you at?' Claudia had slipped into full interrogation mode.

'Robinson,' replied Susie.

Claudia winced. 'Don't you find it ghastly?'

'What?' asked Susie.

'I mean it's a red-brick monstrosity.'

'Oh,' replied Susie.

'In my opinion its worse than Churchill Chapel, the typewriter, or the University Centre combined. In fact, Robinson makes Cripps look like The Parthenon.'

'I like you,' said Susie, with mock frankness. 'Come and sit down with us.'

Claudia assented.

Lucian sighed. He had thought for a split second that this could be his moment. Looking around, it was clear the party was winding up; all that was left in the room was the detritus of a long night, several bodies, a sticky floor and one broken piano.

Lucian certainly did not want to hang around for the

survivors' breakfast, although it was the thing to do. He wanted to invite both ladies back to his room for a nightcap, but then something stopped him. He looked at them with their expensive dresses, the products of expensive education; they both had so much to protect them from what he wanted from them, and even if they were to let him do whatever he liked, they'd probably just turn out to be radical feminists who would scream rape. No, he was going about it all wrong; he needed someone who had no power, who would be dominated and accept her lot. He started to think he was in the wrong place. Perhaps, he thought, not for the first time, that while he was at Cambridge he should remain entirely celibate.

He needed to get his degree completed with no hiccups and no scandals. The two girls were already deep in a drunken conversation with each other, pretending to be best friends, the way rivals do. He excused himself by saying he would get them both another drink. He headed out of the double doors onto the lawn with not the slightest inclination of returning. He saw Johann and the brunette sitting together on the lawns. They would no doubt make the survivors' photo. Lucian went back to his rooms, locked the door and fell onto his bed. He was fast asleep within minutes.

CHAPTER 9

Clementine had not attended the Trinity May Ball, though she guessed that Lucian would have. She couldn't justify the cost, as she was down to her last few pounds and unsure of how she would get through the next two weeks. She couldn't ask her parents for money for the ball as they already thought she had been irresponsible going on the Varsity Trip.

Since her disastrous rendezvous with Lucian, she had contemplated paying him a surprise visit but she doubted that would go down well with him. He would hate his very precise schedule to be interrupted. Days turned to weeks and the start of the summer holiday was suddenly only a fortnight away. She roamed by the river just to catch a glimpse of him in the eight or talking with his teammates outside the boathouse. She drifted through the remaining lecture circuits, fin de siècle, modernism and the short story, she haunted the English Faculty library and the dark corridors and mysterious staircases of the University Library – that large and imposing edifice that looked more like a chocolate factory. She waited in a corner of the Sidgwick Site to watch Lucian pass by each day on his way to the History Faculty. Her heart pounded and she sweated even though she normally didn't sweat at all.

Clementine could not decide what she gained by looking for him every day. It only seemed to bring his presence closer, so much so that she dreamed about him every night. In her dreams she transformed his character into something manageable, but often still in the middle of the dream he did something unnerving and unexpected or another lady arrived on the scene and his attention switched, which Clementine felt like a fist in her gut. She could not understand why she wanted him so very much and found everything he did so interesting and alluring. She tried to beat it out of herself with long hours of study, trying to spend time with her mundane group of friends, all of whom were eminently unattractive to her. She could hardly focus on what they said for more than a few seconds. On and on they droned about something and nothing. She got so bored of their carefulness and their preoccupation with doing well in exams. She hated the way they went to dinner together, yet everybody was there cramming from their books and all you could hear was the slurp of soup or knives and forks grinding against the plates.

She imagined all the things he was doing. Being a rower, he had an active social life, even if he didn't particularly relish it. Whenever she saw a pretty girl near him, her insides turned over. She kept telling herself that this behaviour was not her. She was a watcher of people; she didn't take part in life. Clementine had never been an active participant in life, and up until this moment she had always thought that was perfectly fine. It turned out that in the case of Lucian Dorsey, this long-held assumption about herself no longer held true. Since in reality she had no idea who Lucian truly was, she had created an elaborate fiction bordering on a dark obsession, which compelled her to glimpse at him at least twice a day; otherwise, she felt as if he were slipping away. Her rational brain was laughing at her predicament – if it were anyone else she would have laughed her head off at how pathetic they were.

He probably knew that she was watching him. She was not particularly discreet anymore. Sometimes she thought she saw him shoot her a glance. She couldn't tell if the emotion he expressed was irritation or amusement. There was the girl, Claudia, whom he seemed to be spending more time with. Clementine wished she could be as desirable as her. Admittedly, Claudia probably spent her life at the gym, getting just the right amount of glow on a tanning bed, getting her nails manicured. She had probably had a boob job. She was the type to have got it done between school and the start of university. Her hair was always perfect, her skin clear, without a blemish. She felt the summer holidays rolling towards her – eleven long weeks spanning ahead hopelessly, and all she had planned was an internship. Admittedly, it was an internship with the *FT*, but she could picture herself now daydreaming about Lucian all day, getting no work done, scuppering her chances at a real paid position in the future. And then next year Lucian would be gone – he no doubt already had a job secured with a top firm. He wouldn't look back to his time at Cambridge; he would simply set his sights on the next goal.

Clementine wanted to get Claudia away from him, or him from her, but she still could not figure out how to do that, and anyway there were only a few weeks left before the end of term. She decided on one last throw-caution-to-the-wind visit to Lucian's rooms. A later call would be best, she thought. He had been keeping pretty regular hours of late, always leaving his room at 8.30 am on the dot to make the 9 am lecture circuit at the History Faculty, and nearly always returning to his room after dinner in hall at about 8 pm. He then stayed in; presumably he was still studying for his last few exams. Clementine hung around in his gyp, with the friend, Sam, she kept for convenience's sake, who just happened to be his next-door neighbour. Sam was boring beyond measure, but Clementine kept her supplied with brownies and currant buns from Nadia's bakery. She also fetched her favourite vanilla lattes from Starbucks. As Sam was overweight and beset by insecurities, possibly agoraphobia, she seemed to welcome Clementine's attention. Clementine tried to be as genuine as possible, which was hard, because she veritably despised this type of fat, insecure creature, who slouched around in a leavers' hoodie from her old school. She lived in that old grey thing, and it was stained with flecks of sauce and bits of egg yolk from her rather messy cooked breakfasts.

Clementine kept one ear out for Lucian's door: the exits and entrances that made her spine tingle with excitement. Sometimes, she managed to persuade Sam to invite her to a formal hall, which occurred every night at Peterhouse. The girl was reluctant to go because there were 'too many people' but Clementine reassured her that the hall was candlelit and in the semi-darkness it wouldn't feel like everyone was staring at her. Internally, Clementine scoffed – as if anyone would be looking at her; no one would give her a second glance – she was so dull and frumpy.

When Clementine finally got her wish, it was on a night when most of the Peterhouse rowing squad were dining together. She was thrilled to see Lucian in his blazer, sitting with all the other tall, muscular rowers who look like young gods. Clementine only had eyes for Lucian. She observed the elegant way he ate his first course, smirking at the vulgar jokes made by his companions but never taking part. He was so dignified and mysterious, thought Clementine. She hardly touched her food, as she was so entranced by the way Lucian ate his beef bourguignon, with its little new potatoes and petit pois. He did not shovel the peas like everyone else, but instead decisively pierced them with short, stabbing motions. He ate quickly but not uncouthly, the potatoes disappearing in quick succession, through his lovely lips, touched by his tongue. Clementine found herself extremely jealous of those potatoes. If he had noticed her presence, he made no indication that he had. This was the way it had been between them for weeks now. Clementine got satisfaction from watching and he seemed satisfied in being 'the watched'. She believed now that he did find it oddly satisfying; otherwise, he would surely have said something to her by now. Her propensity to watch, to obsess, was nothing new and by now she knew the signs when somebody was beginning to get uncomfortable.

She decided to make a last attempt to see him in person, face to face. She decided it must be that very day. It seemed she had waited too long already, and her procrastination was not getting her any further in her pursuit.

That evening she selected a dress, something she wouldn't usually dare to wear (thin straps and cut very low). As she got ready there was the sense of it being a ritual. She closed the curtains of her room and lit a few old floating candles she had lying about. She put the candles in a bowl of water so that the reflections cast strange shadows on her wall and watery spirits danced in mad, writhing contortions. She wore no jewellery apart from a chain of silver around her wrist – a present from her father when she finished her A-levels. The silver reminded her of the things she ought to be doing, the ambitions which, for the time being, had fallen by the wayside. She promised herself she would get her life back in order, just as soon as things with Lucian had been clarified. Here she trailed off in thought. She still had no idea if her self-'cure' would work, if all of a sudden she would be released from her fascination, her obsession with Lucian. It was terrible not knowing for sure. At least five times she went to the mirror, looking at herself in the dress, beginning to remove it, then stopping. There was something in her eyes that she had never seen before. It was an aliveness that made her appear more beautiful. Her hair was wavy, on account of her not blow-drying it straight after her shower. She could not decide what Lucian would prefer: straight or wavy. She realised that slowly, obsequiously, everything in her life was being set to Lucian's imagined preferences. In the supermarket earlier that day, she went to pick up an apple and then the thought occurred to her: Lucian preferred the scent of oranges and the zest of lemons. She had put down the apple immediately before fully realising her thought process.

Now, as she stood there contemplating her body, she started to hate the curve of her hips: Lucian would like them to be more defined, to jut out more; she was certain that he preferred thin women. He liked to be in charge, to take command of any situation; he would no doubt find a larger woman intimidating or disgusting. He seemed to prefer his women ultra-feminine and blonde if possible. She loathed the blonde hair on her: it made her dark eyebrows look ridiculous, and even Lucian has said she looked better brunette. However, she had seen the way he looked at blonde women, and she couldn't help but want to be stared at in that way, like when a magpie sets its sights on something shiny and wishes to possess it at any cost. She wanted to arouse that hunger in him.

She barely remembered to extinguish the candles as she left her room, wrapped in her undergraduate gown. The distance between Trinity and Peterhouse was not far; she walked through Trinity Great Court and through Trinity Street, past Great St Mary's and on to King's Parade with its throngs of students meeting, kissing and hugging and going off to bars and parties. There was a celebratory vibe in the air, as finals had almost ended, and everyone wanted to let their hair down and have a good time.

She had to watch where she was going over the cobble stones and uneven paving: she was not used to walking in high heels and felt incredibly conspicuous.

A dozen times she wanted to turn back. She felt the weight of his possible rejection upon her and it was almost unbearable. She managed to get to the front gate at Peterhouse. She took a deep breath and stepped through. The porters recognised her and gave her their usual cool greeting, calling her Miss, using her surname. She didn't like being known by them: it made her feel like they knew her mission and could feel her desperation. She went down the familiar paths and corridors. The courts were quiet and cool. There was a tour taking place in the corner of Great Court. She headed up the staircase and hovered outside Lucian's door. She believed he would be in, but she knew how her heart would sink if he weren't.

She rapped lightly, three times on the white lacquer. She couldn't hear any movement inside. She didn't want to be cornered by Lucian's neighbour, who was clattering about in the gyp. She plucked up the courage and knocked again. The door suddenly burst open, just like a frying pan spits when a drop of water gets into the oil. He was there, looking annoyed and frustrated and sexy as hell. She was almost scared, so she stood there clutching her little handbag, feeling small and weak, now she was in front of his strong, healthy, muscular body.

'For fuck's sake!' He grabbed her hand and this time he was not messing around. He pulled her into the room and her handbag went flying, its contents spilling onto the floor: a tampon, a red lipstick, a set of keys. He was pulling at her gown, which fell down by her ankles. He didn't stop to look at the dress; everything came off. Clementine felt as if she were being skinned alive, peeled like an orange. Before she could say yes or no, she was standing there exposed, naked, in just her ridiculous shoes, which made her nakedness even more pronounced. His mouth was on hers, and then on her collar bones, on her neck, on her breasts. He picked her up like a doll and took her to the bed. She knelt up on the bed, and he did too; she pulled at his sweater like a wild thing, wanting to yank away anything that separated their two skins. He kissed her mouth hard, so hard that their teeth clicked, but he didn't stop to see if she was ok. She felt a slight trickle; her mouth was actually bleeding from the force of the kiss, but Lucian didn't care and nor did she. She had never felt so much desire, so blindingly ravenous, and there was nothing but the physicality of the thing, the urgency of humans who have thrown away any semblance of civilisation. She could not stop herself from moaning out loud and whimpering. He told her to shut up but she continued to make the sounds until he slapped her in the face. She loved the contact of his hand on her cheek, the burning sensation of the blow.

His torso was tanned and he looked like the god Atlas. It was like being devoured by the sun, thought Clementine. She let him do what he wanted, and everything at the speed that he wanted. She did not complain; she became his plaything. Somehow, he could do no wrong; she was annoyed with herself, at becoming so passive, but she could not help herself. He was master of the situation. It seemed to go on and on, different positions, Lucian exploring her body so that he derived maximum pleasure from the experience. She wanted to say 'I love you' over and again and cry and hold him. But she knew how that kind of outburst would be greeted by him, and she knew how pathetic she would feel about it the next day. I am better than that, thought Clementine, and his ego doesn't need any more inflating.

After he had finished, she was sore everywhere; she looked at the red marks on her body and lay there, in Lucian's bed, feeling perfectly content. He turned his back to her, put on his shorts, lit a cigarette and sat back on the pillows. He didn't offer her a cigarette or even a drag. She wanted to cling to his chest, to always feel his skin on hers, but it was clear that he didn't feel that way. His passion was spent and now he just wanted his space and distance, to be his own entity, entirely separate from her. Lucian wanted to rest, he told her; he wanted to sprawl in his big bed by himself, to smoke and go to sleep alone. She didn't want to leave but she wouldn't dream of saying a thing. Meekly she put her dress back on and then her gown over the top; she didn't bother with the heels, and instead carried them by the straps. Now for the walk of shame, thought Clementine.

She returned to her room like a zombie, emotionally weathered, physically aching. She took a long shower and washed the red welts, which were turning blue-black. She would wear those marks with pride. She wished they would never fade – this from the girl who would never have a tattoo. That was the last time she saw Lucian. In that way she left him, forever in that room, with both of their desires aflame and then extinguished. It was not that it was all she needed or wanted from him; it was simply that the end would come sooner or later, and she preferred sooner, having got what she wanted. He never once contacted her again and she never wrote to him or sought him out. Over the following days and weeks, before he left Cambridge for good, she would glimpse him around the town or in a library. Each time that happened she made her feet walk in the opposite direction. If he saw her, he never once acknowledged it. Clementine felt she had had enough of Lucian to last a lifetime. There were undoubtedly times when she wavered, when she thought she might transgress and run to his room during a restless night, or early in the morning, having lain awake thinking about him for hours. But she knew the repercussions would be too much for her; she could never fully have him, nor he her; it would be a fruitless endeavour. No more could be created by the two of them; everything after that moment would have the taste of tragedy about it.

CHAPTER 10

In the final weeks before his exams Lucian gave up everything apart from rowing. He focused on his revision with a ferocity of dedication. It really pissed off Claudia, but he didn't care. She was a fresher who had unlimited time on her hands, whereas he was in his final year. And as for the other girls, he felt he owed them nothing – not even replies to the numerous text messages. He ignored them all. He was in the library at nine o'clock every morning after thoroughly exhausting his body on the river. His effort was like the concentration of light in a pinhole camera and everything on the periphery of his task became dimmed. He lost awareness of other people; he didn't think about women – and they all (apart from Claudia) mostly kept their distance. Once Claudia knocked on his door, all made up with a short, tight dress, but he just acted distant and gave her the brush-off. He loved watching her walk away pissed off – that was priceless. Women always seemed to think that men could not control their animal urges and when they finally met a man who could resist them, they went wild. He knew she would be back again, but for now he had wounded her pride and she would go and seduce someone else – all the while thinking about him. This gave him enormous satisfaction – imagining her fucking someone else while fantasising about him.

He stayed up late every night and, apart from the occasional slip-up, like the May Ball, he abstained from alcohol and drugs. If someone tried to engage him in time-wasting conversation he replied in monosyllables. His tutor was positive about his progress and his coursework was awarded a high First – before moderation. He was on course to get a First – and that was exactly what he needed to get into one of the leading investment banks – Goldman Sachs, Morgan Stanley, Lehman Brothers, or JP Morgan. Nothing else would do. Years ago, during freshers' week, he had put his name down for all the social events held by the big banks and he had attended more than a dozen. Competition was tough – but he had confidence in his abilities. He could imagine nothing better than being a top-shot investment banker with a million-dollar bonus every year. Lucian spent long hours envisioning himself in that position – he believed that the universe could shift according to the direction of one's thought. When his mother rang him to check how revision was going, he was abrupt and always cut the conversation short. He did not need her to feel proud of him. It was not how he measured his self-worth.

Before bed he worked out and focused his mind on the goal. By the time the exams came round he was prepared, more than anyone else he knew. It felt good to narrow his existence down to a focal point, to give up all distractions, to become monk-like. No doubt that was how the most beautiful illuminations were created – men foregoing all distractions to create things like the *Book of Kells*.

The first exam was at nine o'clock on a Monday morning and was to be held in the old Corn Exchange. He got there early with his candidate number, three freshly sharpened pencils and four black pens. He had a bottle of water and some energy sweets. He had had a good night's sleep and he thought the clear blue sky and the fact that he had not seen any friends so far were both good omens – he did not want an encounter with an acquaintance to break his concentration. Unfortunately, a fellow historian who recognised him from lectures at the History Faculty came over to nervously make small talk.

'Prepared?' he asked, anxiously clutching his revision notes.

'Uhuh,' said Lucian, trying to brush him off, but he did not take the hint.

'No notes?' he asked, looking at how empty-handed Lucian appeared.

'No,' said Lucian curtly.

'You look confident; have you revised much?'

Lucian nodded. He wanted this small, bespectacled loser to leave him alone.

'I get so nervous before an exam, I feel like I'm going to be sick.'

At this, Lucian turned away and started to pace up and down the alley. But the man followed him, walking at his side, trying to engage him in small talk as if his life depended on it. It was maddening and distracting, and Lucian wanted to punch him in the face. Usually, people take a hint that someone wants to be left alone, but this guy was unaware of the effect he was having on Lucian.

After four lengths of the alley Lucian turned to the

man and, close in his face, hissed: 'Just piss off will you.' He did not touch him, but his tone clearly scared the man to death, and he mumbled a 'sorry' and then wandered off to find another unfortunate victim to attach himself to. Lucian felt blood beating in his temples. The encounter had thrown him a little off course. He tried to regain his composure and re-focus on all the information he was trying to keep at the forefront of his mind.

The begowned university invigilators, with their lanyards around their necks, were now ushering the students into the exam room. He followed the long queue into the high-ceilinged Town Hall with its shiny wooden floors. Bags and coats were to be left at the back of the room. He looked around for his name and candidate number and found his place in the left-hand corner of the room. It was next to a radiator and below one of the large windows. Lucian seated himself at the desk. The first thing that he noticed was that the desk had a wobble. He was irritated but there was some lined note paper on the desk and so he folded it up repeatedly until he had made a wedge to put under the shorter desk leg. Once that was done, he tested the desk and found that it no longer moved – the first obstacle had been overcome. He arranged his pens and pencils in the groove at the top of the writing desk. The desk itself was made of pine, but its construction and style looked like a Victorian school desk.

After five minutes everyone had found their desks and the exam could begin. The invigilators, all members of the university, were mostly wearing their black MA gowns. They glided between the rows distributing the exam paper face down. At the front of the hall, written on a large blackboard, were the rules of the exam, clearly stated in white chalk. Refrain from talking, raise your hand if you need assistance, do not turn over the exam paper until you are instructed to do so. Lucian could feel little pinpricks of sweat in the palms of his hands. His heart was hammering in his chest, but he did not know why; there was an aura of tension in the air. He kept telling himself that he was thoroughly prepared, that he knew all he was ever going to know of his subjects, that his First was in the bag.

The bearded invigilator at the front of the hall was wearing a mortar board and looked the epitome of the stern, intellectual don. He went through the rules of the exam in a deep and solemn voice, reminding the candidates that they could go for breaks to smoke or use the lavatory, but they had to do so silently and leave their exam papers on the desk. After being switched off or put on silent mode, the mobile phones were duly collected and stored in a large wooden tray at the front of the hall.

Then, as a hush descended on the hall, the begowned invigilator said, 'You may begin'. Lucian felt all the blood drain out of his hands. He flicked over the exam paper; it was on the topics he had studied. He breathed a sigh of relief. He drew up his plan, wrote down his quotes and sources, pulled out the dates and events that he needed – as he had been taught to do at school – formulated his argument and then put his pen to the fresh lined paper. It was a three-and-a-half-hour exam and for the first forty minutes he was completely absorbed in the task. He began to relax into it and instead of feeling pumped he just felt cold. He shivered in his suit.

CHAPTER 11

Lucian arrived at the Senate House alone. It was results day, and everyone would eventually pass through the gates and look at the class lists posted on boards outside the building. Everyone who sat the exams would find their names there under their awarded class. All the Firsts of a particular Tripos were together, as were the 2.1s, the 2.2s and the Thirds, as well as those who had passed but without honours. Lucian's gut twisted a little when he realised that everyone on his course could see his class, but he remained confident that he would attain his First.

Cambridge is the only university in the United Kingdom which does not classify its degrees, rather the honours examinations for each part of the Tripos are classified. Therefore Lucian would have his results for his Part Two History pinned to a board, there for all to see. This was a long-standing tradition, and though not intended to humiliate the graduating cohort, it inevitably led some to despair, some even to suicide. The Maths Tripos famously used to produce a list of undergraduates' attainment to be read out loud in order; the student who achieved the best results was called the senior wrangler and the lowest attaining third class honours received a wooden spoon;

thus ensued a race to the bottom, with the students in the lower attaining third of the cohort vying with each other to receive the worst results and thereby be awarded the spoon. This practice was therefore abandoned in the sixties after the university realised its incentive structure was somewhat misaligned with what was intended.

Lucien had sailed to a first in Part One of the History Tripos the previous year and had thus been elected a Junior Scholar at Peterhouse, entitling him to his fine 'set' in college.

Lucian was dressed in a dark flannel suit with a fresh sea island cotton shirt and college tie. As he approached the boards, he saw some familiar faces from the History Tripos. One girl was holding a bottle of champagne and as she looked closer at the board, she let out a triumphant whoop. All the others around congratulated her by hugging her or shaking her hand. She took her bottle of champagne to the senate lawns and uncorked it, drinking from the neck of the bottle, before a university proctor told her to move away and go and celebrate in a more suitable place. She moved off with her gaggle; their bright smiles and voices masked the disappointment of others who were mournfully looking at the boards, and looking again before retreating to drown their sorrows at one of Cambridge's numerous pubs.

Lucian walked up the white steps to look at the rickety wooden boards covered in dark green felt, with their pieces of paper neatly secured with drawing pins. He looked for his Tripos, and once he had found that he looked for his name among the two marked with a small asterisk – a star that denoted a recipient of a 'Starred

First', the highest scoring undergraduates in the year. No luck, his name was not one of those so marked – but that was by no means a disaster. His eye then fell to skimming quickly through the other names that had achieved Firsts. He scanned right, and left; there were only twelve names there, but no matter which way he read it he could not see his.

His mind stuttered over the realisation: it was as if he could not allow his eyes to fall lower, to look for his precious surname and initial among the students whom he would have deemed the dregs of the course.

His heart sank, believing some prank was taking place; he looked about him to see if someone was sniggering in a dark corner. But there was no one.

Then his eye, accustomed to seeing the familiar arrangement of letters, fell on the next group of names, the 2.1s. There, bold as day, was his – Lucian Dorsey – along with thirty-five or so others. The shock left him winded and staggering; he felt light-headed and needed to sit down but there was nowhere to sit other than the steps of Senate House. He sat down on the cold Ancaster stone and cradled his head in his hands. It was impossible; there had been a mistake. He thought about who he could appeal to and how he would need to get his work re-marked. It was all an enormous headache, and it had completely taken the sheen off his day.

Briefly, the crowd thinned, as the other undergraduates drifted away, sharing commiserations and celebration in equal measure. He could, at least, ensure this matter did not come to the attention of any more of his peers. He walked back to the Class Lists, and, with very little effort he pulled open the glass-fronted door which sheltered the green backing, and the class lists, from the elements, breaking the weather-cracked wood around the lock, ripped out the History class list, and stuffed it into his pocket. He pushed the door back in place – the damage barely showed.

More students arrived at Senate House; they all made their way to the boards. He could hear them whispering, sniggering. Perhaps word had already spread.

'Hey, Lucian man,' said the voice in its accented, stentorian tone.

It was Johann and his usual throng of females (a new set, it seemed).

'Hey, everything ok, man?'

'Yes,' replied Lucian, trying to sit up and look more composed.

'How did you do?' Johann was alarmingly direct- it was his Scandinavian way.

'Not bad, not bad,' replied Lucian, wishing Johann would just move off and leave him alone.

'A Desmond then?' replied one of the girls with a smirk. Lucian's gut twisted – was it shame or anger, or a deadly combination of both? He knew he should get away from people as soon as possible, just in case something happened, something he would regret. He was in a strange position, while a 2:1 was 'respectable', was in fact what most people were more than happy with, Lucian had never considered himself 'most people'. He was Lucian Dorsey – he was extraordinary, mysterious, beguiling, brilliant, all the adjectives he imagined people used to describe him when he was not in the room. Someone had fucked up. Someone needed to pay, but as the person who was responsible could not be known today (he would find out as soon as he could and destroy them) he might just as well take it out on someone who was around: the unfortunate looking girl could be the victim, just as easily as anyone else.

Lucian stared at her little resting bitch face and decided to smile; he stood up and took a bow. Then he held out his hand to shake hers, but instead of shaking it he pressed her little doll hand to his lips and said, '*Enchanté*'. She thought he was cute and forgot about her 2.2 comment. Lucian did not forget. What did it matter, if it was a 2.1 or a 2.2; they were both second-class grades. He looked at the girl's face. It was definitely a resting bitch face.

'Hey, Lucian man, we're going to have a little punt later, fancy joining us?'

'Yes, why not.' He played his role as the handsome, dark, haughty prince – that's what he was – unknown and unknowable.

'And now we're off to celebrate and drown our sorrows,' said the girl, smiling at Lucian. Lucian went along with them, his mind full of a nagging disappointment. They stopped to buy strawberries and champagne on the way to the backs. Lucian made sure to give 'resting bitch face' his undivided attention. She did not know what was going on – she was not used to men being so attentive, as her friends were much fitter than her.

When they sat down on the backs Lucian refilled her glass with champagne and paid attention to her inane drivel (she clearly thought she was Einstein). She was a little on the chubby side, with a spare tyre around her middle, and unlike her friends, who had lovely flawless skin, she had a few pus-filled pimples on her chin. Her hair was mousy-brown and untidy, which she wore in a scruffy bun on top of her head, and a couple of her fingernails were dark with dirt. He found her repulsive. He did not really know what he was doing, but Lucian loved nothing better than crushing fragile people – it engendered a satisfaction within him like no other; plus he was reeling from the news of his 2.1. He kept drinking and chatting, saying, 'Yes,' or 'No,' and all the time the conversation seemed to be taking place extremely far below him as if he were standing on the edge of a precipice just waiting to jump. And then he saw others standing on top of Clare bridge and jumping, and he decided to do it. What the hell. He took a line of ketamine, snorting it off 'resting bitch face's' *War and Peace* tome. And then he stripped off to his boxers, and jumped in. The Cam water shot up his nose and left him gagging but once he resurfaced the ketamine had taken effect and he was feeling all smoothed out. He kept on swimming upstream, past all the punts, the students and the tourists who made the backs so crowded. He didn't care; he swam all the way to the Mill Pond and then realised he had gone too far so he had to swim back to his clothes. The girl was still there, waiting for him, but the others had left.

'Where'd everyone go?' he asked as he climbed out of the water, his boxers dripping water everywhere. He went to lie down beside her on the picnic rug. He knew she could not help noticing his perfectly sculpted abs, his beautiful tan. My god, she was practically drooling. He took out a cigarette from his jacket and offered her one. She took it, trying to appear nonchalant. There was nothing beautiful or alluring in the way she smoked.

She lay back on the rug, her head close to his. She said she thought a cloud looked a bit like a rower – or a dragon – some such fluff. He did not care; he was thinking about his 2.1; it hung about him like a scarlet letter. The shame of having to talk to his parents and tell them that, for the first time in his life, he had failed to make the grade, failed in his endeavours, it was almost too much to bear. His mother would give one of her little exhausted sighs and his father would ask him how he felt about it and remind him that all that was really important in life was to be happy. Worst of all his parents would say it didn't matter. Of course it mattered.

Then there would be neighbour or a close family friend who would be told the 'good' news and they would congratulate him and then tell him about so and so's son who got a starred first in physics while having been in the hospital for the entire year with chronic fatigue syndrome and unable to attend lectures or supervisions – but he was just so natural at everything – a true-born genius. Lucian would have to listen, to his parents' questions without slipping into a complete rage and slamming the phone down. His father would never understand his ambitions. His parents had money but neither had attended Oxbridge, and neither understood his desire to work for a top firm. He loathed their lack of drive and aspiration – in fact, it was this lack of ambition at home that had catapulted him into his highly competitive mindset. He wanted to be different to them, better than them.

He kept thinking back to his exams and the things

that had happened that might have caused him to have a bad day. There were the numerous mobile phone rings in one of his exams because some prat had forgotten to put their phone on silent. In one of his exams, he was seated by a noisy radiator that had an air bubble – perhaps it had distracted him enough to flunk one of his exams. He had always, quite consciously, led his life assured that his own future publications (of which there would be many) would be prefaced with a brief biography, summarising his key achievements, Winchester, Peterhouse, a double-first. It began to dawn on him that this was, perhaps, something he would not be able to 'fix'. He took the bottle of vodka he had in his bag and took a big swig.

'Aren't you going to offer me some?' the girl asked in a whiny unctuous tone. He was suddenly extremely irritated by her; she had already had one of his smokes and now she wanted to take his drink – even though it was the only thing that would take away the pain of his failure.

He turned to look at her suddenly and asked, 'So where did your friends go?' He was ready for the kill: the quick knife in the gut that would rid him of this pointless person.

'Oh, they just went back to their rooms to get ready for tonight.'

'Shame,' said Lucian, twiddling the grass between his fingers.

'Oh,' she said, her face immediately downcast.

'I'm so sorry – you didn't think – I thought you were in on it?' Lucian asked, feigning genuine concern. 'It's Johann – he's such a dick – he told me you were.'

'In on what?' She was more confused than ever.

'Oh god, I don't know how to say this,' said Lucian with faux concern. Then he shrugged. 'But I guess you should know because Johann really is a wanker.'

'What did he tell you?' Her face was full of worry and embarrassment.

'He said you're happy to be a wingman, like the type of girl you go out with and pay attention to in order to make other girls jealous. You see, if they are really fit girls, they just can't understand why they are not getting all the attention – it drives them wild,' he said, trying to explain in terms she would understand.

'Oh, so by talking to me you were just trying to get my friends interested in you.'

'Pretty much, but I swear it was Johann's idea, and he said you were on board with it.'

'Well, I wasn't.'

'Sorry about that. You really should tell Johann it was a dickish thing to do,' said Lucian. 'But hey, if you see your friends, tell them I said hi.'

She gathered up her bag, sandals and sun hat and went off forlornly. It was the first happy feeling Lucian had had that day – it was amazing up until he thought again about his 2.1.

He went back to his rooms and looked in his drinks cabinet; there he found vodka, gin, whisky. He decided to start with the Grey Goose vodka. He got some ice from his icemaker and poured himself a generous measure. It was 2 pm and the sun was streaming in through the windows; he looked out at Old Court, its immaculate rectangle of grass, the undergraduates horsing around on the gravel beside it. Someone was playing *The Moonlight*

Sonata. It was almost perfect. It could have been perfect if he hadn't failed.

He saw a group of Japanese tourists dressed in pastel shades with shorts and t-shirts (some were wearing the ubiquitous facemasks). The undergraduates were becoming rowdy (everyone was lightheaded and giddy after the exams). One of the begowned boys started cartwheeling on the grass – a thing that is completely forbidden at all Cambridge colleges, where grass is treated as holy, like cows in India or cats in ancient Egypt. Lucian was amused; he wondered what would happen. Suddenly a porter ran out of the porters' lodge and rather than shouting at the undergraduate he simply held out a small gun and shot the undergraduate in the chest. The boy fell backwards, blood leaking all over his clothes; he twitched a bit and then he fell back dead. The Japanese tourists who had been watching started running around bumping into one another; they dropped several items like umbrellas, pocket tissues and water bottles and scurried out of the court, some holding hands, some with their hands over their heads. Lucian almost pissed himself laughing. When the last tourist left, the dead boy was resurrected and dusted himself off. The other boy (playing the porter) quickly removed his disguise, and both bolted from the court, laughing, clapping each other on the back.

Lucian had forgotten his problems again momentarily, but then they came back again with a vengeance. He sat on the floor and quickly emptied the glass of vodka. The alcohol he had consumed that day was slowly starting to take effect, but he did not want to go to sleep; he wanted to focus on what his next steps might be. The face of his tutor kept swimming into his line of thought; there was a vague nagging doubt that it was somehow his fault – it had been this tutor that had perhaps lulled Lucian into a false sense of security over the First. He had always made him feel like he had it in the bag. Lucian stumbled to the drawer where he kept his pharma and contemplated its contents; he took out two Pro Plus and some ketamine. He snorted a line of ketamine off his desk and then popped the Pro Plus. He was so sleepy; he fell into his bed waiting for the drugs to take effect.

It was strange because he must have blacked out and then awoken to a slow-moving nightmare. His body was moving but he was struggling to stay focused on his actions. He felt incensed and his body was moving according to its own whimsical fancy. In his hands was a cricket bat – he would later find out that he had broken into the room below his, which belonged to a keen sportsman, to lay his hands on this weapon, and the next thing he knew he was walking into the alumni parking lot looking for his tutor's Mercedes – a silver c-class sedan produced in the nineties. Once he found it, he quickly smashed in the lights and rear-view mirrors, which set off the alarm, and then he smashed through the windscreen. It made a satisfying crash – the car alarm kept on blaring and soon enough a couple of porters ran out to disarm him. Cambridge porters are all ex-army and sturdy. They disarmed him quickly and efficiently and frogmarched him back to the porters' lodge. Lucian lay on the floor in the lodge, his intoxication suddenly overcoming him. It was decided that he would be taken back to his rooms to sleep it off.

When Lucian awoke the next day, it was already three

o'clock; he looked about him filled with the awful recollection of what he had done. His head was pulsating like it had swallowed an alien life form. His contact lenses had fallen out and shrivelled up on the carpet, so he staggered around for a moment trying to locate his glasses. He found his glasses in the bathroom, next to his toothpaste. He put them on and surveyed the damage. His arms felt sore; no doubt the disarming of his person had been a little heavy-handed. He stroked the stubble that was beginning to form on his chin and opened his bathroom cabinet. He took a codeine and washed it down with a glass of water. Then he returned to his rooms.

At once he noticed that a note had been placed under his door. It was a blue folded bit of paper, and when Lucian opened it, he saw it was a summons to the dean's office. Lucian picked up one of his crystal glasses and threw it at the wall. The sound prompted his downstairs neighbour to come knocking on the door to enquire if he was ok. Lucian called out, 'Yes, fine, glass just slipped.'

'Ok, let me know if you need anything.' The tone was one of neighbourly concern for his welfare, indicating to Lucian that his neighbour was aware of what had taken place the previous evening. In fact, Lucian guessed that by now the whole college knew – as Peterhouse is the smallest of the Cambridge colleges and gossip spreads like wildfire up its stairwells and through its shady cloisters.

Lucian could not believe how unfair it all was – he would try to explain. Really his supervisor deserved everything he got after misleading Lucian so spectacularly. His 2.1 was his supervisor's fault entirely – Lucian had been on course for a First, so what had gone wrong?

Lucian showered and spruced himself up. He wanted to look so immaculate and come across so well that the dean would not believe he was capable of the deed that he had been accused of. He left his rooms and walked brusquely through the college. He noticed all the little side glances and sniggers as he passed. A girl walked out in front of him and said, 'I just want you to know…' She paused, staring at him with her big, baby-blue eyes and pouty mouth. '…I just want you to know, Lucian, that as a peer mentor here in college, I'm here for you. Ready to listen.'

Lucian did not know who she was, but she was pretty enough to get his attention for a few minutes. 'Thanks ever so much,' he said in his best solemn-distressed tone, looking deep into her eyes for a moment. He could see her visibly swoon and, as he began to walk away, she floated off in a fantasy of her own making.

When he arrived at the dean's heavy grey-lacquered door, Lucian prepared his face and his bearing. He was a good actor and could play the part that was needed.

He knocked. A voice boomed out, 'Enter,' and Lucian obeyed.

Inside, it was the usual type of professor's room but slightly larger and with a perfect view of the Fellows' Garden. The walls heaved with books with distracting titles on the theme of masculinity and modernism. Lucian was also very distracted by the gold stud in the dean's left ear. The man was in his fifties but obviously took care of his appearance. Oh, thought Lucian, I know how I can play this – he has left himself wide open.

'Please be seated,' said the dean his tongue practically lolling out of his mouth. Lucian held out the blue slip in his hand.

'About this, sir.'

'Oh, no need for those formalities here,' said the dean. 'Please, call me Allan.'

'Well, I'm afraid it was all a misunderstanding,' said Lucian, removing his spectacles to wipe a moist corner of his eye. Then he quickly popped the spectacles into his breast pocket and looked the dean in the eye.

The dean was clearly affected by this action; he got all jittery and red-faced. A vein popped up in his temple – sitting across from Lucian was the most fun he had had all year. His hands passed over the spines of a stack of books on his desk. He stroked the edge of a picture frame, which contained a black and white photo of his Cavalier King Charles Spaniel named 'Mephistopheles'. Then he cleared his throat. 'Clearly there was some damage done to a member of staff's car last night.'

Lucian shook his head as if he could hardly believe that something so heinous could happen. Then he looked up with a pure and unaffected earnestness in his face. 'I am fully responsible for my actions and deeply sorry that those actions have affected the lives of others. If I could take back those actions, I undoubtedly would,' said Lucian with tears in his eyes.

'My dear boy,' said the dean, awed by the deep guilt that was on display. 'My dear boy, please don't upset yourself.'

'No, no, I must continue.' Lucian dabbed a pocket tissue on his wet eyelashes. 'I just wanted to say that if I can make recompense I shall. I have been suffering from several stresses and disappointments of late. I have been over-indulging and living a life altogether too demanding for my delicate constitution.'

'There, there, my boy. There is no need to go any further; the college understands that you have been a model student and is therefore willing to foot the bill for the damage to Mr Andrews's car. I have been reliably informed that the car can be repaired for a modest sum and the college has the funds necessary for such little accidents, or shall we say minor lapses of judgement.'

Lucian could not believe what he was hearing but he stuck to his character and sobbed a little more as if the relief of what he had just heard were almost too much to bear. 'But I am so afraid that this might go down on my record.'

'Oh, dear no!' cried the dean. 'Make your mind easy on that score. Mr Andrews has agreed, out of the goodness of his heart, not to press charges.'

Again, Lucian was astounded. He had obviously chosen his victim very wisely.

The dean offered him a glass of sherry, which Lucian accepted. He still had a splitting headache, and his fingers shook as he took the glass, but it felt good to have the alcohol – it was his first hair of the dog.

Allan pulled up a chair close to Lucian's and spoke in his most supportive tones. 'And Lucian, if there is anything I can help you with, and I do mean anything, then please consider my door always open.'

Lucian nodded and inched his knees away from the encroaching hands of dean Allan. After downing two glasses of sherry, he made his excuses, saying he was still very tired and needed to return to his bed.

'Then I must bid you adieu,' said the dean.

Lucian went back to his rooms, relieved that he had gotten away with everything. After that little excitement things seemed a lot better than they had been just twenty-four hours ago when he had received the bad news about his class. What did it matter? The city would still take him – the class didn't matter that much. His first city interview was in a few days. He would destroy the competition.

PART III

CHAPTER 1

The interview was over. The alarm had rung.
Lucian pressed his hand against the glass, looking at Clementine, and without thinking Clementine pressed her hand back.

'It was good to remember with you,' said Lucian.

'Do you think it was Cambridge that did it?' he joked as the orderly entered the room behind him to unlock his chains and lead him away.

'No,' she replied. 'It wasn't Cambridge.'

'Well, I guess you better come back for the next instalment: we'll be talking about London and Hong Kong and working for Goldman Sachs. Less about you, but you don't mind if I get all egocentric, do you?'

'I'll be back in two weeks,' Clementine confirmed.

The guard was already unlocking the shackles from the ring on the wall and leading Lucian away. Lucian winked at her with his beautiful, mischievous eyes. She hoped that no one noticed that she was blushing as she packed her notes back into the leather case.

It was horrible to feel enthralled all over again and to have shared so much with him. She had not planned to reveal so much but Lucian had a way of extracting information so that she forgot the promise she had made herself.

Clementine got a taxi back to The Peninsula and ordered a large whisky in her room. She looked out of her window over Victoria Harbour and brooded. Clementine took out her notes and read through them; she decided to type them all up that evening. She questioned herself about whether she would really return in two weeks. But really, she knew the answer. There was nothing that could stop her looking at that cruel face again. She wanted to hear and feel his malice. She wondered what he would reveal next time.

The weeks passed slowly. They did not exist to Clementine. She wrote a dozen articles. She also completed the draft article about Lucian. It would no doubt have to be changed.

Then the day came, and she was back in a taxi, then in the car with the police driver. The whole journey she imagined his eyes smiling at her in that mischievous, cruel way that so attracted her to him. She arrived, had her bag searched, submitted to the pat down and entered the visiting room.

The bell rang and the door opened. Lucian was there again, looking even slimmer. Clementine could tell that he was eager to begin speaking. As he sat down, he said, 'Don't let's waste time. I have been thinking about what I wanted to say. I'll tell you about London first.'

Clementine nodded; she noticed that Lucian's demeanour had changed considerably since the last interview. It was as if there were things that had been playing on his mind, things that he needed to explain. Clementine was ready. It would be her last opportunity to see Lucian for a long time, perhaps forever.

Lucian began to speak. He took her back to the streets of London, to the life he led in his early twenties. Clementine listened, her hand hovering over the page making her shorthand notes in quick, confident strokes. She was concentrating hard and trying to get all the details as Lucian spoke. Lucian spoke rapidly and without pausing. Clementine tried to keep her gaze on Lucian's face. Each time they made eye contact a shiver ran down her spine. His voice moved her, coaxed her out of herself, re-established the bond between them that had never truly died.

CHAPTER 2

London

Lunch in the city was a solemn ritual. There were an array of places that advertised their lunchtime fare, and these places only ever did lunch, never dinner. The establishments were for the city gents, the businessmen of a bygone era who still wore pin-striped suits, and bowler hats and carried umbrellas. Sweetings was still filled with these on a daily basis, and it was only open from 11 am to 3 pm, Monday to Friday. Bookings were never accepted. They sold simple seafood and were famous for their silver tankards filled with black velvet: a mix of Guinness and champagne. In season, it was one of the few places where Lucian could eat gulls' eggs, which he discovered were delicious. The bills were not itemized, and when they came, delivered by a stalwart waiter in pristine uniform, they simply read 'Luncheon'. This came in handy when Lucian had ordered a bottle or two and didn't want to let his boss find out. Crammed onto long benches with fellow bankers, eating elbow to elbow, the windows outside were piled high with that day's catch, fresh from the North Sea: lobsters, oysters, crab, and, for special celebrations, Dover sole. Lucian felt at home in this world.

The puddings were the same ones that the clientele would have enjoyed at boarding school: bread and butter pudding, spotted dick, everything covered in generous, gelatinous dollops of custard and cream.

They still sold savouries, dishes that had gone out of fashion so long ago that nobody nowadays would know their names: roes on toast, devils on horseback, scotch woodcock, welsh rarebit, buck rarebit. Each morsel contained just the right amount of lemon and salt and really cut through the haze of a boozy afternoon.

Then there was Simpsons in the City, which offered a type of Dickensian fare, where everything was served with sausage, along with its stewed cheese challenge: the person who consumed the greatest amount of stewed cheese after a full meal and then lived ten consecutive days afterwards was hailed the winner.

Le Caprice in the West End, hidden behind the Ritz Hotel, was always a favourite haunt for Lucian. It was also the restaurant where bankers would go to have a couple of drinks for Dutch courage and then hurl themselves off the roof if a deal went south or they got fired. On bad days Lucian thought about those suicides a lot; he was getting a taste of the hopelessness of a city analyst.

The days were long and disagreeable, and when he was at work Lucian did not feel at all special. It was only on the late-night taxi ride to a bar that he threw off his melancholy and thought himself a very fine fellow. Slowly his ego beat back into life, pulsating with a hollow pride. Yes, among these mere mortals – the barmaids, the touts, the rickshaw drivers, the world's small fry – he cut a very impressive figure: his suits on trend, his hair immaculate. Lucian had not gone for the conservative look – Henry Poole suits or Gieves & Hawkes – but wore instead Richard James and Alexander McQueen. In these expensive materials Lucian felt like a god. Of course, his shirts and ties were from Turnbull & Asser.

At work there was a hierarchy that was adhered to with military precision. Step out of line and you were swiftly knocked back in your place with a force that could take your breath away. Lucian had a hide like a hippopotamus and was extremely meticulous. He didn't make stupid mistakes, and he held in contempt all those who had lapses and made errors of judgement.

As an analyst he was still low in the pecking order. The VP would summon them all to the long boardroom every morning, with its view of the metal-grey city, and grill them over their results. If there were failure it would be rooted out. If there was success, praise was meted out grudgingly, often in the form of mockery. There was always room for improvement. It was a macho, boisterous atmosphere where Lucian felt at ease. It was like school, and he had got used to that alien atmosphere by the time he was seven years old.

There were a few women, and as much as they tried to fit in with the public-school atmosphere, few succeeded. They started off being sweet, pretty, feminine things, and then they either crumbled or turned into bullish harpies.

It was always Annabel's on a Friday and afterwards Aspinall's for blackjack and roulette. It took stamina to keep up, and if you didn't make it in your twenties, you didn't make it. Once you had commitments – children, a spouse – you were not going to be going out every night, having worked all day to get hammered until 3 am, go home to collapse for a couple of hours and then be back in the office for 7 am. And everyone, it seemed, who was anyone, was in this game.

A few days into the job, Lucian's boss had taken him aside in the boardroom after a meeting and told him a joke. Lucian was always suspicious about his boss's motivations for doing anything; it seemed that everything, even one's reaction to a joke, was a kind of covert test to see if you really had the mettle to get on in the business. If you failed, then whenever the VP looked at you, he would make you feel like there was an invisible black cross hovering beside your head. Lucian had to think quickly and decided to find the joke excessively funny and then tell a sexist joke of his own (since no women were present and he wanted to impress this macho VP). The VP's joke went as follows. There's this registry office in Chelsea: a young man registers to get married, lists his occupation as banker and the registrar says, 'Banker? And what bank do you own?'

God, Lucian laughed so hard it made his jaw ache, and then he told his own dumb blonde joke. The VP looked at him like he had gone mad and for a moment Lucian thought he might have monumentally stuffed up. But then the VP put on his 'just kidding' face and laughed and slapped Lucian on the back. This is the way things are meant to be, thought Lucian. A little banter between men, a little back slapping and, hey ho, I'm on my way for a raise and a bonus. I can do the work, now he just has to like me, thought Lucian. I need to be his go-to man, his confidant. What else has the man got, thought Lucian? Nothing apart from a bed full of high-class hookers when he desires it, and all the booze and drugs a person could ever want. He doesn't have freedom or friends and probably hasn't seen a family member for years. He's vulnerable really; he just wants people to be impressed.

Lucian had developed a tough exterior at school, where jokes could quickly turn to cruelty. He thought little of the initiation ceremonies designed to cow and humiliate new boys. He went through these little tortures just like the best of them and didn't complain. Even at a young age he was able to put it all in perspective and eagerly await his own chance to make the younger boys' lives a misery. He couldn't stand the snivellers and mummy's boys who cried with indignation and whined at the system. So, when justice was meted out in the office, Lucian tended to think it was right and proper. It bred either acceptance or defiance; those who were too defiant often walked.

When he stepped into the office one morning with the mother of all hangovers, he could see from the VP's expression that someone's head was for the block. There was a hush in the room, and Lucian, through his migraine haze, could make out the rattish face of a new analyst who wasn't keeping up. This small, prematurely balding man with a comb-over sat down and began to shuffle papers, avoiding eye contact with everyone. The VP was in a mood; his nostrils were unmistakably flared, and his eyes were burning with an inner hellfire – a type of brimstone reserved for those who made him recklessly angry.

He sat down at the head of the table and his eyes bore down on the rat-faced man; he did not even blink. This should be fun, thought Lucian, squinting at the brightness of the room. At least there's going to be a show today; otherwise, I might have just fallen asleep from boredom.

'Mr Samuels,' the VP began, 'how many months have you worked here? Please enlighten us.'

The man turned crimson and could hardly drag his eyes from the papers he had been religiously shuffling. After a couple of seconds, he pulled himself together and replied, 'Six months, sir.'

'Six months, you say, Mr Samuels, six whole months, in which you have shown not one modicum of improvement. In fact, if we are to go by the latest work you submitted it would seem that you are unravelling. The work is even more shoddy than when you began with us. What have you got to say, Mr Samuels?'

'I have tried to implement all the suggested corrections,' the man pleaded.

'Implement, my fucking arse!' The VP, by this point incensed, suddenly leapt up from his chair and marched round the room to stand directly behind Lucian and launch a tirade against the terrified man from across the board table. 'Your work is a fucking dog's breakfast. My god, man, you can't even write a sentence in fucking plain English without cocksucking it up.'

Lucian was annoyed that his suit was getting covered in spittle, but apart from that he was thoroughly enjoying the morning so far, as much as was possible with a complete bitch of a headache and his boss shouting right next to his ear.

'Mr Samuels, I'm going to give you a choice, you piece of shit analyst, either you pack up your sad existence and get the fuck out of my office today, and I mean now, or get down on your hands and knees and pray to mother fucking Christ and do your penance. So, what will it be? Are you gone or are you going to stay, you cocksucker?'

Mr Samuels looked left, and right, stuttered and mumbled. 'I'm staying.'

'Are you sure?' barked the VP.

'I'm…'

'You're what…?'

'I'm…'

'Come on, Mr Samuels, there's only so much moral cowardice I can take in the mornings!'

'I, I, I'll stay!' shouted the man, and instantly looked shocked that the words had left his mouth. Lucian was shocked: it didn't seem that Mr Samuels would have much of a future at the firm.

'Oh, you'll stay, will you?' spat the VP. Now he was incandescent with rage, that this slug was defying him, showing some courage and saying he would remain when most would have started to pack up immediately. 'Well, for starters, you don't deserve to be sat on a chair. So, get the hell off my furniture and get on the floor.'

Now the VP charged around the large table; several of the women's mouths were contorting in looks of fear and disbelief. They lowered their heavily mascaraed lashes and started to contemplate their fake nails.

Mr Samuels had got up from his chair but seemed unable to navigate his way in this new and hostile situation.

In a split second the VP, a tall, broad guy, a bodybuilder type, was looming over the runty Mr Samuels. 'I said get on the fucking floor, you cocksucker.'

At this point Lucian had to jam his knuckles in his mouth to suppress a snort of laughter.

'On your knees, Mr Samuels.'

Lucian, like everyone else, was half-expecting the VP to whip out his dick and give Mr Samuels a crack over the cheek with it. Mr Samuels was now on his knees, his face pale, unsure if he should just get up and leave. Instead, the VP hooked up one of his trouser legs to reveal his gleaming black brogue – an expensive soft leather shoe that he had bought from Loakes and had polished by his valet, who inserted cedar shoe trees into them at night to give them a nice woody fragrance. Then he turned the sole to face Mr Samuels.

'Since nothing else has worked, Mr Samuels, I'm going to suggest this is our new method of instruction. Let's see how many fucking mistakes you make after this; now get your tongue out and lick my goddam shoe, you cocksucker.'

There was no way that Mr Samuels could refuse this time and suddenly everyone over the opposite side of the table was standing up to get a good view. If they could have dared to take photos with their phones they would have, but everyone was too caught up in the moment.

Mr Samuels shook his head.

'Well then, get out of my goddam office, you slimy sonofabitch.' The VP raised his hand as if he were about to hit Mr Samuels and the man flinched in fear. The VP laughed a hard, mocking, falsetto laugh as Mr Samuels crawled out of the room on all fours.

'Keep crawling, motherfucker!' screamed the VP, who then turned round to the ten faces in the room and smoothed down his waistcoat, slightly loosening his tie. 'And that's what will happen if another one of you fucks up again. Understood!'

He took a deep breath and walked back to his chair at the head of the table.

Lucian muttered a voiceless 'Bravo'. He loved that this guy kept no hangers-on, he just disposed of what was left of a person and moved on. Lucian wanted to spend more time with the VP, to learn how all this was done. Imagine what he was like with women, thought Lucian – he was not some sap who would treat them like princesses and take all their shit. I bet he doesn't have a girlfriend, thought Lucian, just a phone full of numbers – a different girl every day of the week.

'Lucian,' said the VP, 'I'd like you to take us through the data from the Merriman portfolio; I assume I can rely on you for some clean, well-ordered stats.'

And with that Lucian knew, and everyone in the room knew, that he was the VP's star, the one to set an example for the rest of them. One of the women rolled her eyes and bit the rubber on the top of her pencil. Lucian would not forget her look, and he thought, I'll nail that bitch. Lucian smiled, showing his perfect top row of teeth, opened his laptop and gave everyone a lesson in doing the job well. Later, when they were on a coffee break, the VP came up to him and took out a small flask. He added a shot of whisky to his and Lucian's coffee and told Lucian to come to his office.

The office had a large white orchid in a vase on the desk. The view from the window was the panorama of the city. The table was modern, eccentric, with brass chicken feet on the ends of the table legs and an ebony bust of an Ethiopian woman on a side table, her breasts conical, jutting when seen in profile.

The VP sat on the desk. 'Lucian, Lucian, Lucian,' he sighed. 'I think we need some chill time.' His hands were folded over his broad chest. Lucian, seated on the black ergonomic chair in front of his desk, smiled with the corners of his mouth.

'I like you, Lucian. I think you're going to go far.'

'Thank you.'

'Don't fucking thank me; I'm not doing the work for you. What I'm saying is you've got to get into the lifestyle, or you'll never be accepted here. Get out a bit, spend the cash, have some fun, go to the right bars, drink, get laid. You know, lad's stuff.'

'Well, to tell you the truth, I needed a few painkillers this morning.'

'Painkillers!' scoffed the VP. 'Are you nine? We don't take painkillers; we have things that are much better here, and that essentially means more fun and games, and less pain!'

Lucian smirked, but he wanted the guy to like him, so he pretended to be the apprentice willing to learn the trade from this old wise guy.

'There's a couple of us going out on Friday. Why don't you join us? Look, you've got this lot licked; they'll all be here Friday night crunching numbers. But if I know you, you will be done by then; you won't let work get in the way of play like this bunch of saddos. You've not been associating with the right types, but we're going to remedy that. Come on, what do you say?'

'Yes,' said Lucian simply, but inside it was a resounding 'Yes'. Things were really moving forward for him. He could feel that a promotion or a bonus beckoned, or maybe both. He got a hard-on just thinking about it.

CHAPTER 3

Lucian killed himself getting the work done so he could go on a complete bender on Friday night. He knew that was what the VP expected. He put in two all-nighters and became well acquainted with the horrors of the magic roundabout. The taxi took him home, waited outside for Lucian to shower and get changed, and then he was driven back to the office for another full day's work. It made Lucian's brain feel murky, as if the lack of sleep was like a lack of shower for the mind.

No one worked as hard as him that week, and he went home early on Friday, proud of what he had accomplished. Home was a one-bedroom apartment in Dolphin Square, Pimlico. The owner of his flat was a fit twenty-year-old who lived in a larger apartment below his, and who kept inviting Lucian round for drinks. He always made up some excuse because he did not want something to happen and for her to get the wrong idea and then ask him to leave. He liked the place and for now he wanted to stay. He wished she would have a bit more self-respect; after all, if he really wanted her, he would have her; she shouldn't act so desperate. At home he put his sound system on and listened to "Drive" by

The Cars. Nothing could beat the sound of that eighties synth. Lucian wished he had been a city banker back then; he imagined the times they must have had in the Thatcherite years. There was so much energy and cash slopping around.

He took a shower, got out, wrapped a towel around his waist and combed his wet hair in the mirror. He then got dressed in a more casual beige suit while watching the six o'clock news. He dabbed a little Floris No. 89 on his wrists, fastened his Patek Philippe and then checked his smile in the mirror. It was all good; he was just as handsome with no sleep. He hadn't eaten all day and he was starving. He was going to meet the boys at Coq d'Argent. They were to meet there at 6.45 pm. The VP had made a private booking for fifteen on the upper terrace. Lucian ran down the steps and jumped in his Lotus. He kept the hatch down. It was a pleasant summer evening. He loved the sound of the engine as it roared into life. He reversed out of the parking space while checking out a blonde walking her Shih Tzu. The dog did a crap on the pavement in front of his house.

'Fucking clean that up,' he shouted at her.

The woman gave him the finger.

'Bitch!' he screamed back at her as he accelerated down the road. An elderly couple looked at him in horror as he roared past them at fifty miles per hour. He wasn't going to let it get to him. These fucking people. Sometimes he didn't want to be a part of this disgusting world.

He was the first to arrive at the restaurant. He gave the name at the front desk and was led up to the terrace by a nice-looking waitress with blonde hair and blue eyes.

When he saw that he was the first one to arrive, he was a little embarrassed. The waitress took his jacket to hang in the cloakroom and then he watched her leave, staring at the way her tight black skirt accentuated her pert bottom and muscular thighs. With that physique she could be a ballet dancer or a gymnast.

Another waitress came to his table and asked if he would like to order anything while he waited. There was a slight smile on her face and Lucian interpreted it as some form of subtle mockery – for the fact he was alone and seemingly friendless. For a few minutes he thought about the possibility that this was some bizarre company initiation – where a new analyst was invited out to dinner with the VPs only for nobody to turn up. It was perfectly possible. Luckily Lucian did not have to wait much longer and the VPs began to arrive. They came to the table in groups, laughing loudly, showing that they were a bonded pack. Lucian stood up and shook hands with them one by one. He introduced himself fourteen times and each time felt the pressure of their handshakes. He felt as if this were all a big test and he had to judge the situation and act accordingly. Lucian's VP was the last to arrive; he bounded into the room and apologised loudly for his tardiness. He sat opposite Lucian and offered his hand across the table.

They didn't need to look at the menus. When the waitress returned every man asked for his usual fare – she understood this. Lucian asked what he should eat and one of the men recommended the jugged hare, another the steak. Lucian went for the steak, and to his surprise when the food came he saw that most of the bankers had chosen the same thing. Good call, thought Lucian. They drank and talked shop and then the conversation moved onto women. As far as Lucian could tell only one of the VPs was married and this was an endless source of mockery. The chap was in his mid-thirties and he took the jokes on the chin, but some of them were very crude. Lucian could see it was best not to be committed to anything but work, at any rate before you were forty. And what was the hurry anyway? Women had to think about their ticking body clocks but it was different for men – men only had to think about the size of their wallets. So, thought Lucian, it was better to wait for all that, if it was what one wanted. Lucian could see that type of life, the life of matrimony, in the very distant future. He never gave up hope that there would be a perfect 'one' whom he would give up the chase for. She would have to be really something, that much he knew. But for now, Lucian could think of nothing worse than being trapped and having to provide for a wife and children. Now was his time, and his time was precious and not to be used up on days of self-sacrifice or boredom.

The conversation took the usual diversion at some point in the evening, and they all got to comparing the size of their dicks. It was decided almost unanimously that a guy called Piers Elliot had the biggest wang. And because they were all pissed, they started thumping on the table and screaming at Piers to show it. 'Out with it!' they chanted, and they didn't stop while the waitresses cleared the table. Piers pretended to be bashful around the waitress, but he wasn't capable of maintaining that demeanour for long. When the good-looking blonde waitress returned, he made a show of standing up and unzipping his flies. She smiled like she was used to this behaviour. Then he whipped it out. Lucian was smiling and looking through his fingers, trying not to appear too interested in another man's dick. Everyone was laughing and stamping their feet. And they were right, it was huge, maybe the biggest Lucian had ever seen (even taking into account all the dicks he'd seen at boarding school). Then, while still unzipped, and flowing free, Piers grabbed the blonde by both ears and pushed his tongue into her mouth. Lucian expected her to punch him. Piers's dick was pressed against her short, tight black skirt.

'Knee him in the bollocks!' shouted the married guy. But, to Lucian's surprise, she kissed him back. Maybe she liked Piers, maybe she was used to the Friday-night high jinx. She let him grope her thigh and then he hugged her, and she patted her hair and laughed with her pretty teeth, though her red lipstick was smudged all over her face. Piers took out a few notes from his trouser pocket and stuffed them in her skirt at the top. Then he rested his head against her beautiful flat stomach and the others pelted him with napkins. Lucian enjoyed that moment. He saw the power of these city men, the space they occupied at the top of the food chain. They could do anything they wanted and women still flocked around them. Even with fifty years of feminism, this was how it was. In fact, women, like the barmaid, probably enjoyed these little displays. She could go back to her co-workers and boast about what had happened in that faux shocked way that women describe things like that. I bet she went straight to the other waitresses and showed them the money, thought Lucian. The other girls were probably envious too, asking her to tell them all the details, hoping that next time they would be chosen. Of course, Piers had chosen the blonde: she was by far the best-looking bird in the place, and she had a sense of humour, you could tell, thought Lucian.

Lucian felt a strange yearning to be like Piers, to be so confident with members of the opposite sex and just do exactly as he pleased with them. Money talks, thought Lucian; if you have a fat wad of cash and everybody knows it, then women just act differently. It's in their nature to go after the alpha male. It's instinctive, primal. They're not going to flock round some no-hoper deadbeat. They want a thrill, just like men, something to brighten the dullness of everyday life. Lucian decided that Piers would be his new guru. He would follow this glorious man and try to emulate his every move and hope that one day he could be just like him.

Later that night they moved onto Annabel's – Lucian hadn't yet got his membership to the club but Piers told him he would 'do right by him'. When they arrived, Piers had a word with the doorman and Lucian's night was made. Of course, all the VPs had membership; Piers even said he would try and make sure Lucian's came through in the next few weeks.

Lucian entered with the rest and tried his hardest not to gawp at all the oddly familiar faces (famous actors, models, singers). Someone whispered that Kate Moss was sitting at the bar with some friends of Piers. Lucian half-looked and out of the corner of his eye saw the gamine beauty, her face in profile. She was no doubt still exquisite but there was no point staring – she was here to escape the riff raff, not to be ogled by lowly analysts. He heard her laughing in a high-pitched shrieking manner and saw the cigarette held nonchalantly in her bony hand. There was a pang of disappointment somewhere right in Lucian's core. He wondered if it was because of his own failings or the fact that a mythical beauty was now before him in the flesh and blood. He did not like to go too close because he didn't want to see her faults or let her see his.

Lucian ordered a gin and tonic and sat with Piers and another guy at a table. There was some live piano music, jazz of some description, and the vibe was good and mellow. Piers reached into his breast pocket and brought out a little metal box; it looked like a box where a grandmother might store her peppermints. He flicked it open and offered it to Lucian, very calmly and casually. A little 'e' to get the party started.

Once he had popped that pill, the night really took off. He was dancing, he was hugging his fellow men, he even managed to snog Kate Moss (or maybe it was just his imagination); anyhow, it felt real enough at the time. They were all going at it, full tilt and somehow, they all ended up at Aspinalls. From there on, Lucian only had vague recollections of being at the roulette table, his arm around some Scandinavian model who had taken a shine to him that evening. Her cocktail dress was very tight over her small breasts and her décolletage was a perfect milky white; she had a boyish body with incredibly long legs and her ankles were deer-like. He couldn't wait to get her on her own; he wanted to take off her heels and examine those fine-boned calves. Piers was off somewhere else, cheating at Baccarat – he too had picked up a gorgeous red-head, with a mass of curly locks that cascaded off her shoulders and reminded Lucian of Julia Roberts in *Pretty Woman*.

Lucian kept drinking; the VPs made sure the libations kept flowing, and pretty soon Lucian's head was spinning like the roulette wheel, with a croupier's gloved hands on either side of his temples. Everything was a blur, like the reels of a bizarre fantasy movie or whacky trip. Lucian remembered bundling into a Bentley with Piers and the two women – Piers had taken control of the situation, which was necessary, given Lucian's state – and Piers's driver took them to leafy Hampshire, back to Piers's pad, which was a sizeable country estate.

Once they arrived at the gatehouse at Wyfold, a servant was there to greet them and let them through the huge wrought-iron gates. Lucian remembered seeing a huge statue of a lion situated in the parkland that surrounded Piers's house, and Piers said something about deer roaming around freely. The blonde was asleep on his shoulder, her body wrapped in a fur coat, white as ermine; in the darkness Lucian could see her perfect lips slightly parted, with the slight gap between her teeth visible. What a mouth she had – it was all natural, no doubt, and beyond perfection.

He must have passed out again because his next memory was of being carried up a huge staircase by some strangers and placed in a bed. The blonde was placed beside him and at dawn he woke with the worst headache of his life, but the only thought in his mind was the need to relieve himself. He stumbled out of bed, hoping that a bathroom was situated somewhere close by. He found one adjacent to the bedchamber, immense and totally pristine, and as he relieved himself the pressure inside his head seemed to increase – he needed something to take away the hammering in his brain and he thought about the things he was carrying with him the previous evening. He had a packet of codeine in his jacket pocket. He stumbled back to the room to look for the pills and as he did so something caught him in the back of the neck. He was thrown to the ground with the shock of it. Someone was kneeling on his back trying to throttle him with a tie, screaming, 'Fucking bastard!' in a very feminine voice.

Lucian involuntarily dropped to the floor, trying to loosen the tie around his neck. As he did so the door to the room swung open and Piers stepped in. He immediately rushed to Lucian's aid and prized the woman away, carrying her, kicking, screaming and spitting, to the bed.

'Shhhh,' he said in his calmest, most condescending tone. 'Please,' he said as she swatted away his hands, 'Please tell me what is wrong, darling. Did he do something bad to you?'

Once she was free to move again, she backed herself into the corner of the bed and tucked her arms around her bare legs just as a scared child would do.

'So, what happened?' asked Piers again. As he said this, he looked across the room at Lucian, who was sitting on the floor, trying to catch his breath and get his pulse rate back to normal. Piers winked and Lucian half-smiled. The girl had not seen the wink.

'I just woke up in this bed with him,' she said in her Swedish accent.

'And?' Piers enquired.

'And I don't know this sonofabitch,' she screamed. 'I don't know what he did to me.'

'Why don't you know what he did?'

'Because I can't remember.'

'Ok, why can't you remember?' Piers shot Lucian a grin.

'I don't know,' she replied, putting her head down on her knees.

'Could it be that you had a few too many drinks?'

She shot Piers a withering glance.

Lucian had by this time recovered himself. 'Look,' he said, getting to his feet. 'Nothing happened here, we never did anything. I promise you. We were both way too wasted. I don't even know how I ended up in this bed, let alone how you got here.' As she turned her back, Lucian winked at Piers, who smirked back.

'Hey, you both told me you wanted an after-party,' said Piers. 'It wasn't my fault that you were both unconscious when we got here, and my gardener and my valet had to carry you to your rooms. And you,' Piers looked over at the Swedish girl, 'you looked like you were having fun with him.' Piers gestured towards Lucian.

'I don't remember anything,' she said again, looking like she was going to cry.

'Can I give you some advice, honey?' Piers said, stroking her bare ankle. 'Next time, don't drink so much. It really doesn't suit you.'

'Fuck you!' she shouted.

'No, fuck you,' said Piers. 'Now get out of my damn house.'

Piers grabbed both her legs and pulled her off the bed so that she crumpled to the floor. The Swedish girl started yammering in Ukrainian which made Lucian realise that perhaps she wasn't Scandinavian after all.

'She's not happy,' said Lucian, sniggering.

'Yup, the thing is,' said Piers, as he collected various items of the girl's clothing and her purse. 'These girls are all the same.'

Piers took out his wallet and the girl quietened down. 'So how much to settle this? One hundred?'

'One thousand,' she replied, now eager, now sane, the talk of money having whetted her appetite.

'Oh, I like a little haggling in the morning,' said Piers. amused. 'Five hundred, and not a penny more.'

The girl nodded.

'Done,' said Piers. 'And here's a little extra to spend on yourself.' Piers counted out the notes and gave her the fat wad of cash.

Lucian laughed.

'What can I say, I'm a generous guy.'

The woman put on her dress and gathered up her things before hurrying out of the room.

'Phewee,' said Piers. 'That one was highly strung. I promise you, man, they're not all like that.'

'Yeah, thanks for dropping me in the shit like that,' said Lucian.

'What do you mean?'

'Oh, just fucking putting a drunk girl in bed with me, naked, when we're both out of our minds.'

'God, man, you worry way too much. Lighten up,' said Piers. 'You said you didn't do anything, and she can't remember shit.'

'Yeah, well I'll lighten up as soon as I have a painkiller and a shot of something strong.'

'Well, I have just the thing,' said Piers, taking a packet of white powder from his pocket.

Lucian now recollected some of the previous night, and the memory of it made him very glad that the girl had just accepted the money and left. He had been rough with her and at one point she had hit her head. Well, no matter, he thought, she woke up, she's alive – no lawsuit there, no murder trial.

CHAPTER 4

It had all been going well. Lucian had proven himself repeatedly, both at work and elsewhere. He was one of the lads, and they all liked him. He had made associate with relative ease. They thought he was made of the right stuff.

He had been working relentlessly, and it had begun to take its toll. His hair was receding around his temples and when he let his beard grow for a couple of days on leave, he noticed the sprouts of grey hair coming through. As soon as he noticed them, he got his razor out and was determined to stay clean shaven for the foreseeable future. He put eye drops in his eyes to keep them clear and prevent the bloodshot look he got after spending upwards of fourteen hours a day staring at a screen. Lucian had been to all the social events he had been invited to, which meant buying almost a whole new wardrobe to change into after work every day. This, coupled with all the other expenses he had incurred 'living the life' meant that his take-home pay barely covered any costs.

But Lucian was fortunate. All it took was one pleading phone call to his mother to ensure that his bank account got topped up and his rent was paid in full, and on time.

Lucian never considered what it would be like to not have this back-up option. He hated the other members of the team who were always having to say no to going out because otherwise they would not be able to pay their rent. He called them grubbers or penny pinchers and sought to undermine them at work as much as possible. He was determined to succeed, and if that meant highlighting others' flaws, so be it. When Summers said he was feeling under the weather at work Lucian worked a little criticism of him into a passing comment to Piers. Piers thought Summers was good and Lucian could see that he might be in line for a promotion if he continued in that vein. Lucian could not tolerate the idea that an associate in his cohort might be getting a promotion to VP before he did. It wasn't right. So, when Piers suggested to Lucian that he and Summers and another guy, Jackson, go for a drink together after work, Lucian was ready with an offhand comment about Summers having a delicate stomach and having to go home early most days. Lucian didn't even perceive how petty this might sound; he was thinking about number one – and to him, that was the way to play the game.

Summers got his promotion, and it was Piers who gave it to him. For at least two weeks at work, Lucian could not look Piers in the eye. Lucian felt a great sense of betrayal. Piers had to tell him to get a grip and lighten up. The whole thing put a great strain on their friendship. Piers called him an arsehole. Lucian couldn't come up with a comeback – and was mildly afraid to do so. So Lucian buried himself in work. He worked harder and longer than anyone else. He didn't go home at night. He fell asleep at his desk. He stored clean suits and shirts in his car. He drained a full jug of coffee from the percolator each morning and still felt like shit. His skin was grey and his visual near-sightedness worsened so much that he needed a new set of lenses. His optician told him he needed to stop looking at screens. Lucian laughed in his face. It was too funny.

It was also at this point that Lucian met someone who he never expected to meet. Lucian had all but given up on relationships and decided to live as a confirmed bachelor with a string of ladies on call, should he need a date, a fuck or someone to relieve his boredom. Then one evening he went out to a company event and met 'the one'. It was a river cruise on the Thames with a formal dinner and free bar. He was still trying to avoid Piers and all the rest, but he knew his future depended on his ability to navigate these schmooze fests.

As soon as Lucian embarked and was given his first glass of champagne and a blini covered in crab and caviar, he could see Piers making a beeline for him. In fact, Piers was with a tall blonde woman and the two glided towards him ethereally as if their bodies possessed no weight at all but were only airy shapes.

'Lucian!' cried Piers, the tone indicating that their previous conversations about Summers had all but been forgotten. 'Lucian, my dear fellow, let me introduce you to Marcia Maddern.'

Lucian looked up into the frank, clear stare of Miss Maddern, a willowy and exquisitely featured woman in her late twenties.

'Miss Maddern is a bit of a superstar at The Golden

Sacs in New York City.' Piers never called it Goldman Sachs on principle. 'In charge of a two-trillion-dollar project.'

'Three actually,' said Marcia.

'Impressive,' said Lucian, feeling the sweat start to prick at the back of his neck. Perfect women like Marcia made him feel uncomfortable.

'Anyhow, I just thought you two should meet. Something tells me you're going to get along just great. Lucian, mind your manners.'

And then he disappeared. Was this a set-up, wondered Lucian? Piers never did anything randomly. Everything was part of the game plan, although Piers made things look so effortless that few were aware of it.

They sat down with their drinks in the stern of the boat and Marcia crossed her endless legs. Her stockinged thighs were almost fully visible, curving from the short, tight cocktail dress. She wore diamond teardrops in her ears and a diamond-encrusted choker around her neck. Her watch was exquisite and also set with diamonds. She looked like the angel atop the Christmas tree. She sparkled and shimmered as the light reflected from a million tiny perfectly cut surfaces. She was luminous. Lucian had a hard time trying to make conversation with her and was about to make his excuses (as he hated feeling inferior to any woman) when she kissed him. He was taken aback. As they were temporarily alone, the kiss lasted a good five minutes. Afterwards, Lucian knew he couldn't ever think about another woman. Lucian also felt that Piers had put this gorgeous woman in his path as a kind of consolation prize. It would be churlish to refuse the gift. This was the type of unspoken generosity that passed between the men in the company. By taking Marcia home, Lucian was accepted back into the fold. His problem with Summers' promotion would be water under the bridge. Lucian felt he had lucked out.

That night, Marcia and Lucian went back to her serviced apartment in Bloomsbury – a two-floor penthouse situated near The British Museum. The night was a blur of skin and ecstasy.

Lucian woke early but Marcia was already up. Her live-in maid had begun cooking breakfast. A steaming cup of coffee was waiting for Lucian. He looked about him and tried to figure out how much she must be making annually. Knowing that her salary may be quadruple his (that was even before one got onto the topic of bonuses) made him feel a little queasy. Lucian hated to feel inferior, but Marcia was so perfect he decided to overlook that. They started seeing each other. First, they met for coffee during the workday and then they started going for dinner twice a week. Marcia was witty, straight-talking, very American, but feminine at the same time. Lucian did not know what to do with her. He had never felt these emotions before; he baulked at the thought of calling them 'love'. Lucian was a pessimist; he didn't believe in true love. But once or twice, he caught himself genuinely smiling and feeling that warmth in his insides that he had heard people refer to as love.

Marcia liked to think of herself as a patron of the arts. She donated generously to the Royal Opera House and The Globe Theatre, and in return she was given tickets to see whichever performances she wanted and access to all of the performers. She loved to talk about her special relationship with so-and-so musical director or the A-list celebrity playing Richard III in an all-new production at The Globe. Lucian was impressed by her passion, and he enjoyed being taken to full dress rehearsals when only he and Marcia and the director would be sitting in the audience, sipping champagne.

Marcia also believed in spending time in nature. She always wanted to wander around Kew Gardens or Hampstead Heath with Lucian. She told Lucian that he was too pale, that he needed to get outside more, to smell the flowers. She prescribed him a vegan diet, monthly detox drips, wheatgrass drinks, yoga and meditation. Lucian listened to Marcia like she was his new guru. He looked at her life and thought, I want to be like that. He couldn't help it; her brash but kind American ways had completely won him over. Finally, here is a woman who understands ambition but isn't a total bitch. He started thinking about committing to Marcia; sometimes he even caught himself thinking about marriage. But he knew he would need to become a lot more successful before she would ever accept his hand in marriage.

Of course, he was not quite as on top of his work as he should have been. It was a dangerous thing to have a distraction. One morning Piers rounded on him, demanding to know why his stats had been submitted half an hour late. Lucian hated that Piers could lord it over him, but he knew his work had been getting scrappier.

'You need to reassess your priorities, man,' said Piers. 'Get yourself free of whatever is holding you back.'

This advice angered Lucian and he took that anger

to dinner with him that night. Marcia was organising a skiing holiday to Verbier to coincide with Easter. Lucian remained non-committal when she suggested the dates and his strange attitude annoyed Marcia. The dinner ended abruptly with a few bitter words on both sides.

The next day at work Piers seemed to know all about it. Marcia had rung a girlfriend, who had then spoken to Piers (with whom she had an ongoing understanding).

'It's just better this way,' said Piers. 'She's got her career, and you've got yours. It's far too early to settle down.'

Lucian wanted to appear indifferent. He shrugged his shoulders and said, 'You're right'. Inside, Lucian was terrified at the prospect of never seeing Marcia again and even more terrified at the prospect of seeing her somewhere with another man. He tried to reason with himself and remind himself that he was going places but the question, 'Why not with her?' kept popping up in his mind. After all, they weren't so different – they were both ruthlessly ambitious. That shared trait would be an excellent foundation in a relationship. So, Lucian decided to ignore Piers and his more rational self. He phoned Marcia and tried to get her to meet him for lunch at Simpson's in the Strand. The phone rang several times and went to voicemail. Maybe she is in a meeting, thought Lucian, so he decided to ring later. Again, she did not pick up. Lucian left a couple of mumbled messages, but they were met with a wall of silence. Marcia was completely unresponsive to his attempts to win her back. She broke off all contact with him, until six months later she needed someone to look over some stats for her. Then she pretended nothing had happened between them and showed off her enormous diamond engagement ring. She was set to marry a billionaire financier in the spring. She invited Lucian to the reception.

So, Lucian got back into the normal rhythm of his days and tried to put all thoughts of Marcia to the back of his mind. But he could never truly forget her. Often it was late at night, when he was sitting alone at home, with a vodka in his hand, that he thought about her and was filled with anger, envy and lust. He decided that never again would he be with such a woman, not for love or money. It was too risky.

CHAPTER 5

Samuel Johnson once said: 'When a man is tired of London, he is tired of life.' After six long years, Lucian had done his time in London. He had exhausted all the bars, all the women, all the life one could live there. He was twenty-seven years old, and he had finally been given the promotion that had eluded him at Goldman Sachs: a VP position in the Hong Kong branch of Merrill Lynch.

Though he had made associate very swiftly at Goldman Sachs, the promotion to VP had slipped through his fingers. Lucian could not understand why he had been kept back while other, less talented individuals had been promoted. He had gone through the gamut of emotions over the past two years, from disappointment, to rage, and finally to acceptance, and it was then that he had begun to look around for other opportunities abroad. The bank of Merrill Lynch was more than happy to take him on, with a promotion and a significant pay rise.

Now he felt he could start his life over again – the life he was supposed to lead. His colleagues threw one hell of a goodbye party for him at the firm – it was practically a three-day bender. Piers brought in a few high-class hookers and a lot of coke; they rented a Georgian manor house and went wild. When the owners returned, they were horrified by the state of things. How did vomit end up on the three-metre-high ceiling of the drawing room? They paid their dues and in the end no one was sued for vandalism. He felt a little sad to be leaving his London wolf pack (that was how they referred to themselves) but he was on his way up to brighter and better things. He had avoided long-term girlfriends and anything that might be construed as 'baggage'. He was, to all intents and purposes, a free agent. Piers told him that the women in Hong Kong were top notch.

It was a long flight, but of course he flew business class, so that eased the discomfort a little. He ate his in-flight meal and washed it down with plenty of Meursault, vodka tonics and Glenfiddich. It was the A380 so the whole of the upper deck was designated to business and first-class passengers. There was also a sizeable bar area where passengers could mingle. Lucian took himself to the bar and sat looking on; the air hostess was very amenable. He asked her where she was from and she replied – with her beautiful Slavic accent – that she was from Estonia. One of the things Lucian wanted to do was to join the mile-high club. He was twenty-seven years old and he still hadn't banged an air-hostess mid-flight. It was definitely something that was missing from his bucket list. He tried to sweet-talk her; he was still handsome, though considerably stockier. He looked like a fully grown man now, no longer a boy. She smiled, her teeth very white between the beautifully rouged lips. Lucian thought she was one of the most exquisite women he had ever seen and the modest uniform somehow made her all the more alluring: the light-brown skirt came down below the knee, she wore a fitted blouse and a tunic, and a little hat with a scarf down one side, which veiled her face magically from one side. He had never got used to the effect of a beautiful woman – maybe it's the altitude, he thought, or maybe it's fate.

She gave him a lot of attention on that flight, and she certainly seemed interested in him, but she remained poised and professional throughout. When he disembarked, Lucian gave her his card just in case she found herself at a loose end in Hong Kong. Why not, he thought? Maybe she will, maybe she won't, but for weeks and even months after, he kept hoping for her to call. She never did. Maybe she knew all it would be with Lucian was a traveller's tryst, and that's not what she was looking for.

When Lucian arrived in Hong Kong he made his way to the Grand Hyatt, situated in the metropolitan area of Wan Chai. Lucian had chosen this particular hotel as a base, as it was a five-star, modern hotel overlooking Victoria Harbour. It had everything he would need for a few weeks while he got to grips with his new job and started looking for a suitable apartment. Once he had checked in and the bell boy had deposited his two large cream and blue globetrotter cases (made of vulcanized fibreboard) in the room, he locked the door of his suite, sat down on the bed, loosened his tie and began to take in the magnificent sunset over the harbour. The glass on the skyscrapers appeared to be on fire as the sun set lower and lower, and the crepuscular hour began. He ordered room service and ate while checking his emails. After catching up he decided to check out the night life on Lockhart Road. Piers had recommended this area to him as a good-time place with plenty of attractions.

As he walked down Lockhart Road, Lucian noticed the dark alleys branching off the street, he smelled the sweet scents of cooking and observed the duck carcasses on spits in the windows of the restaurants. Everything was bright, neon and garish; there were too many people walking down the pavement so sometimes he needed to neatly side-step to avoid brushing against them. He walked past The Queen Victoria with its loud drum n' bass beats, a crowd of drunk, middle-aged Caucasian men standing around with pints outside. Everything was noisy, including the crossings, which made a tinny ringing sound when pedestrians were permitted to walk. Men and women were walking up and down, going about their business, men carrying big crates of fruit, women out shopping with their girlfriends. There were many young women milling around dressed in miniskirts and crop tops. On their tiny feet were huge chunky wedge shoes or stiletto heels. As Lucian passed, they made eye contact with him and jutted their hips out, pouting their lips. Lucian found the experience very provocative. They could see he was a white male, well dressed, out on his own at night on Lockhart Road, and to them this meant he was only looking for one thing.

Lucian was not overly keen to prove them wrong. He had no idea where the night would take him; sometimes he just liked to leave all that up to fate. He looked at the heavily made-up faces and slowed his pace; some pawed at his arms and sleeves with their long, sharp nails. He gave one of the prettier ones a wink and then almost instantly regretted it, as she had taken it as a sign that he wanted her. But as she walked alongside him, her narrow hips swaying, her small breasts almost visible through the thin material of her top, he thought why not, it might as well be her. As they walked together she gave him her patter, the list of things on the menu, and their prices, and things that were off the menu. But Lucian had been developing his tastes and he took her by her slim wrist and pulled her towards him so that they were walking down the street like a happy pair, although from the looks of the older street hawkers, most people doubted their legitimacy as a couple.

She said her name was Sally, after Mustang Sally. He laughed and started to sing the song. She put her hands over her cheeks in a very girlish coquettish way, which he liked. After that first meeting, they played at being boyfriend and girlfriend for four days while he was settling into his new abode. He didn't take her back to his room, but they hung out on Lockhart Road and Lucian gambled at the dimly lit poker tables, flashed his cash and generally had as good a time as possible. Sally was an invaluable guide to the seedier side of Hong Kong, and for this information he rewarded her handsomely. She also had many other talents, which he discovered in one of the many cheap hotel rooms that are rented out by the hour. It was his first taste of the Asian way of doing things and after his first experience, he was an addict. Sally introduced him to some dealers, and during those first few days on the island he spent his time in a state of happy intoxication.

When they ate, they went to the big food stalls known

as Dai pai dong, where hygiene was circumspect, but the fare was hot and delicious. Seated at battered wooden tables next to the panoply of life that the underbelly of Hong Kong had to offer – toothless old women, men wrinkled as dried prunes – Lucian felt a mixture of disgust and curiosity, but he was high as a kite and simply followed Sally to the places she dined at. He was getting his bearings, trying to figure out where he would fit in. The city beckoned him with all the gold of Midas. He felt a wild abandon – here at last was a place where he could do exactly as he pleased unfettered by the standards of Western society. The steamed rice rolls and congee really hit the spot in the morning after an all-nighter. Then Lucian would return to his neat and orderly hotel suite and grab a few hours' sleep before his revelries started again after dark. He and Sally walked hand in hand around Victoria Harbour, taking in the city lights and fireworks in celebration of Chinese Year. She never said much, and Lucian liked that. Also, she never asked him questions. This was good, he thought – as she would never learn about his life and never seemed concerned that everything in her life was on a temporary rental basis.

Then, all too suddenly, he was standing in an ice-cold shower at 7 am trying to clear his brain before he stepped into his new role at the office. He put himself together with all of the usual fastidiousness, hair neatly cut and groomed, face clean shaven, collar starched, bone collar straighteners, mother of pearl cufflinks, shoes polished to a deep sheen, teeth brushed, flossed, aftershave applied sparingly, nails trimmed, suit pressed; but with all this, after four days of gritty debauchery, he felt like an alien in the bright, clean world of corporate finance. He shook hands with the MD and hoped that the man did not notice his red-rimmed eyes, the look of exhaustion before he had even done a day's work. Also, after a brief hiatus of several months when he had tried to cut down on alcohol and other substances, his self-control had waned considerably over the past few days. Sally had hooked him up with the dealers he would need to continue to function at his job while intoxicated. He had parted ways with Sally on the best of terms. No doubt he would see her around Wan Chai. It was an area that held a deep fascination for him. He steeled himself, put on the bullish front, met the team, led the meetings, told them about himself and remained professional at all times. That first week he created quite an impression – the reports from London had been very favourable and everyone seemed happy to have him on board.

Lucian's days were filled for him, and his evenings too. His secretary, a half-Chinese, half-Portuguese woman in her mid-forties from Macau, was extremely diligent in her mission to pack his every waking hour with important meetings. Within his first week at Merrill Lynch he had been taken to a black-tie dinner and ball at The Peninsula held for the Oxford and Cambridge Society. There he had been paraded around by the MD, also a Cambridge man, and had shaken hands with all the great and good of Hong Kong society. As most of the VPs at Merrill Lynch were Oxbridge graduates, Lucian came to understand that these soirées would become a regular part of his life. He felt at ease in these arenas; he understood the protocol and could blend in seamlessly or choose to be the centre of attention if he had a mind to be.

A beautiful Chinese lady dressed in a Versace gown, with long white gloves, asked him for a dance, and he impressed her with his dancing abilities: he had joined the ballroom dancing society at Cambridge in his first year and had become so good that he had competed a number of times. Lucian never let a skill set go to waste; he always tried to use his talents to his advantage. After the dance, the lady gave him her card, and he was surprised to read on it that she was chief executive at Next Media: Hong Kong's largest media company. He was pleased that almost immediately he was being accepted into the upper echelons of Hong Kong society. It felt, thought Lucian, like the natural order of things, how things were supposed to be in his life. The lady, whose name was Li Lau, went so far as to personally invite Lucian to a meeting with the ex-governor of Hong Kong the next day. Lucian was charmed.

So, the next day, Lucian put on his most expensive suit and got his driver to take him to the China Club. As Li was a member of the club, Lucian was permitted to enter as her guest. He was able to shake hands with the ex-governor and say a few words before they all sat down to dinner at a large table. As Lucian was seated quite far away from Li and the ex-governor, he was not included in their conversation. Instead, he was forced to make small talk with other club members who were seated next to him. This greatly annoyed him and, although the food was excellent and the atmosphere created by the dark wood furnishings and the Chinese paintings was welcoming, Lucian felt disappointed. After he had eaten as much dim sum, braised beef and scallops as he could manage, he made his excuses and left the club. Li would later contact him and ask if he was unwell, but he would reply that he was fine and was simply adjusting to being in a different time zone. That was Lucian's last communication with Li.

After a full two months of making good impressions, networking and schmoozing, Lucian was chomping at the bit. He knew what he needed to do to regain his equilibrium. So, two months after he arrived in Hong Kong, he allowed himself to have a weekend to himself. He was ready to let loose. He was wound up so tight that the release could not happen soon enough. He dressed down and went out and had dim sum and chai on Jaffe Road; then he headed back to the earthly delights on Lockhart Road.

A full weekend passed in this way, and then the next after that. Lucian slid into a satisfying routine of living monk-like during the week and letting all hell break loose at the weekends. But slowly, as the weeks passed, and then months, it was the weekend that became the dominant factor. First, it encroached upon his Monday mornings and started to make him late into the office. Then, a couple of times, the weekend swallowed Monday before Lucian even realised that it had begun. He chastised the weekend, but the weekend had the upper hand and soon it was making him take a half-day on Friday just so that he could get to happy hour. He cultivated a reputation for himself as a generous guy – a big spender. He would buy rounds for everyone at the bars and flash his cash at the hookers. At the dance clubs he would ask for lap dances and then throw notes onto the floor, or stuff them into the girl's G-strings. His largesse knew no limits.

CHAPTER 6

The Old China Junk was a British-style pub with a garish neon sign that buzzed on and off continuously because of a short circuit. Lucian frequented this place on an almost daily basis. It was two years since his arrival in Hong Kong. Lucian never cooked at home, so this was where he filled up on heavily battered cod and cold, limp chips. He couldn't stand all that foreign stuff anymore, laced with chillies, which disagreed with his gut. He was snorting a lot, and it gave him an insatiable appetite but an overly sensitive digestion; he was not above sneaking a chip off another customer's plate if he felt peckish and couldn't be bothered to wait half an hour for his own food to arrive. The old reserve was slipping – he used to be so poised. After a few beers and chasers, he would either sit listlessly, legs splayed out in a dark niche of the pub, or lazily pursue some pretty little thing at the bar by staring at her and beckoning her with his index finger. He could have whatever he wanted here on the island; it was all up for grabs, and the little girls all tried to please him. He felt like a fisherman whose luck for the catch never runs dry. He didn't have to waste energy pursuing some haughty female. They came to him begging to be his lover for just one alcohol and drug-fuelled night of fucking. Sometimes he took one home, sometimes four or five. They knew he was good for it.

'Mista, yu so rich, yu ca ha waddeva yu wunt.' That was what one of his favourites; Petal had said it, and it was true. Here he was an overweight god, and even his weight seemed to carry an aura of importance. 'Yu bi stron maan, yu ea well, it meen yu tak care o yu wimmen.' He was overindulgent with them at times, giving them an extra wad of cash if they told him their little sob stories, giving his favourites ostentatious jewellery for their birthdays. He liked the idea of providing, but he liked the idea that he had the power to stop these small generosities even more, the idea that he was the prize pig, and that each girl coveted her place at the table with him.

There were other men at the 'Junk' but he tried to pretend they didn't exist. He had his little harem around him and as long as they only looked his way, he was partially content. Sometimes he saw one of the prettier ones eyeing up another man – it was a big mistake on the girl's part, especially if she was obvious about it. When this happened, he made sure he won her attention back, showered her with gifts and compliments (got her hooked on the promise of more) and then took her home, had sex with her and told her how crap she was in bed and how he never wanted to see her again. This was his little revenge for any of these whores having wandering eyes. He would also make sure the sex was really rough, enough to put her off for a few weeks at least. These girls, he thought, they have to know who's in charge, who calls the shots. If they didn't already know it, then Lucian was always happy to provide a refresher course.

All the women he went with were petite and feminine, but Tiny was the most beautiful. Her presence after a long day at the office was like some fragrant strain from the wooded mountains, or fresh laundry strung up on a camomile meadow. Or rather, that was what he fancied she smelt like when she was close by – perhaps even that was an artfully constructed illusion. These women, he often thought, have ways to make one an addict. Tiny would sit on the floor at his feet and massage his toes. She was always keen to sit on his lap and feed him crisps, and she would shoo any other girls away when she provided this service. She was submissive in the extreme. Lucian did not know if she had been taught to be this way by her pimp or if it just came naturally to her. It was an intoxicating experience for Lucian. This was the first time a woman had truly surrendered, powerless to him – like a rag doll. She didn't seem to mind if she left with bruises all over her body after a night spent in his bed. She was just as polite after rough sex as she had been before. Tiny was an addict, but it was not immediately obvious when you met her. She still kept herself immaculately presentable, her long black hair, dyed dark chestnut, hung thick as a horse's tail down her back. She wore crop tops that accentuated her wasp waist and skyscraper heels that raised her four-foot-eleven frame to a height where she could see over the bar.

'What would you like, Tiny?' he asked her before the Christmas holidays began and he reluctantly took his annual pilgrimage back to the UK to visit his parents. She looked at him wide-eyed, the white eyeliner on her lower lids making her gaze look huge and child-like. She shrugged and turned away coyly. She was not the type to make her wishes known. Lucian felt she was allowing him to make the decision for her as a way of showing her respect and affection. He decided to buy her a Tiffany eternity bracelet. It was something that he knew the other women in his 'harem' coveted in the extreme; he would watch them fascinated by the way they could spend hour after hour on their phones scrolling through the most desirous objects of the season, imagining spending vast amounts of money that they would never have.

When Tiny was given the present, she unwrapped the crepe paper very carefully and her long flame-coloured fingernails moved over the box, caressing the sides. It was like a child opening a gift from Santa. As she opened the box, she gave a gasp of delight. She shut the box immediately and then went through the process of opening and shutting the box four times as if to maximise the pleasure she had felt on first discovering its contents. Of course, he gave it to her in front of all the others – just to amplify the effect. They all rallied around him and Tiny, craning to see the sparkly object.

'You gunna marry her,' said Petal, and Tiny beamed – a genuine smile that was so rare in these parts that Lucian could hardly bear to look at it. Lucian sat and watched her wondering when he had last derived such pleasure from a material possession. It seemed unfair to him that Tiny should be so happy and not fully share her happiness with him. He took her aside and asked her what she would be willing to do to keep the bracelet. Her face changed but almost imperceptibly. Tiny had thought the gift was already hers to keep. Lucian had changed the rules of the game, but that was his right. She recovered quickly and didn't let anyone see her disappointment. Tiny was used to the whims of men. Her calm passivity was born out of the many trials and hardships she had already faced. Ultimately, it was better to go along than to resist. She thought Lucian was an attentive lover and a good man, most of the time. He didn't hurt her maliciously. She mistook his strength and ardour for passion. She thought he favoured her above any of the other girls that hung about The Junk, and although she was not manipulative, she was keen to make some money. Tiny, though she looked like a borderline malnourished fifteen-year-old, was actually a twenty-five year-old with a six-year-old daughter. The daughter lived with her parents in a slum district in Jakarta.

Tiny sent back as much as she could afford, but her pimp took the majority of her earnings. His name was Tao, and until a few years ago Tiny had called him her boyfriend. He had met her five years ago when she was new to the city, hungry and looking for extra work. She had a part-time job as a manicurist. He took her out on the town, was nice to her. She told him about her daughter, and he seemed sympathetic. He bought her new sexy clothes and took her to bars to show her off. He was very protective and wouldn't even let other men look at her without threatening to punch them.

A few weeks later, after he had moved her into an apartment owned by his father, he seemed glum when they went out for dinner. He said that his father's restaurant business wasn't going so well and that he was terribly short of money. She felt sorry for him, asked him if there was anything she could do. He told her that one of the men his father owed money to was a very rich, important man and that if he said she would go and have dinner and drinks with him it might sweeten things up.

Sweeten things up – it was a phrase Tiny would come to know well; it didn't mean what she thought it did, and in time she would come to hate anyone who uttered it. Tao said he would be there too but there was nothing like a pretty face helping to smooth things over. At the time Tiny was delighted that Tao would have thought of her for such important work.

Mr Sing was a rich business owner with powerful links to several crime syndicates. He expected his employees and those under his protection to pay their dues; if not, it was well known that the penalty would be severe. Tao and Tiny met Mr Sing at his nightclub in the French Quarter. The neon cocktail glass glowed and pulsated above the entrance where a bald, two-hundred-and-fifty-pound bouncer stood before a line of scantily clad girls and suited men waiting to get in. Tao and Tiny were ushered through the VIP entrance.

Once inside, they were taken to a small table at the back of the club, ringed in by ropes and dimly lit. A waitress in a white mini dress took their drinks order; Tao ordered two French martinis. Mr Sing kept them waiting for quite some time. Tao looked nervous, his eyes skimming past the bodies of the pole dancers writhing to k-pop beats on the podium. Tiny smoothed down her silver skirt and adjusted her white top to show a little cleavage. Eventually, Mr Sing arrived, flanked by two bodyguards with earpieces. He sat down at their table and greeted Tao like an old friend. This greeting surprised Tiny a little but she kept quiet about it and sipped her French martini. She swung her hair over her shoulder, showing off its shininess and thickness. Mr Sing was a short but stocky man, with a balding head and tiny pinprick eyes, which seemed to have sunk into his round cheeks. When he smiled he displayed a neat row of top teeth, the canines of which glinted in the light, as they had been capped with gold. Mr Sing was full of boisterous, violent energy, which he showed with his exaggerated movements and the way he forcefully embraced Tao when they greeted.

The two men chatted and Tiny let her eyes flick over the room; she looked at the face of the dancers, the weariness behind their heavily made-up masks. Mr Sing soon switched his attention to her, and after that Tao seemed to fade into the background. He was no longer much interested in staying at the table; he excused himself to go to the bathroom and then did not reappear for an hour. By this time Tiny had been plied with more French martinis and she had had a line of coke, which she snorted right there at the table as if it were completely legal to do so. But Mr Sing was there so it must be alright – she thought innocently. Mr Sing moved his ringed fingers onto hers, pressing them against the glass of the table. When she tried to reclaim her fingers, a smile fixed on her face all the while, he took her hand forcefully and pressed it to his chest.

'My heart is beating for you,' he whispered in her ear when he had pulled her closer, his breath stinking of halitosis and cigarettes. She allowed a small smile to flicker at the corners of her lips. Then Tao was shaking his hand and suddenly they were leaving. Tiny was relieved. She did not like being close to Mr Sing; he scared her with his hard, beaming smile and his strong, cruel hands.

On the way home Tao's mood changed into one of abject despair; he told Tiny that he would lose everything, that Mr Sing was so powerful he could swallow small businesses whole, and people too. Tiny did not like this metaphor at all; it filled her with terror.

'Is there anything I can do to help?' These words that she uttered in sympathy for Tao were later to echo in her mind, to haunt her on a daily basis. It was at this point that Tao wiped away his tears and looked at her, with the look of a sailor who has been lost at sea for many weeks and has suddenly spotted sweet, dry land.

'There might be a way you could help, Tiny,' he looked at her eagerly in the back of the chauffeur-driven car that belonged to Tao's father. 'But,' he continued, 'it might be too much to ask.'

'Please, I want to help.' Again, Tiny would rue these words.

'You are such a good little girl, Tiny.' Tao pressed her to his chest, so tight that she could feel his ribcage beneath his shirt. 'You know Mr Sing really enjoyed meeting you, and he wants to see you again.' Tao paused, looking out at the passing traffic, the red and white lights of the cars' headlights and break lights. He looked at her with his smooth handsome face. 'Tiny, would you meet Mr Sing again, for me?'

'Of course,' she found herself saying, though there was

a lump in her throat and her insides felt like they were sinking.

Tao beamed back at her, his former anxiety all but forgotten. 'Great, because he wants to see you again tomorrow night, at his apartment.'

And that was it. Tiny did not remember many of the details of the next day or of the weeks that preceded this discussion. Tao must have slipped something into her drink before he escorted her to Mr Sing's the next day, something to make her more pliable. She had some memories of a bluish liquid, which was served to her by a servant while Mr Sing finished in the shower. She remembered the steam that rose from his skin as he entered the room in nothing more than a fluffy white towel around his midsection, and the way he offered her a pill. Then nothing, blackness and heat for hours, maybe days.

When she woke up, she was in a bed, undressed, in one of the rooms in Mr Sing's apartment perhaps. Her jaw ached and when she pulled the white bedsheet down she saw the bruises all over her thighs purpling beneath the pale skin, blooming like lilies.

Then she was kept prisoner in that room for a couple of months. Various men visited her during those months. Rich men who were married, powerful bosses that Mr Sing liked to keep sweet. Tao even visited her, protesting his innocence, saying that he didn't know it would end up like this, asking her to forgive him. Tiny, in her half-drugged and dazed state, fully believed his protestations of innocence. She believed it right up until the point when she was allowed to leave, barely human, utterly addicted to the drugs they had been feeding her for months.

Tao took her back, but everything had changed between them. He acted like it was her fault that she had been kept away from him for so long; she must have wanted to stay because Mr Sing was such a rich man. Tiny did not have the will to argue with him. He was also now often seen with another young girl, a beautiful Filipina. Tiny was no longer much on his radar, although she now knew what her job was. She was allowed very little time off, but at least she was not incarcerated. Tao would introduce her to various clients for a fee, and as long as she paid him a certain amount of money each month there was no trouble.

The Old China Junk became her usual haunt, and it was there that Lucian first laid eyes on her. He seemed very shy and reserved on that first meeting when she went over to him and asked if she could get a light. She lit her cigarette and looked deep into his eyes as Tao had taught her to do. He immediately invited her to sit down for a drink with him. He didn't say much to her that evening. He was new in town and without many friends; they drank a lot of shots together. He told her they could party at his flat. She agreed, and that night they slept together for the first time. He was strong but tender, a good lover, thought Tiny. He was full of praise for her, and his flat was very modern and expensively furnished. She told him she needed money to send back home and he gave it to her without question. She thought he was gentle and kind and, compared to men like Mr Sing, he was a saint. She wanted to keep Lucian interested; she wanted him as her boyfriend, or as close to a boyfriend as was possible for what she and he were: a junkie whore and a junkie banker.

CHAPTER 7

Angeles City in The Philippines had become one of Lucian's favourite playgrounds. He flew out with a suitcase full of cash to go and visit the hordes of women who would welcome him. Each time he went there he rented the prime minister's suite at the Angeles Beach Club Hotel. It was an enormous suite of rooms with a bed large enough for ten people. He spent his days wallowing in the pool, drinking beer and snorting cocaine. When he arrived, Lucian handed out money and sex toys to his favourites, and the throng of scantily clad women around him only increased. He gained a reputation for his decadence and all-night orgies. The other men who stayed at the Beach Club Hotel looked on with envy and jealousy. They could not afford his excesses. But Lucian liked to splash his cash – and he had plenty of it.

Lucian would have fun with the girls. Every day he instructed them to wear a certain colour bikini for the evening: Monday was white, Tuesday green. If the girls did not have the right colour bikini, he would send them on a shopping spree in the afternoon. Having them all in one colour made him feel even more god-like. He would also have favourites whom he showered in gifts so that there became a sort of struggle between the girls to assume the top position in the hierarchy. He was kind, but his kindness always came at a price. He would give a girl something and then she would have to act out a specific fantasy he had been concocting. Once or twice, it meant that the girls needed medical attention. But he paid for all that, and none of them would dare mention it to anyone – especially not the police, who were violent and corrupt.

There would be all sorts of competitions for the girls that Lucian devised for his own entertainment. There was jelly wrestling, which involved the staff at the hotel making vast quantities of the stuff and filling a large paddling pool. Then two women would enter 'the ring', as Lucian called it, and try to wrestle each other into the jelly. This almost always resulted in one or both women losing their bikini tops, or bottoms, and so Lucian thought it made for an excellent spectator sport. A lot of the other men at the hotel thought so too and they would come to cheer on their favourites. Although he didn't like the other men being there, he made sure, by generously tipping the hotel security guards, that they were kept in order. In the privacy of his own suite Lucian made the girls compete for 'trinkets', as he called them. Sometimes the competition grew fierce and there was a cat-fight with lots of hissing, pulling of hair and scratching. Lucian was secretly thrilled when blood was drawn because of him.

After having eight women for a 'sleepover' one night, he awoke with the jitters in the morning, so he told them all to leave because he needed space 'to hear myself think'. Women were good for one thing and it was no use trying to think of work with them chirruping around him. Then he washed, took more cocaine and lay on the bed waiting for the rush of ego and energy. He began to plan his day according to his mood. First a massage, followed by a pedicure, and then he would get his beard washed and trimmed. After that he would dress and head out.

He had a girl he always visited at her place above a convenience store, in Fields Avenue, which was just down the road from his hotel. Lucian had discovered Fields Avenue after it was recommended to him by a fellow Hong Kong banker as a good place for some R&R. It wasn't long before he had met Angel, who was working as a stripper and escort at that time. She was a great dancer, and an in-demand stripper, but she always talked about wanting to move on and run her own business. Lucian respected something about her ambition and the two became close. She made him laugh, and he always looked forward to returning to Angeles City and spending a few days in her company. Angel knew he had dozens of other women, but she didn't seem to mind. Even Lucian acknowledged that over the past year the relationship seemed to be becoming more serious. She had been living in a partitioned room in a run-down high-rise, but Lucian had started paying the rent for her to live alone. The last time he visited her she had talked wistfully of settling down and having a family. To his surprise, her talk did not repulse Lucian as he thought it would and he ended up agreeing that he would like to have children in the future. But he told her that he did not want babies right now. Lucian was still climbing the greasy pole to the top of the corporate ladder and he couldn't handle the level of responsibility required by a wife and children. He told her he would like to get married as well, but really this was just to soften her up a bit more and get the love hormones flowing. He didn't know why but sex was always better after one had these little romantic conversations about babies and marriage. It was like he could cast a spell over these women with the merest hint that he would one day like to settle down and play house.

However, although the women got a kick out of it, Lucian had the recurring feeling that everything he was getting was still not enough. It was like there was an itch that he just couldn't scratch, and every time he thought about what the itch might symbolise, he was drawn back to a selection of violent porn scenes that he had been watching more and more on the dark web. It was as if only when another felt pain could he truly feel any pleasure. So, after these jaunts to Sin City, he always went home depressed and deflated – feeling there could have been some other way to maximise his pleasure, which he had not achieved.

He returned to his office at the firm and started on the backlog of work feeling like he was missing out on something. Lucian felt like his work was beneath him and he started treating it accordingly. He would be late to meetings and his work was sloppy – not meticulous like in his London days. He would leer at the pretty women in the office just to make them feel intimidated and uncomfortable; he was disparaging of the junior staff and planned nasty, vindictive punishments if their work fell short. He actively encouraged a toxic rivalry between all members of the team and enjoyed watching the devastation it wreaked on their health.

His friends, the other VPs, were shunning him. Lucian had noticed it in the way they would no longer discuss their weekend plans in public, or at least when he was present. Byron from mergers and acquisitions had stopped making filthy jokes when they met at random at the water dispenser. People like Richard from accounts, who had clamoured to shake his hand when he had just started at the firm, were now avoiding eye contact. But nobody said anything. They just moved around him awkwardly, and conversations died when he entered a room. As Lucian looked at himself in the polished surface of the plush, corporate bathroom, its urinal sparkling, its soap and hand lotion dispensers full of some designer gloop, he tried to see what they saw.

His transformation had been rapid and drastic. Gone was the taut-chested, tanned youth who strutted around with a preternatural sense of his own entitlement, and now here was a pot-bellied, sad-faced man who, though he had just turned thirty, was looking well into middle age. But there was more than that. There was a blankness to his stare. He did not respond to people in a friendly manner. He had become abrupt, sarcastic, cutting, and with the loss of his looks people found these negative traits less easy to ignore or forgive.

In the beginning they would go out as a pack, five of them every Friday night. The drinks would flow, and the women would flock. Byron had a couple of girls who he would take back to his place (a penthouse overlooking the water) and they would all just fool around together. Byron was a senior VP and said he would make the board in five years. He was tall, self-assured, good-looking and silk-tongued. He had a good tan, which stayed put all year round.

A month ago, Lucian had stayed at Byron's all weekend. It was a two-day bender, the details of which Lucian still couldn't recall clearly. A lot of yayo had been snorted, and they had gone through crates of Belgian blonde beer. He and Byron had had an orgy with three Filipinas. Lucian could not remember if he ate anything that weekend. He had a vague recollection of a man showing up with eighty fresh oysters, some French cheese and baguettes (typical Byron fodder). And the girls were so compliant, so un-Western in their bearing. But it was after that weekend that Byron and Lucian's relationship cooled down a few degrees. Even Lucian, who was not astute in these matters, felt the chill. Lucian thought hard about what happened on that particular weekend that might have led to things souring between them. It was dreadful to have only hazy recollections of things that seemed to have had an impact on his whole existence at the firm. There were vague snapshots of legs and tongues and hips grinding over his body. There was one tongue that Lucian remembered in particular – it was healthy and pink, long like an eel. It belonged to Byron's favourite Filipina, and she had used her tongue on both of them but seemed to give Lucian more attention.

Images of that beautiful tongue covered in blood still haunted Lucian, but the details escaped him. He couldn't remember what he had done. But gradually as the days and weeks passed Lucian began to remember more. Lucian and the Filipina had been in the bathroom, laughing at the contents of Byron's vanity kit. The man had everything from nostril-hair trimmers to surgical sutures. The instruments disgusted and fascinated Lucian. Perhaps he had tried a few of them out, just to see if he needed them in his life. He had recorded it on his phone as well. At the time it seemed like a good idea. He liked to watch his videos when he was back home – it helped him to fill in the missing gaps.

However, it was a week before Lucian remembered that he had made the video of the beautiful Filipina in the bathroom at Byron's. When he did get around to watching it, it was more because of the nagging absence in his mind of any details from the weekend, coupled with the fact that Byron had taken Richard, and Rohan (a new Afrikaner), on a lads' weekend to Macau and had not invited him.

The footage was terrible quality and the audio even worse. He saw her face, and her lips, and for an instant the tongue flashed sensuously over the bottom lip; then it disappeared and all he could see were Byron's pristine white tiles, with the immaculate grout in between. There were sounds of scuffling and moaning in the background and then a scream.

A few moments later and the camera refocused on the girl, who was staring into the bathroom mirror picking at the corner of her mouth where bright red beads of blood were forming and dripping onto the white basin, covering it in what looked to Lucian like a mass of poppies. Lucian zoomed in to the perfect mouth, which had been messily sutured together on one side. Two little blue stitches. And a long thread trailing down to her naked breast. Hammering on the door there was Byron's voice. Lucian was mumbling something about blood on the bathroom carpet. 'Who has fucking cream carpet in their bathroom?' Lucian could hear himself shout. The video ended. Lucian couldn't remember what happened after that, but he remembered having an incredibly sore jaw for a few days after the party at Byron's.

He was in work on time on Monday, with a freshly pressed suit and starched collar, clean-shaven. He drank two pots of Ethiopian coffee that morning, took two Pro Plus, brushed his teeth twice and scrubbed his tongue, flossed and put a little yayo on his gums. He felt like he was on fire. Two boardroom meetings and one presentation later, his cock was so hard that he had to go and jerk off in the men's.

He had begun watching porn more often; he needed it to calm down at the end of the day. Of course, his addiction had started long ago, during one of those empty summers back home from boarding school. Maybe he was fourteen and it was a Sunday morning so his parents were out at church and he didn't have any commitments, no rugby practice or extra maths tuition. And he had been curious for a while (such things were forbidden at school; not that it really stopped the other boys). He would begin by locking his bedroom door (he had only recently been allowed to lock his own door) and then he lowered the blackout blinds. In the darkness of his room one could not tell if it was day or night, summer or winter. The AC was kept at a reliable twenty degrees Celsius. His bed was always made, the sheets tightly folded and tucked in below the mattress. The duvet was blue and white; it smelled of citrus and mimosa. He only allowed the maids in three times a week, at times that he would specify. He did not want to be unexpectedly disturbed. It all started with the soft stuff – and then he began to let his imagination run wild. There were things he had seen while staring into the screen at night that still haunted his dreams. He didn't think about the impact of all those images on whatever was still pristine and untouched within him.

School was like a ferris wheel. Always the same view from the top. Night or day, he would have the same feeling of being glued in place – that place being a particularly foul and uncomfortable dorm. He was called 'beast', having earned his nickname from his placid demeanour, which changed utterly when he got onto the river or competed on the racetrack. He excelled at cross country and won a few county-level competitions. Then he got bigger and heavier and started getting second and third place – he couldn't understand why. His coach told him he didn't have a long-distance-runner's physique. He punched a hole in the changing room door when nobody was there. He never owned up to that crime. On the water he grew more aggressive, pushed himself to the edge of endurance; often it made him vomit. And he expected no less from the other rowers in his team. If they couldn't keep up, he would beast them until they gave up. Setting ever-more demanding tasks on the ergs, singling them out to do Herculean numbers of press-ups and burpees. He watched his time for the 10k go down. Lower and lower, as his body became leaner. Then he plateaued. He was getting good times for an amateur but he knew it would never be good enough to get into the Boat Race at Cambridge. That was what he wanted, to row in the Boat Race with the Light-Blues. His coach tried to keep that passion alive for him but he had an overwhelming sense of dread: that he just wasn't good enough.

There was no question in Lucian's mind that he would get into Cambridge. He had always had the top marks in a class where excellence was the norm. The other boys respected him, feared him perhaps. He had a way of going quiet, which was more menacing than any rage-filled tirade. His lips compressèd, his eyes glazed over in hate if the rowers in his boat did not push hard enough, if his debating team lost, if he was ever asked to work with a group of sub-standard individuals who would jeopardise his academic advance. His mother once said it didn't matter if he didn't go to Cambridge. As the words left her tongue, he was already slicing off his filial emotion, viewing her as a stranger, a woman who had never understood the breadth and depth of his talent.

There was a time at school when he had not been the 'beast'; in fact, that time had seemed unrelentingly long. He was a puppy-faced thirteen-year-old, not having gone through his growth spurt yet. The other boys in his year seemed tougher, older, and he had to jump and skip to keep up. Intellectually, he was their superior; he knew that in his Maths class, and Physics and History. He always had the answer, even if he was sometimes reluctant to speak up in class. If the teacher went too slowly, he became morose, and he would make snide comments under his breath to the boy next to him. Of course, this behaviour meant that the teacher would fire an unexpected question in his direction. He would flick off the interrogative stare, like one flicks a fly, and answer the teacher with an obnoxious surety that would make the teacher question whether he had really seen him chatting in the first place. Lucian could simultaneously hold conversations and listen with the acuity of a translator to what was going on. Maybe it was because nothing interested him apart from the thing that interested him; therefore, there could be no distractions in his life.

He did not miss his parents. He had already boarded from the age of seven at prep. He knew intimately the morning schedules, the need to make one's bed, to keep one's clothes folded or hung up, to perform brief but thorough morning ablutions, to not hog the showers. He mocked any boys who didn't know these life lessons and wondered what mollycoddled existences they had led back home, going to their day schools. His parents were kind but unambitious; they had not understood how to nurture Lucian's growing aspirations and capabilities. They did their best to provide him with the material things that Lucian requested: musical instruments, a telescope for his interest in astronomy, the latest ski equipment for the annual school trip to the Alps, flying lessons, diving lessons, a sportscar when he passed his driving test at seventeen. They were perfectly willing to pour money into the education of their only son, their only child, and they always followed Lucian's advice on what he needed to become more successful and to have an edge over his peers. Lucian felt that they gave him what he wanted in return for love, but he would never agree to that. Whatever was given to him he accepted politely but the more he received, the colder and more distant he felt towards them both.

Before prep he had a nanny, now long gone; she was the person he had gone furthest with, in terms of giving and receiving love. The year before he was sent to prep he cut out his feelings for her as one might core an apple, with a slicing and gutting motion. Then there were the holidays when he would return and his mother and father would be eager to spend time with him. But because he regarded them both as intellectually inferior, he would hole himself up in the attic of their beautiful Grade II listed house and play video games all night so that he looked like a zombie during the six weeks, so that he always missed breakfast and put his head on the table during lunch, one eye on the bubbles in his glass of mineral water. His father would suggest some activity that they could do together, like going for a walk, or going fishing, but Lucian just gave him a withering glance and asked, 'How will you manage that when you can't use your legs?' Lucian always made sure that his father's disability was a well-hidden secret. His father could never understand why his own son was so ashamed of him.

School was, Lucian assured himself, a short blip, a minor inconvenience in what would be a successful life. Even if everything turned against him, he would bulldoze through. Never mind the casualties or the carnage. There had been an incident, when he first arrived at the age of thirteen. He never spoke about it and the thing became so wrapped in shame and loathing that it calcified like a stone baby lodged in a womb. No one must know, apart from himself and the other boy. No, he was not gay, that he was sure of. But at school you took what you could get when it was offered. Lucian was not hard to convince. The other boy was older, and he never referred to it after it had happened, never looked Lucian's way again. The two avoided walking the same way, avoided each other's friendship groups, which, given the age gap, was not too difficult, and they never uttered the other's name.

Lucian remembered being cornered by the boy but not wanting to run. He felt as a deer might feel in the sights of the hunter. And there was an all-consuming curiosity. Up until that point he had been a virgin. Albeit one who drooled over any lads' magazine he could get his hands on, and whose gaze followed the young female teachers at the school with an intensity that they would find unnerving. But with this tougher, stronger boy he could be himself. He could be strong; he could hurt and no one was going to go crying to a teacher or a parent. Lucian enjoyed looking at the wounds on the secret places on his body. He watched as his own body began to gain in definition; the muscles on his biceps and forearms came to prominence after months of rowing. His legs became tougher and he lost all the puppy fat that had once clung about his middle.

They found the dark, secluded places to meet. In the care-taker's cupboards with old mops, buckets and floor polish. In the boys' lavatories late in the evening. If someone came in when they were together in a cubicle they held their breath. The older boy put his hands around Lucian's throat. There was a certain thrill to the possibility of being found out. Lucian brooded over his actions for a long time. Had he been the victim or the perpetrator?

Was it something that would stay with him forever, like a tar stain on a cream carpet? Would it at some point need to be cut out? He always wanted to know if it had happened to other boys, so he stood listening to all their dark conversations, the hushed giggles, the huddle of smokers hiding on the school grounds. There was a lot of salacious stuff, but no one ever mentioned the other boy by name. Lucian started to wonder if it was him they talked about when he was just out of earshot. Were the stifled laughs, boys stuffing their school scarfs into their mouth to stop the explosions of merriment, about him? He began to feel small, but it did not turn him into a frail, whimpering thing. He adopted his cold haughtiness and thought that if he could just despise them all then his secret would be protected. He poured all his hate and malice into being the best Lucian he could be, and as the school only valued sportsmanship and academic prowess, these were the things he mastered.

Then came the fateful day when the school admissions advisor asked him if he had considered making an application to Durham or Bristol. He laughed so hard he turned purple and almost fell off his chair. 'All this,' he wheezed at her between gasps, 'to go to some mediocre establishment for Oxbridge failures.' She looked shocked. 'No thank you, miss; I would rather be dead.'

As a result, Lucian put all his eggs in one basket and applied only to Cambridge. He had his interview in November, in which he excelled, even when asked, 'What was Blake's opinion of Milton in the metaphysical context?' On New Years' Day he received the crisp white letter, just heavy enough for him to know before he opened it that it was not a rejection. That evening was a bit of a blur; nothing that happened could dampen his mood, though he was with his unedifying fellow students holed up in a dingy local pub, where the publican asked them rather rudely to prove they were eighteen. Lucian had grabbed the guy and threatened to stab him in the eye.

And now, he thought, all these years later, I am here. Hong Kong was always going to be my final destination. Hong Kong: the fragrant harbour, the pearl of the orient, the land where the air smells of money. But here he was failing too, slowly but surely; each day at the office produced in Lucian a greater certainty that he was floundering. His dependence on cocaine and alcohol, the fact he looked more and more unkempt. He was not completely immune to the stares and looks of contempt or disgust. Occasionally a female colleague would try to show some genuine concern, would try to mother him. Lucian hated that almost more than anything because he knew they thought he was weak. His male colleagues circled him like he was fresh meat thrown into the water. Every time Lucian was called for a meeting with the MD he steeled himself for the moment when he would be handed his marching orders.

Lucian had gone too far down the rabbit hole to believe that he could ever scramble out again. He was on a one-way journey, tumbling down with Alice to a nonsense world where time and morality worked very differently. After one particularly brutal day at the office, where a fellow senior VP had chewed him up in front of the boardroom for not getting his subordinates to complete an analysis on time, Lucian decided to leave the office early (at 7 pm) and take a taxi to the Tsing Ma Bridge. He had been thinking a lot about the bridge lately after he read about a spate of suicides that had taken place there, in *The South China Post*. He wasn't planning on taking his life just at this moment, but he thought it would be prudent to check out the location to see if it would really be feasible to jump and make an end of oneself. If, Lucian thought, he was going to do it at some future juncture, then he must know exactly where to do it. The bridge crosses the Ma Wan Channel and connects two islands, Tsing Yi and Ma Wan, as well as the richly forested Lantau Island. Lucian found himself looking at the picture of the bridge next to the suicide article in the *Post*. He liked the particular hue of the water so much that he cut out the picture and asked his secretary to have it framed. So, for weeks before his trip he had been gazing at this miracle of engineering, the two-legged towers with their trusses, their sinewy cables.

It was a forty-five-minute journey over to the bridge and he took a red taxi: a Toyota crown comfort. It was stuffy in the car and the AC wasn't working. The traffic out to Lantau Island was sluggish and the heavy vehicles belched out their noxious, leaded fumes. As he wound down the window to get a breath of air Lucian gulped down the heavy oily stench. He looked at the traffic. He was still undecided. Perhaps today was the day he would finally do it – finally put his hands up and say enough is enough. He imagined taking that first step into oblivion. What did one feel the moment one realised there was no going back. Of course, jumping from a high precipice made death all the more likely. You could be more certain with jumping than, say, an overdose. A few years ago Lucian would have laughed at himself – this maudlin frame of mind that had consumed him lately was uncharacteristic. Lucian was indomitable; he had often thought of himself as the devil (and the devil never dies). But lately his corporeal existence had lost its sheen. He was poisoning himself every day and he didn't know how to stop. And there was no one to help him get out of his rut. All his friends outside work were caught up in their sordid existence on and around Lockhart Road. It was in their interests to keep him an addict. This was why he had begun to hate everyone who milled around in the bars and clubs. He had even begun to find fault with the women in his harem. He took his frustrations and insecurities and poured them into their ears, or the ears of anyone willing to listen. Sometimes he used his fists.

They were approaching the bridge. The green neon arrows overhead pointed to the 'If you drink do not drive' sign. Lucian asked the driver to drive in the slow lane. He was still unsure if he was going to get out. It was dark but he might arouse suspicion. There was no middle option for Lucian. It was either do it or don't do it. Getting caught trying to attempt suicide and it being splashed all over the papers was a horrifying thought. Some of his colleagues would find it downright shameful. He would be forced into some rehab programme. His fall from grace would be dissected in the court of public opinion.

The view from the bridge was beautiful – the water beneath was light with a coating of mist, and dark green hills spanned all around. The barriers looked low and easy to climb. He wanted to ask the driver to stop but it would be difficult to explain why. The cars were moving quickly over the bridge, and slowing down might even cause an accident. So, the end is not today, thought Lucian, but I'll save it for another day. I'm still too attached to this life, it seems. I have more excuses for not doing it than I imagined.

Lucian returned home. He ate takeaway noodles, drank two Heineken beers and popped a sleeping tablet. He curled up under the duvet and slept as deeply as a hibernating bear. He did not wake up until twenty hours had passed. His dreams were full of women tumbling from the sky and piling up over the land. Their limbs and hair linked together formed a soft carpet on which he walked. The dream was strange and oddly comforting. He enjoyed looking down and stepping on the side of a made-up face, or leaving a shoe imprint on a buttock. Fingers and bones crunched beneath him. It was highly erotic. In the distance women continued falling from clouds onto a vivid cityscape. As they fell, they were impaled on the glittering pinnacles, their torsos sliding down – forming a red mist. Their mouths were wide open in screams but everything was silent. He awoke with a warm, good feeling in his belly like he had just swallowed a bowl of manna.

Lucian lay in bed not moving, soaking up the feeling. The long sleep had given him a new perspective. He knew that something needed to be done and finally he had settled on a course of action. But the haze of sleepy contentment did not last long. Within half an hour his body had started to kick into action and make demands. First, he was insanely hungry. So hungry that he couldn't wait for a delivery to be made. He went to the kitchen and opened the fridge, almost vomiting at the detritus that had built up in there. No, there was nothing in there. The freezer was almost barren apart from a large tub of cookie-dough ice-cream. He cleaned a spoon, as he had no clean spoons left in the cutlery drawer, and tucked into the hard, icy surface, digging so deep that the spoon almost bent in two. He finished the entire pot and then remembered he had a packet of biscuits in the cupboard. As he was beginning to get the sweats, he took the biscuits back to his bed, where he ate them huddled in his duvet.

He had been contemplating getting clean – going cold turkey. But every time he stopped using, the effects made him feel like hurling himself off the balcony. Slowly, reluctantly, he reached into his bedside drawer. He took the bag of white powder in his hands and put a pinch on the back of his hand and then snorted it into one nostril. He repeated the process for the other nostril. White powder coated his nose and lips. He lay back in bed knowing that the whole world was about to come right again. He got a bottle of vodka and took a swig. Then everything refocused. He was himself again, full of energy and resolve, full of the feeling that he was the only thing that was truly magnificent in a sick and venal world. He moved towards his computer and switched it on. He had decided to take a break from the rat race – to spend some time nourishing himself. He changed the automatic response on his email: 'Off dancing with the devil. I may be away for some time.' He had decided not to go into work on Monday morning. He would surrender himself to the pursuit of pleasure.

CHAPTER 8

Lucian paused in his narrative. He took a sip of water from the plastic cup sitting on his right. 'You're disgusted, right?'

'Yes,' replied Clementine. 'But it doesn't matter. It's just a story.'

'Perhaps you've heard worse.'

'Perhaps,' she admitted.

'This is where you come into the story,' he said, a slight smile on his lips.

'It's not necessary,' she said. 'I have enough.' Clementine pointed to the copious notes she had already made.

'But this is the best part,' said Lucian.

'In fact, one could say that this is the crucial part.'

Clementine had not expected that they would focus on her trip to Hong Kong six months ago. She had thought there would be enough material to focus on in Lucian's early life. She checked her watch; there was still half an hour to go.

'I want to hear about your trip to visit me,' said Lucian.

'It wasn't that long ago,' replied Clementine. 'Surely you remember.'

'Oh, I'm just a bit hazy on one or two points,' he said.

Again, there was a smile at play, now at the corners of his mouth.

Clementine wanted to leave, but she also wanted to remain in Lucian's presence. She looked into his eyes and saw a look of expectation. Again, she felt compelled to speak, to tell him everything. He once more had a terrible, overpowering hold over her and she felt like she must obey. Clementine placed her notepad and pen on the table beside her and clasped her hands together in her lap. She lowered her eyes and shut them.

'Don't look so stressed,' said Lucian. 'I won't bite. You may as well tell me the truth.'

The truth, thought Clementine, was not always something she was proud of. She felt stupid and petty. It would be horrible to reveal her insecurities, her fragility, to Lucian, but that was what he wanted. She lifted her head and said simply, 'Ok, I'll tell you.'

Her heart was racing. It was dreadful to feel completely compelled to tell her story. But at the same time she wanted to share everything with Lucian. She was grateful for his honesty thus far and she wanted to reciprocate in some way. Clearing the air between them might be just what was needed, she mused. Well, whatever happened he couldn't kill her now.

Clementine began. Her voice was small and unconfident, but Lucian's smile was friendly, encouraging. Maybe it will all be fine, she thought.

CHAPTER 9

Clementine had heard through the grapevine that Lucian had changed a great deal since his time at Cambridge. She kept a vague eye on his progress, a google search here and there to see what he was up to, a chat with Claudia over the phone, only, of course, if she had completed all her work. She used these little updates as incentives to reward herself for a job well done. In the early years there wasn't much that he shared, and what he did share was all quite good and proper. There were pictures of Lucian at his new firm, dressed in a suit, beautifully turned out. She heard that he had a girlfriend. Later, she heard that his girlfriend had left him. This pattern repeated itself several times, and all the while the names of the women involved became less familiar, less Cambridge, and more part of the other world in which he now moved.

Of course, she had her fair share of boyfriends too: there were those who were fleeting and unmemorable, and those who stayed and became boring. No one came close to breaking her heart – or even getting close – and she was very proud of that. Clementine was content in her career, in her progression to the top: ruthless and with an eye for deception, she became one of the paper's finest columnists. She had her flat overlooking Green Park. She had books, friends, holidays and time to indulge her passions for her own pleasure. Never once did she trouble herself to think about the welfare or happiness of another. But nobody seemed to notice or care that Clementine was Clementine's number one priority. All of her friends conducted themselves that way in the city.

There was of course the veneer of chumminess, friendliness, the things you do to get into the social bubble that they deemed acceptable. For example, going to a friend's exhibition launch at the Tate, or holding a banner outside parliament to score points with an individual who was going to give her an interesting piece on the Israel/Palestine conflict. These things were easy, and living in London, everything was only a stone's throw away. There were nights at the BFI, long walks along the Thames with new boyfriends, breaking up in an adult fashion under a streetlamp on London Bridge. There was getting engaged and getting unengaged, all without the hint of desire or hysteria. All without a trace of passion or madness. She complimented herself on the way she handled her personal relations so coolly.

As the years turned into almost a decade since that night she had spent with Lucian, Clementine began to find her feelings towards him change. She saw him now as more of a boy than a man, with little knowledge and far less experience of women. She saw his frailties as she could never have seen them at the age of nineteen; she also saw the seeds that were present, even then, of something malicious, something more malicious than she had ever known or experienced since.

He still came to her in dreams, or rather she went to him. She wandered a towpath not unlike the towpath of her Cambridge days, but it was changed, as dreams tend to change reality. Lucian was always close at hand, rowing out on the river, due back at the boathouse or at some rendezvous that they had agreed upon. Then there would be the lapse of time and either he wouldn't show up, or he would turn up aloof, his thoughts preoccupied with something else. Sometimes they would be in a room, either in a big stately home that she had dreamed up or in a potting shed. There would always be some issue, someone was going to be arriving so she couldn't be there now, or the bed was too small, or they would start kissing and then his real girlfriend (someone who was almost always a lot hotter than Clementine) would turn up and his attention would drift. There was always a barrier between them, but it didn't stop Clementine's subconscious bringing them together, sometimes once or twice a week.

The dreams left her with a deep sense of dissatisfaction – a hole in her heart that could not be filled – so she overloaded it at night, almost as systematically as she had packed it, it would unpack itself, and there would be her big, ugly, gaping hole, with nothing in the world to satisfy it, and nothing that ever would, now or in the future. Sometimes this hit her pretty hard on those cold, damp, November mornings when one needed to be hooked up to an IV of coffee to make it out of bed. But as the day progressed, she always started to feel better, or at least she thought she did. Yes, she was a little angry with Lucian, and it was irrational. It became clearer to her as the years passed that he was so damaged, so unlike a normal functioning person, that she wondered how he coped out there in the world. Did he simply build up more layers to deceive people, did he cover himself in a veneer of normality, and just do the things others did to fit in? Maybe he had found 'the right girl', who had broken down the terrible castle he had built around himself. God knows, maybe he was planning to have children and perhaps that would save him. Save him – yes, there was the growing feeling that she had been close to something diabolical; she knew she was no saint but at least she could mask her feelings adequately and interact with people without having a permanent look of disdain or even hatred on her face. Clementine did not hate people; instead she had a complete disregard for the feelings of most people.

Lucian, however, had the type of hatred that would fester and turn gangrenous with age. What would it lead him to? Religion? Drugs? Drugs almost certainly. He was already a user at Cambridge and, although controlled with his alcohol intake, he did drink to excess. How would the years have gone for him, Clementine found herself wondering, on an almost daily basis, at moments when she was supposed to be concentrating.

At some point after his move to Hong Kong, Lucian started sharing snaps of his life on Facebook, surrounded by half-dressed women. Evidently, he thought he was living the life, but to most of his friends from Cambridge his exhaustive debaucheries were becoming a cause for concern. Even the lads from rowing referred to him as that sad case, so and so. Lucian could not see (or did not care) how far he had fallen from grace. Clementine could see from the pictures that he had grown fat and puffy-faced. It amused her to see that he was no longer the god he had been at Cambridge.

Clementine decided that she must see it for herself; she must see him in the flesh. It was almost a sense of schadenfreude: if Lucian had been rich, successful, and happy, it would have burned her insides. Now that he was rich, fat and unhappy, she could view herself as his superior. She felt she should have a little gloat. He was so much like Dorian Grey: a perfect young man, slowly turned into a monster by his constant excesses. Clementine took a week off work. This was something she had never done before, as she lived and breathed her job as a journalist. She booked her ticket to Hong Kong. She decided to fly business class as a treat. She was smug at the thought of discovering him in some seedy bar, on a cocaine binge, a half-clad prostitute draped over his thigh, as fat as a whale. She wanted to sit across the table from him and let him see the look of pity on her face. Also, she was much more attractive these days and had really grown into her skin. There were no vestiges of the awkward teenager of their Cambridge days. When she walked into a room, men noticed; she was always catching someone staring at her in a shy, flirtatious way.

Hong Kong Island was bustling at night. Clementine booked a room at The Peninsula, with views over Victoria Harbour. She was told by a friend where she was likely to meet Lucian these days. He stuck to two or three old haunts in the evenings: The Old China Junk and a couple of seedy nightclubs.

She decided to try The Old China Junk first. She

would sit at the bar and order a cocktail. No doubt, she thought, she would have some drinks ordered for her. Her hair was now an expensive viking blonde, cut into a sharp bob, and with her blue silk dress she looked like a Hollywood siren of the silver screen.

The bar was full of westerners drinking. There were small groups jammed together at red plastic tables, and some men who sat alone. There were very few women around, and almost all of them looked Filipino. On one table, three middle-aged, suited men sat in a booth with a girl who looked no more than seventeen wedged between them. She had long, very straight, black hair and was wearing an orange halter neck top. She had eyelash extensions and white eyeliner, which made her gaze look huge and childlike. Her nails were adorned with neon acrylics. She didn't say much but she laughed when the men laughed, seeming to take her cues from the intonation of their voices and the expression on their faces. Clementine thought she understood very little English. A large man with a sweaty face had hold of the girl's left hand. He appeared to have ensnared her delicate fingers in his meaty paw, by simply clasping her hand down on the table. At times the girl looked extremely uncomfortable with the pressure of his hand. The man leaned into her, nuzzling her cheek and neck. He appeared pleased as punch that he had acquired such a nubile young thing for the evening. His companions looked on with envy.

As she took in the scene around her, Clementine realised that no one, not one man, was looking at her. She felt piqued, and the irritation led her to be abrupt with the waiter, who was taking a good deal too long to serve her. Eventually the martini arrived but he had drowned it in vermouth, even after she had specifically told him to make it dry. She knew that her voice, and her annoyance, along with her blue dress and peroxide hair, were out of place here. Maybe they were wondering if she were some kind of new European high-class prostitute.

The barman apologised and made another martini in front of her, so that she could give instructions. Clementine felt embarrassed. Already an older gentleman had decided to seat himself at the bar, only one bar stool away from her – evidently he wished to start a conversation. He had an expensive watch, which dangled from his wrist below his silver cufflinks. Clementine decided that if the man spoke to her she would try to squeeze him for some information about Lucian.

The man leant in, took a packet of cigarettes from his back pocket, and offered her one. She accepted. She had long since given up smoking habitually; now she was a social smoker only. She held the filter in her left hand, between her thumb and forefinger. The man informed her that his name was Ian. Clementine didn't want to give him too much encouragement, so she nodded and smiled at his comments but offered little in return. She let the burden of the conversation lie on his shoulders. He asked her what brought her to 'the island'.

She shrugged. 'Work, mainly. Visiting friends.'

He nodded enthusiastically and complimented her dress and her elegant style. 'You don't see much of that here,' he grimaced, nodding to some of the other ladies in the pub. The lights at the back of the room suddenly blazed into life and the karaoke began. Two girls in super-short shorts and bra-lets were singing along to a song by Cher. They were wildly out of tune, but they tried to make the performance as sexy as possible, wiggling their bums and flicking their long, dark hair. A group of men suddenly appeared around them, clamouring for their attention, making song requests.

'Ah, the locals' favourites,' said Ian. 'Twins, and they do everything together, so they say.'

Clementine smiled a weak smile and turned back to her martini. Noticing that it was empty, she promptly ordered another. 'Do you come here often?' she enquired.

'Is that your chat-up line?' he joked, which threw her off guard. She really didn't want to give him the wrong impression. He obviously saw her embarrassment, so he answered her question frankly. 'On Friday nights mostly, to catch up with a few friends who often lurk about these parts. I guess we expats do seem to stick together – more fool us! There's really so much more to see once you get out of the quagmire.' He smiled and looked wistful for a moment.

She decided to be frank too. 'I'm looking for an old acquaintance; you might know him?'

He nodded with encouragement but looked a little wounded that she was here to pursue another. 'His name?' he asked wryly.

'Lucian Dorsey.' She managed to say the two words together, without the usual sneer that accompanied them.

'Lou? You know Lou?' Ian's response surprised her, as she has never heard Lucian referred to by a nickname – he was just not that type of man.

'Well, I never knew him by that name, but yes, if his

full name is Lucian Dorsey.'

'Well, you're in luck: our Lou is a frequent visitor to The Old Junk. In fact, you see the reservation on that table? That's his. He always sits at that table so he gets a good view of who comes in. Know what I mean.' Ian winked.

Clementine eyed the little plastic reservation sign, sitting like a bad omen on a chequered plastic table-top cover.

'But he never arrives early – probably something to do with his work. Earliest he gets here is 11 pm. Want to go for dinner? It'll be a long wait otherwise.' He was trying his luck again, but unfortunately for Ian, Clementine had no interest in men who were even vaguely over the hill. She preferred twenty-year-olds, and plenty of them.

'You know what, I think I'll call it a night. I'm very weary after the flight; I must rest. Lovely to meet you, Mr...?'

'Oh please, call me Ian, let's be on first-name terms.'

'Well, goodbye Ian, and goodnight.' Clementine exited the bar as regally as possible with her head held high. Once out on the street, breathing the night-time air, she realised how sour and close the air was inside The Old China Junk. On the short walk home, she almost convinced herself to give up on seeing Lucian again. After all, what was the point? He was now the type of man who had a nightly reservation at a seedy nightclub. But then the feeling that had been nagging her surged up again in her mind. It was a feeling that had started during their encounter at Cambridge and had built up over the years. Lucian wasn't right, he was a man on the edge.

With the wisdom of age Clementine could look back and see the nastiness that was eclipsed by his good looks. Now his looks were gone, his nastiness would surely remain, stronger and uglier than ever. And here in Hong Kong, among the nightclubs and bars, the women and drugs, that could all be obtained for a price – there were no limitations to the damage he could cause. Clementine questioned herself, if she really did care all that much about the havoc Lucian could wreak. She had never felt the burden of people's misdeeds much before, but lately she was beginning to feel a genuine remorse for people she had wounded. But then, of course, she had not been able to wound Lucian, and maybe that was what irked her. Maybe she just wanted to see his beauty gone – and gloat. But perhaps his beauty didn't mean all that much to him anyway. Maybe his only priorities in life now were drugs and women, and any man with money can have those.

Before she got to her hotel, she passed a throng of scantily clad girls who were standing outside the front of a bar. Techno music was pumping out from inside the venue. They were trying to get punters inside. Their faces were heavily painted and their already thick hair was adorned with neon-coloured hair extensions. She saw the desperation in their eyes, and the rough-looking men who stood partly in the shadows of the club's exterior, watching their every move. Clementine watched as one of the pimps took a girl by the scruff of the neck down an alley. If she were not such an alien here, she might have said something, but she felt out of her depth and alone. It felt so very far from the seemingly emancipated world in which she lived and worked. At that very moment she decided she would try to see Lucian in the flesh, even if it were a brief look. She decided that it must be done.

At 11.30 pm the next day, Clementine turned up again at The Old China Junk. She was wearing a strapless red dress, which fell in folds below the knee, and red high heels. She wore a lot of make-up. She felt it was part of her protection against Lucian. It was like a mask that would hide her real emotions. She doubted he would recognise her, as her face and hair were so different to the way she wore them back in their Cambridge days.

Entering the bar at this time of night was a completely different experience, she soon found out. The music was on full volume and the lights were dimmed, with only plastic LED lights that changed colour in the centre of the tables. There were a lot of men and plenty of scantily clad women too. The girls clung onto the arms of the men. Some of the men wore casual jackets and chinos; others wore t-shirts and shorts with flip-flops. She couldn't immediately see Lucian's 'usual' table, on account of the number of people in the room. However, once she'd made it to the bar she glanced over. It was then that her stomach seemed to do a somersault. Lucian was there, lolling back in a chair. Three women were seated around him, and one small girl was sitting on his lap. On the table, there was a large platter of nachos with melted cheese and salsa. The girl on his lap would scoop salsa onto a nacho and guide it to his mouth. He was very bloated and pale – totally unlike the tanned Greek god that he had been at Cambridge. His skin had a gleam of sweat on it, as if his organs were strained by all the excess baggage they were carrying. He looked really spaced out.

It didn't look like he was talking much, and the women seemed to be gossiping with one another. Occasionally he would paw at the girl on his lap and pull her hair so that she leaned over and he could say something in her ear. She was such a slender-looking creature that it looked like just one of his massive hands could break her in two. While the other women in his 'harem' looked cheerful, this waif-like girl looked sullen and downcast. It was immediately clear to Clementine that she was his favourite. Lucian kept a possessive hand around her waist as if he were worried that if he let go of her she might fly away like an untethered helium balloon.

Somehow Clementine knew, just from looking at the scene, that Lucian's petite mistress would be the key to inflicting pain on Lucian. She had a good instinct for these things. Clementine wanted revenge, although she did not quite know why. She tried to justify it with feminist ideas about his machismo and patriarchal nature; she even tried to convince herself that she just wanted to help a vulnerable young woman escape the clutches of a controlling man. In the end Clementine decided to be honest with herself, as there was very little to gain if one were not. She wanted to cause Lucian pain and her observation of Lucian and his little quartet of women had given her a few ideas about how this might be achieved.

Clementine waited until Lucian's favourite was given permission to use the bathroom and decided to follow her. The girl meandered through the crowd of men. Clementine watched the men's eyes swivel as she passed. They were all checking out her backside, encased as it was in a short, tight-fitting silver dress. The female lavatory was situated down a narrow corridor. Tiny disappeared through a frosted glass door. Clementine entered closely behind her. Once inside, Tiny opened the silver clutch bag she was carrying and began to take out various make-up items. She fixed her hair back and took out a bronze powder and a brush, which she dabbed over her cheekbones and nose. Clementine looked in the mirror and likewise rummaged in her bag for her cosmetics. She retouched her lips and redid her eyeliner.

Tiny seemed completely preoccupied with her reflection in the mirror. Clementine felt that she could not intrude on this sacred ritual of make-up application. Clementine switched on the faucet and a rush of water cascaded from the tap, covering the front of her dress. The water reached Tiny and she gasped, hopping backwards from the mirror. Clementine apologised profusely, pulled some paper towels from their holder and offered them to Tiny. The woman smiled but looked worried that the water had got on her dress. Clementine now had a rather large, dark wet patch on the front of her red dress. She laughed out loud as she considered how she would manage to get back to the bar without anyone noticing.

'Hold your dress under dryer.' Tiny offered this advice as she stationed herself back in front of the mirror. 'It only take a few minutes to dry,' she added.

'Thank you,' said Clementine. 'Good advice.' Clementine felt like an idiot, but perhaps this was necessary to break the ice. 'Guess I won't be going back out there in a hurry.' And then she added, 'Is it always like this, y'know, so many men?'

'Always like this,' said Tiny, 'but it good, lots of men

mean lots of fun for us.'

Clementine wondered if 'fun' was the right word to describe the trade in flesh taking place at the bar. 'Do you come here often?' she asked. Now she was trying to coax the woman out of her shell. After all, this woman might be Lucian's closest companion; she must know things about him.

'Most times,' replied Tiny, shrugging. 'It not as nice as Bella or Mode, but it ok.'

It looked like Tiny was putting the finishing touches to her make-up. Finally, she pulled out a tortoiseshell comb and brushed the long mane of hair.

Clementine decided to take a risk, more out of a sense that the woman before her was scared and weary in some way. The way she sighed at the end of each sentence was as if she were ready to lay down and curl up asleep. 'I know the man that you're with; his name is Lucian, but you might know him as Lou.'

Tiny spun around. 'So what, you know him, all people know Lou round here, he very popular guy. You his old girlfriend?'

'No, I just knew him once,' said Clementine, reeling at Tiny's insight.

'Oh,' said Tiny, shrugging again. Maybe she was ever so slightly jealous; she was trying to imagine another woman knowing Lucian.

'Can I ask your name?' Clementine tried not to sound patronising but inevitably it came out wrong.

'Why you wanna know my name?' Now Tiny sounded fearful.

'It doesn't matter,' said Clementine. 'I just wanted to

say that I know Lou, and he's not a nice person. He could hurt you.'

Tiny gave a short chuckle as if she were very knowledgeable on the subject of how men could hurt women. 'He never hurt me, lady,' she said with her own tone of superiority. 'I must go now; Lou's waiting for me.'

Tiny brushed past her on the way to the door. A sudden impulse made Clementine grab her arm before she left. Tiny recoiled from the touch. She clearly thought Clementine might be crazy.

'I can help you,' said Clementine. 'Get you out of this situation. I have money, contacts. You don't have to say yes now, but call me, or write to me. My details are on this business card; I'm staying at The Peninsula Hotel.'

'Lady, you don't know me, why you help me?'

'Because it's a sisterhood, right?' said Clementine, trying to sound convincing. 'And we should all look out for one another.' God, thought Clementine, she even sounded like she believed that crap. She sounded exactly like a feminist. Bea would be so proud.

'I don't need your help; Lou is good to me. He's a good man.'

'You don't know him like I do,' protested Clementine. 'Just take the card, please.' Tiny stared at her then pushed past Clementine and left. But she took the card, despite her reluctance.

Oh shit, thought Clementine. Now I've done it. She would probably blab to Lucian about the strange lady she had met in the loo, and then he would get all defensive. Clementine put her hands on either side of the basin and looked hard at her reflection. What are you doing? She wanted to scream at herself. What had she just offered that woman? Friendship, financial support? Would she really give money to an unknown woman just to fuck up Lucian's life? Hell yes, she would, if she believed it would get him in the soft spot, right on the Achilles heel! He liked that little girl, probably relied on her for all sorts of things, the disgusting pig. Imagine if one day she just didn't show up, to feed him nachos or jerk him off? Imagine that? Clementine was almost rubbing her hands in glee at the prospect. Of course, he'd find another 'girl' in a week, but she would have put a spanner in the works.

Clementine left the bathroom after drying her dress. She was careful to avoid Lucian's table, as a confrontation with the girl now would be a disaster. She enquired at the bar and found out her name. She fought hard to hide the smirk when the bar man told her. After casting one more sideways look at Lucian and his 'friends' she departed, walking swiftly out into the close humidity of the island night.

★★★

When she awoke the next morning all she could think of was the great stupidity of her actions. Perhaps Tiny was in love with Lucian, besotted by the attention he lavished upon her. Perhaps compared to other men she had encountered in her life he was a model of kindness. Yet, Clementine could not erase the old feelings of hurt and anger she harboured for Lucian. His passive aggression, and discarding her like a used tissue. She hated that she felt anything for Lucian, but she could not deny that she did feel a lot. And whatever that was had remained with her ever since her first encounter with Lucian.

Would Tiny call her, or would she simply throw her business card away? Perhaps she had even shown it to Lucian. Clementine could only imagine Lucian's horrid, fat smirk as he read her name on the bone-coloured card. Clementine fell asleep with a thousand images of young Lucian in her mind.

To take her mind off things the next day, Clementine decided to go sightseeing. After a dim sum breakfast at a restaurant next to her hotel she took the funicular railway to Victoria Peak, to take in the panorama of Hong Kong Island from its vantage point. She stood for a long time on the terrace gazing down at Victoria Harbour, watching the tourist boats chugging to and fro. She wanted to keep moving, she decided, after a cup of jasmine tea at the Peak Cafe, to make the descent down to the harbour and take a ferry to Kowloon. It wasn't the clearest of days and the air was heavy with heat and pollution but she stood on the top deck notwithstanding, with the wind messing her hair and the salt spray from the harbour water getting into her mouth and eyes. When she returned to the hotel at around 6 pm she was so tired that she went straight up to her room. Clementine drew a bath and lay in the soothing warm water, playing with the bubbles from the complimentary bath soak.

At 8 pm, when Clementine was in her bathrobe, lying on her bed, flicking through shopping channels on the TV, the phone on her bedside table began to ring. She picked up the phone. It was the concierge to tell her that she had visitors waiting for her in the lobby. Clementine was curious; she told the concierge to ask her guests to wait for her at the hotel bar. She hurriedly put on a dress and fixed her make-up, which had mostly perspired away in the heat of the bath.

The elevator seemed to take forever as she descended to the ground floor. Clementine walked through the ostentatiously decorated lobby with its gold candelabras and plush sofas, and onto the bar. She almost didn't recognise Tiny, who was wearing her own version of business dress: a miniskirt with nude tights, skyscraper heels and a black blazer with a white blouse, the buttons on which lay undone to her cleavage. She was not alone. Another woman, equally smartened up, was by her side. Both women had downcast faces and dark glasses. Clementine decided to buy them a whisky. When the barman put down the tumblers, each of the women cradled the glass like a prized possession.

Tiny did not talk.

Instead, the woman next to her (who looked older and more used up) spoke on her behalf. 'You meet this girl yesterday in bar, yes?' she asked in a brusque tone.

'Yes,' replied Clementine, fully prepared to go into battle with this old hag should it be necessary.

'She say, you make her money offer.'

Clementine stifled a grimace. She did not like the woman's tone and she couldn't figure out why she seemed to be negotiating with her so she decided to play along. 'Yes, I might be willing to help her, but there is a price. She must leave Hong Kong.'

The woman inhaled sharply. 'She canna do that, she work here.'

'Well then, I can't help her.' Clementine was annoyed at how this woman was speaking to her. 'What's it got to do with you anyway?' she asked. 'It's not up to you; it's up to her.'

Tiny had not uttered a word, so Clementine turned to her and asked her directly, 'Do you want my help?'

Tiny nodded and the woman beside her tutted.

'Well then, you must do as I say. Please trust me. I just want to get you out of this situation. I know Lucian and he's not a good person; he has the ability to cause lots of pain and upset.'

Tiny's head drooped so that a curtain of hair fell across it. Something had happened to her, thought Clementine, and she was running scared.

'So why are you here?' Clementine demanded, deciding to be combative to scare off the other woman.

'Oh, we like sisters; I take care of her.'

Yes, yes, thought Clementine, a likely story, more like a vulture and her victim. Though she never mentioned wanting a cut of the money, Clementine could feel that this woman was hovering around just so that she might get an opportunity for a windfall too.

'Can you pack up and leave by tomorrow evening?' asked Clementine.

Tiny nodded.

'Where are your family?'

'Jakarta.'

'Right.' Clementine took out her smart phone to look for a flight from Hong Kong to Jakarta.

'There's a 6.30 pm flight; I can book that now if we're agreed?'

'What about the muni?' shrieked the woman by Tiny's side.

'I will give her the money at the airport, once she has checked in and I'm convinced that she will truly fulfil her side of the bargain.'

'She very scared,' the woman replied. 'She work for bad men.'

'Well,' said Clementine, 'all the more reason to escape while she can.' Then, mustering all her female sympathies, Clementine stretched her hand over the table and placed it lightly on Tiny's bird-like fingers. Tiny shuddered, but Clementine did not let this reaction put her off. 'Do you have children?'

'Yea,' replied Tiny.

'Don't you want to see them grow up?'

'Yea,' whispered Tiny.

'I will give you five thousand US dollars to take home with you. And I promise I will send you a hundred dollars every month for the next year if you provide me with a bank account once you are back.'

'Why're you doin this for me?' asked Tiny.

'It's only what women should do for one another,' replied Clementine, with her most convincing 'we're all part of the sisterhood' voice.

Part of her couldn't believe her hastily concocted plan was going ahead. Clementine knew it was a significant amount of money to shell out (after all, she was far from being rich) but she justified it by thinking of all the stupid charities she'd thrown money at in the past just to get some annoying street collector to stop begging at her ear in public. Now, I can tell those smug bastards at home that I really helped someone get their life back on track. She would make sure they felt bad too, about not really knowing where their hard-earned cash was ending up when they 'generously' put a fiver in some do-gooder's collection box.

The only problem was that Tiny really couldn't return to Tao that evening; there was too much at stake. It was decided that 'the woman' would return and use her contacts to get Tiny's passport back. The woman told Clementine that she would need money for a bribe. Clementine reluctantly parted with two hundred and fifty dollars and the woman disappeared. Clementine made sure that the woman knew she would have two hundred and fifty dollars more once she returned with the passport. Clever woman, she thought; she knew she would get her cut and that's why she's along for the ride. Clementine booked a second single room for Tiny that night. Both went to bed early with the agreement that they would meet for breakfast the next morning. Clementine hoped to goodness that nobody would be looking for Tiny and that her departure would not lead to any violence.

The woman was supposed to meet them the next day to hand over the passport. Clementine slept very little. She was buzzing with adrenaline. Excited about paying Lucian back in some small, perverse way, and now surprisingly gratified by her act of kindness, which would be a direct action, actually performing some good in the world. This second sentiment surprised Clementine, as she was used to doing this for reasons of complete selfishness or maliciousness, and though this act had its origins in such feelings the result was starting to look a lot more altruistic (very much in spite of herself).

At breakfast Tiny looked even smaller than before. She was dressed in the same clothes she had been wearing the day before and her face looked ashen. Clementine had considered lending her some of her own clothes but as they would have swamped her small frame Clementine thought it would be a waste of good fabric (once Tiny had departed, she would not be likely to see the clothes again).

So, there she sat, fiddling with the edge of her croissant, taking small sips of her freshly squeezed orange juice. It was only 9.30 am, but 'the woman' was late. She had said she would be there by 9 am. Clementine was beginning to get impatient and Tiny had a look of resignation on her face. Of course, thought Clementine, if this doesn't work out, she's going to be well and truly stuck. Clementine did not happen to feel any responsibility for Tiny if her plan were not to work out. She would most likely simply shrug and move on, leaving Tiny to the chaos that would ensue.

After an agonising wait of over an hour 'the woman' finally turned up. She was wearing huge dark glasses and a scarf over her head, like a femme fatale from a Hitchcock movie. She glided over to the table, never allowing her gaze to fall anywhere else in the breakfast room.

'Do you have the passport?' Clementine demanded.

'Yes,' replied the woman. 'But it was very difficult to obtain. I need more money for my trouble.'

Clementine almost hit the roof with rage that this woman was fleecing her for yet more money.

'You'll get the two hundred and fifty dollars, as agreed.

'No,' the woman replied sharply. 'Not enough; must be five hundred dollars or no deal.'

She had to admit that the woman had really got her in a tight spot, but as it was really of no consequence to Clementine, she decided to drive a hard bargain.

'Two hundred and fifty dollars, as we agreed; I'm not about to negotiate. Why should I anyway, the first offer was more than generous. By demanding more you are simply jeopardising the welfare of your young friend here. Does she really deserve that?'

The woman seemed taken aback by Clementine's tirade. She relented. 'Ok, two hundred and fifty is ok, not enough but ok.'

'Hand over the passport,' Clementine said sternly.

The woman produced the passport from inside her handbag. Clementine checked the photo page and asked Tiny to confirm it was the original document that had been confiscated from her. Tiny nodded and said that it was.

'Do you think you were followed?' asked Clementine.

The woman shook her head.

Clementine pushed an envelope towards the woman with the cash. She hoped it would be her final contact with this woman, who was clearly a slippery individual.

The woman departed quickly, stuffing the envelope in her bag. Clementine noticed that Tiny did not say goodbye to her. Another extortionist, thought Clementine, and felt a pang of sympathy for the shy and sullen Tiny, who seemed not to have a friend in the world.

After lunch at the hotel, they departed for Chek Lap Kok Airport. Clementine let Tiny make calls on her phone to her family. She spoke in a half-whisper, shed a few tears and whispered some more. After the calls she didn't look happy. Clementine asked her what was wrong. Tiny shrugged but Clementine persisted. Eventually, Tiny said that her family were worried that she was stopping work (they thought she worked in a laundry). They were worried that they would not have enough money to pay Tiny's daughter's school fees.

'Don't feel bad,' Clementine said. 'The money I give you will tie you over, and in the future you might go abroad to make money again, but next time you won't make the same mistakes, will you?'

Tiny shook her head, tears dripping from the end of her nose.

At the airport Clementine took Tiny straight to the check-in. As all she had was hand luggage, the whole process barely took two minutes. It was all so easy that Clementine wondered where the catch would be.

In order to give Tiny the money, Clementine needed to use a cash machine. As she couldn't go airside with Tiny because of the security restrictions, the two of them had to wander through the queues of people waiting to check in to find one. Clementine maxed out the amount she could take out on one of her cards and then she used her credit card. Ah well, she thought, as she handed the money to Tiny, it's for a good cause. But she was really thinking about Lucian's face when Tiny failed to return. He'd probably wind up on a coke binge that would see him hospitalised.

Clementine's thoughts were interrupted by a gasp from Tiny.

'What?' she asked. 'What's wrong?'

'I've seen him; he's here,' said Tiny.

'Who's here?'

'Tao. Please, please, I must hide.'

'Which one is he?' asked Clementine.

'The guy with the short hair and black leather jacket.'

'Ok, let's just rest here for a moment; here, put on this cap.' Clementine handed Tiny a baseball cap from a store and slammed five dollars into the shopkeeper's hand. She positioned herself so that she was physically blocking Tao's view of Tiny.

'Look, we need to get you past security.' Clementine was trying to appear calm for Tiny's sake. 'You must follow the signs to security, keep the hat down low, and here, take this cardigan.'

Clementine was wearing a long-sleeved pale-pink cardigan, which came down past her knees and was distinctly un-Tiny. He won't recognise her in all these clothes, Clementine thought, rather cynically. 'Once you're through security and immigration, head straight for your gate, don't stop for anything.'

'Ok,' whispered Tiny. She seemed very young and very afraid.

She said goodbye to Tiny and let her go to the security check. Once she's through it will probably be ok, thought Clementine. She could see Tao milling around keeping his eye on everyone that passed close by. Luckily, the airport was packed so Tiny could effectively blend in, shrouded as she was in the huge pink cardigan and baseball cap.

Clementine had asked Tiny to give her a ring when

she had successfully boarded the plane. She sat in the airport coffee shop, twiddling her rings, picking at her cuticles. She had no idea why the idea of this small, unfortunate woman getting on a plane and leaving Hong Kong meant so much to her but her heart was pounding.

And then the call came. Tiny was onboard – she was escaping – and for a moment Clementine felt as though she had achieved something of real significance. She hated to admit it, but it felt good.

CHAPTER 10

Clementine was about to leave Hong Kong, but then she felt a strange urge to see Lucian and judge for herself how he had changed. She decided to extend her trip. It couldn't hurt. She convinced herself that she could not leave without having spoken to him, without telling him what she had done to Tiny. What she dearly wanted to see was a flicker of pain across his chubby face – to see a moment of sorrow and true humanity in that impenetrable mask. Also, the idea that she had in some small way changed the course of the future, that it was down to her actions alone and that she was no longer helpless, made her feel powerful.

This time she decided to contact Lucian directly. She sent him a message on Facebook and waited to see if he would respond.

Although he kept her waiting an hour, the response finally came. 'Hey beautiful, I want to see you too. Let's meet somewhere nice.'

He suggested a bar in Soho and asked to meet her there at eight o'clock in the evening. Clementine replied, saying she would be delighted to see him there. Immediately after sending the message, she regretted her decision. What if he already knows what I have done? What if he was involved in Tao's business in some way? She could be in danger, but for Clementine there was a thrill to the danger. She decided to risk it, as they were meeting in a public place and surely no harm could come to her there.

When she arrived at the bar by taxi, she asked herself again if she wanted to take the risk. Clementine was not foolhardy, but she was insatiably curious about Lucian and his life and, more than that, she still harboured feelings for Lucian, even if they were more overwhelmingly negative than positive. The feelings of nearly ten years ago were stirring within her and she opened the taxi door as if in a trance. She barely noticed the pinch of her stiletto heels or the constrictive tightness of her short skirt. She was wearing a black leather miniskirt with stockings and a too-tight red halter neck top. Why had she dressed like this? With her peroxide blonde hair and heels she looked like a hooker. The questions spun around her mind. She wanted him to see her with her shit together: better-looking, better-dressed and focused on her career. She felt he had left her in a formless mush and, now that she was recovered, she wanted him to see it with his own eyes. Now she prepared herself; she would enter alone and own that place. All eyes would be on her.

As she entered the bar with its low lighting and immaculately dressed waitresses, she suddenly felt older and more ridiculous. The waitresses all had the complexions of fifteen-year-olds, though they were probably in their mid-twenties. She asked for the table under Lucian's name and was led through a series of dimly lit rooms with low ceilings by a waitress with crimson lips and heavily kohled eyes. The room she was led to was empty; there was a low table and cushions spread on the floor. It felt like a secret place, tucked away from view. On the walls were silk tapestries displaying rural life, men in the fields with oxen, women in traditional dress, working in paddy fields.

Lucian had not arrived yet. The waitress graciously took her shawl to the cloakroom and provided her with a leather-bound menu. A moment later the waitress returned.

'Mista Lucian say he will be a little late; he sends his apologies.'

Clementine wondered if the reason why Lucian was delayed was because of Tiny. She almost got up to leave the restaurant but then decided against it.

'Well, do you think I might be able to get another table, one by the window at the front?'

'Of course, that should be possible,' replied the waitress politely.

Clementine had a strange sinking feeling when she considered the room's isolation, and these days she listened to the little warning signs without trying to ignore them as she would have done in the past.

The waitress led her back through to the main dining area and this time Clementine selected her own seat, with a view over the busy Soho Street and a small candle in the shape of a lotus flower. That's better, she thought, and suddenly her feeling of control was restored. She ordered a whisky sour but turned down the raw egg yolk; she could not afford to risk food poisoning, and another delay to her flight. She waited for half an hour, taking her time with the whisky sour. The waitress then brought her a glass of champagne, which she said was from Mr Dorsey, with his compliments, and an apology that he was running late. Another fifteen minutes elapsed and by this time Clementine was thoroughly bored. She was about to ask the waitress for the bill when she saw a bulky figure come through the door. His hair was damp and matted and his glasses were fogged. He loomed large above the waitress as he spoke to her and she guided him to Clementine's table.

He took off his light rain-mac and thrust it into the hand of the waitress. Then, without looking Clementine in the eye, he sat down wearily in the chair next to her. There was an odour of sweat and stale beer, which reached Clementine's nostrils and struck her as odd, before Lucian had said one word. The old Lucian was always scrupulously clean and fragrant with designer scent.

When Lucian looked up again, he removed his glasses and placed them, dripping, on the table. Suddenly Clementine saw the old Lucian of the past. The mischievous gleam in the green-blue eyes was still there and the undoubted air of arrogance.

'So, you decided to change tables? You didn't like my choice?' His voice low and sensuous.

Suddenly, Clementine felt her face and neck becoming hotter. He exuded a type of masculinity that made even a grown woman feel girlish, and he had perfected the art of playfulness and intimidation. Damn, she thought, to blush in front of this creature is really embarrassing. Why does he still have such a hold over me?

What was worse was that he commented on this.

'That's a nice shade of peony; it suits you, makes you look younger.'

There was the familiar compliment, coupled with the barb.

'I'm glad not to be that young anymore,' she said breezily, shrugging off his comment but knowing she sounded hurt.

'Ageing is hard for women,' he said, matter-of-factly. Already, in a few short sentences, they had arrived at his views on women. His words told her how much he despised the ageing female body, but she decided not to make a big deal of it.

'I don't know what that means,' she replied, her feathers clearly ruffled.

Then he smiled, like everything was a big joke and the joke was on her for being so highly strung. He clicked his fingers for the waitress and Clementine nearly died from embarrassment. 'Two vodkas.'

'On the rocks?' asked the waitress.

'No, just as they are.' His glance lingered for a second longer than was appropriate on the form of the beautiful young waitress taking his order back to the bar. When he turned back to her, Clementine couldn't be sure if he had done that because he couldn't help himself or to insult her. With Lucian either scenario was possible.

'I don't like vodka,' said Clementine.

'Loosen up a bit,' he said. 'I think we need it, or I do. I've had a hell of a day.'

'Work?' she enquired.

He said nothing, just raised his eyebrows and smiled. It was a smile without a trace of happiness behind it. There were beads of perspiration on his forehead and Clementine could see the sweat forming rivulets down his pink shirt front. His face was unhealthily pale and he looked ten years older than his age. The way he looked at her had changed from the way he would look at her in the old days. When she first met him he was haughty and there was no eagerness until he pounced like a tiger in for the kill. Now he looked ravenous and she could see him undressing her with his eyes, and there was a sleaziness about him that had formed like a grime over his bearing and manner.

The vodkas arrived. Clementine picked hers up; it was very cold to the touch, as if the bottle had been stored in a freezer. They clinked glasses.

'Salut,' he said, looking into her eyes, his spectacles still on the table, his small, feral eyes watching her neck move as she swallowed the shot. 'You know I missed you,' he said, his voice silky, playful.

'Is that so?' she enquired, not looking surprised.

'Yes,' and then he laid all ten of his thick fingers on the table. 'Still a little obsessed with me, are you?' His words caught her off guard.

'What?' she stammered. 'I was never...'

'Oh, come on,' he said, teasing, 'you were practically my stalker at Cambridge; it took you ages to pluck up the courage to say one word to me.'

It was strange to be confronted with the truth by such a specimen as Lucian. She did not know what to say; she flushed again bright red and hated herself for it. This meeting was not going as she had planned; she was supposed to be the sassy one. But Clementine had the feeling that he was beyond the realm of hurt or pain. Nothing she had done, even the debacle with Tiny, would stir in him ordinary human emotions.

'So, did you come out here on business or just to see me?' He continued, enjoying watching her squirm. He took a fistful of smoked almonds from the bowl in the centre of the table and chewed them while looking at her with his mouth open. Little white flecks of almond escaped his mouth as he chewed and landed on the white linen tablecloth.

'There was some business, but I've always wanted to see Hong Kong.' She knew he saw straight through her lies.

With the drinks gone, the little waitress lost no time coming over to take another order. Her jet-black eyes flicked over him. Huh, thought Clementine, no one is immune, even now he looks like a lump of lard, sweaty and unhealthy. That's what it is, he brings out the nurturing instinct. There is going to be some poor fool who'll think she can make him change. But maybe more than this, there is the fact that he looks like he makes money. The Patek Philippe on his wrist must have set him back at least five digits, and he made sure he wore it visibly, frequently pulling up the wet sleeve to look at the time.

Lucian ordered more rounds of vodka and all of a sudden Clementine was in a panic about getting drunk in front of him. There was something in his manner tonight that unnerved her. She had wanted to add 'and a glass of water please' when the waitress came to the table, but she had felt her voice box squeeze shut as if under the weight of some invisible pressure. It reminded her of childhood.

When the vodka was placed in front of her, she apologised but said she really shouldn't, as her flight was scheduled for early the next day.

'So, you'll have a hangover on the flight; so what?' he said with a nonchalant tone. 'You didn't use to be such a goody two shoes.'

'Well, we all change.' She said that as she eyed his body, trying to make him feel small.

'Yep, I guess I certainly have,' he replied, stroking his belly and laughing with a hint of menace.

She was mesmerised by his confidence; he didn't seem to care what she thought.

'How about you come back to mine?' he asked with a smile.

'I'm afraid I have a flight to catch,' she said, surprised by the suggestion.

'I want to show you my place,' he pleaded. 'It has a great view.'

Her curiosity was about to get the better of her. She imagined sex with him would feel very different now that he wasn't the sculpted god he had been before.

'I would love to, but I can't.'

'Suit yourself; I guess I'll be home alone tonight.'

'I doubt that very much,' she said with a smile.

'Ah, you know me too well.'

'Now I must go; I'm a nervous traveller so I need to pack and re-pack and stay focused before I fly.'

'Before you go, let's have one more vodka for the road.'

Clementine agreed. It couldn't hurt. She desperately needed to pee, so she asked Lucian where the bathroom was. She followed his directions to the small washroom, which was covered in garish purple tiles. She was a little unsteady on her feet because of the alcohol, and once she had finished she stood with both hands on the sink to steady herself. She stared hard at her complexion in the mirror. She saw the dehydrated skin, the yellowish eye whites, the redness of her eyelids barely disguised by eyeliner and mascara. She was past her prime at twenty-eight. It was a challenging thing to acknowledge. She knew on a good day she could pass for twenty-five, but she remembered a drinking game she had played with a couple of friends and some guys they had just met about a month ago. One of the men had been asked to guess her age. He'd said thirty-five and sexy. But it didn't feel so sexy, a man thinking she was seven years older than her actual age. Not that it mattered to her, not that she valued herself less for it. It was just strange to see all at once the effects of ageing. The fine lines between her eyebrows, the creases at the corners of her eyes. I am mortal and here are the reminders, she said to herself. There is no shame in mortality, or ageing.

This little mantra she had learnt from her yoga teacher – a woman with a sparse covering of grey hair, which she did not try to conceal. Clementine admired and pitied her at the same time, although she secretly conceded that one of the reasons she had declined Lucian's proposal was because she felt unfit to be seen unclothed. She certainly hadn't worked out recently, or shaved. Why should she care, when his body was in such ruins? And yet she did. He never needs to know the real reason; it will simply be my rejection of him, and he'll be none the wiser, she thought. In some way, having this not so perfect ageing body protects me from repeating some of the mistakes I made in my youth.

Looking closer at her reflection, she saw her pupils were dilated; they looked like huge saucers. She kept one hand on the wall, to steady herself, as she walked back to Lucian. He was sitting observing the street. She followed his gaze out to two schoolgirls who were laughing together, under a Hello Kitty umbrella.

The vodka shots were on the table and the candlelight was beginning to make the restaurant look romantic in the half-light. One shot, she told herself, and then she would go back to the hotel. She was surprised by the force of his presence. It did not matter greatly that he was changed, she decided. She had not expected to feel just as drawn to Lucian now as she had when he was young and perfect.

She sat down and Lucian's eyes flicked back to hers. 'To us,' he said, picking up his shot glass.

She did not repeat the words but raised the glass and gulped down the liquid, trying not to splutter. The warm feeling of the vodka travelled down to her toes. She realised she was smiling at Lucian and she suddenly felt so relaxed and at ease in his company. Her tongue and her cheeks were a little numb and although she had been sitting bolt upright all evening, with a lady-like pose, legs neatly folded and on display, she now had the sudden urge to slouch forward on the table. She rested her heavy head on her cupped palms. Somewhere in the distance she heard a soft voice, telling her to leave, to get away, but she shooed it away like a distracting insect.

Lucian was chuckling, his eyes moist with tears.

No, she thought, can he be crying?

Two tequilas arrived, with salt and lime.

Lucian took her hand across the table and stroked it; then he turned it palm down. He put his index finger in his mouth, suggestively sucking it, and took the moistened finger and drew a short line beneath her index finger. He then took a pinch of salt and put it on the lubricated patch. 'Lick it,' he told her.

She giggled, and her voice seemed to echo around her skull. She stuck her tongue out. It felt very disconnected from the rest of her body, and then she touched it to the salt. It made her nose ache. Then he held the shot of tequila to her lips. She was somehow grateful for the assistance, as her hand felt clumsy. The tequila slipped down her throat, severing an additional slice of her rational brain. The green wedge of lime was then between her teeth and she sucked hard at it. Lucian clapped his hands, slowly, deliberately, and she giggled again. Everything was extremely amusing.

His shot quickly disappeared and immediately he ordered the bill, paid and suddenly she had on her shawl and Lucian was carrying his rain-mac and supporting her with his other hand. When he opened the taxi door for her, she slipped in obediently and rested her head on the window. A light rain had begun to fall, and a flurry of umbrellas opened up on the street.

Lucian was then beside her, giving the taxi driver instructions. Then his hand was on her knee, moving higher up. His hand rested on the soft inside of her right thigh and his thumb caressed the warm skin there. She enjoyed the sensation; she had apparently lost the ability to feel fear and it was a wonderful release. Maybe this is what I need, she thought. I've just got to get him out of my system. This was always going to end up with us sleeping together; there were simply too many feelings left unexpressed. She put her own hand on his and he linked their fingers together and brought her hand to his mouth, where she felt the graze of his unshaven face against her cheek.

She would have jumped on top of him in the back of the taxi, her inhibitions were so lowered, but he leaned over and whispered in her ear, 'Be patient, we're almost there.' And then she slumped back, enjoying the feeling that she was on her way to have a night of sex with a man she completely despised, and afterwards she would leave and never think about him again.

She must have fallen asleep in the taxi. When she woke up, she had vague recollections of Lucian breathing heavily as he carried her through the lobby and into the elevator of his apartment building. She remembered the garish light of the corridor hurting her eyes, and then once Lucian had tapped his card, they entered the womb-like dark of his living room. There was a jolt as he threw her down on the sofa and went to the bathroom to relieve himself. If being thrown onto the sofa had caused her any injury, she would have been completely unaware, as much of her body still felt anesthetised by the alcohol.

She could remember the sound of him urinating and the flush of the toilet. She now felt sick to her stomach, and it wasn't long before she was crawling on her hands and knees to find somewhere to throw up. Somewhere in her mind, she remembered that it wasn't polite to vomit over a cream carpet. She was still trying to play the part of a lady – hair dishevelled, mascara running, gagging on her own bile.

She didn't make it to the loo, but she did find a large pot with a gangly rubber plant sprouting out of it, and as she held onto its reassuring sturdy edge, she proceeded to heave her guts up. When she no longer felt the waves of nausea squeezing her stomach she sat back on her haunches and found a box of Kleenex on a low table and proceeded to wipe her mouth. It was at this point that she began to take stock of her surroundings and to wonder where the hell Lucian had disappeared to. Her head, though painful, felt a lot clearer and the buoyant, invincible feeling of intoxication was beginning to wear off, leaving her with a knot in her throat.

What was she doing? She went through the list of drinks she had consumed and came to the conclusion that something was amiss. She could, on a good day, consume twice as much and still find her way home through London and have a perfect recall of what had happened. It was then that her pulse began to race. Had she been spiked? Her adrenaline kicked in and suddenly she knew that she had to leave immediately. She picked herself up, unsteadily, and went back to the sofa, where she found her bag, and her shoes, which she decided not to attempt to put on. She opened her bag to find her phone; it was still there.

Then Lucian appeared in the doorway. 'Jesus! What the fuck?' he shouted, as he covered his mouth and nose with his hand and looked at the mess she had left in his rubber plant pot. Gone was the soft-spoken sensualist she had met in the bar a few hours earlier and here, in its place, was the beast, clothed in only the vaguest layer of humanity. She noticed now that he was only wearing his boxer shorts and there was a streak of white powder below his nose.

'I've got to go now,' she said, moving towards where she guessed the front door was.

'What? So soon? Come on, baby, you want to be here with me, don't you?' It was not a rhetorical question. 'Don't you?' He snarled, and flecks of his spit got her in the eye.

She made for the hallway, which she could see behind the living room door, hoping it was the right way to escape. Lucian blocked her path and shook his head. 'So, I've been meaning to ask you,' he said calmly, holding her arms and guiding her back towards to the white leather sofa.

'Yes,' she replied, trying to keep her voice steady.

'Were you jealous of Tiny?'

'What?' she faltered, feeling her heartbeat accelerate in her chest.

'Well, why would you go and take her away from me, if you weren't a bit jealous.'

She did not reply. In truth she did not know if it were better to confess some sort of jealousy on her part or simply deny having ever heard of Tiny.

'We're going to play a game now,' he said, with a wide, friendly smile. 'Sit down on the sofa and I'll tell you all about it.'

Clementine sat down on the sofa; all her feistiness had left her. She knew she was in the presence of a madman and that, if necessary, she might have to debase herself to survive. 'Lucian, what do you want? I'm here for you; I thought we were just going to fuck for old times' sake. If you don't want that, I can just leave now.'

'I don't want you to leave yet.' He had moved to the corner of the room and returned with a pair of plyers.

'Show me your tits,' he ordered.

'Lucian, look, I'm going to tell you everything you want to know; I'm an open book.'

He ignored her and yanked at her halter neck top. It was so low cut that it was easy for him to slide one of her breasts out, exposing the pink nipple with the piercing she had had done a few years ago. He cupped the breast in his hand. 'This is new,' he said, sneering. He pulled a little at the ring. 'Curious,' he said, 'why would you have something done like that? Is it a fashion thing?'

'No,' she replied, trying to stay calm. 'It was done on a whim while I was out with my friend; she had hers done too.'

'Clementine has friends now?' he smiled. 'You always seemed like a bit of a loner to me. Eating alone in the Sidgwick cafeteria, scared to catch anyone's eye.'

So, he wanted to humiliate her. That was not so bad, Clementine told herself. She could put up with that. She tried to look hurt by his words. He felt her breast again.

'A bit saggier than I remember, but the nipple's hard. You should do some chest exercises, might tighten up your bust. Do I turn you on?' He now had a strong grip on her right arm and in his left he wielded the plyers. His pupils were so wide, they had turned his green eyes black. He scuffed her nipple with the plyers.

She flinched.

'Don't worry,' he said, 'just tell the truth.'

'You turn me on,' she said.

He sniggered. 'You know I just don't believe you.' Then he opened the plyer handles and placed the metal jaws around her nipple. 'You don't want children, do you?'

'No,' she replied.

'That was honest at least. I'd say best you don't, you're the type that's too selfish, too wrapped up in themselves to be able to look after children.'

'What do you want?' she burst out, real tears now falling down her cheeks.

'That, just that,' he said. 'One moment of truth. Let me ask you again, were you jealous of Tiny?'

She paused, tears falling, feeling the grip on her nipple tighten. 'Yes, yes, I was.'

'You wanted me?' he asked.

'Yes.'

'Look at me,' he said.

She looked up into his face.

He searched her eyes and said, 'Yes, I think you're telling the truth.' He removed the plyers and pulled up her top. 'I'm sorry,' he said, 'but I don't feel the same way. I have never felt like that about you. In the beginning, you were just not my type, but you hung around, so I thought, why not. But now, you're older and I'm going to be frank, I don't like the feel of older women's bodies, they're off-putting. You know, maybe you should try to find someone to settle down with. You're not going to turn heads for much longer, and wouldn't it be sad if you turned out to just be an old spinster?' He searched for her reply with his eyes.

'Yes,' she said, brushing the tears from her eyes.

She said yes, knowing that she was defeated. She would not leave the room with her head held high; yet again, Lucian had triumphed over her, and again, for the second time in her life, she had been faced with the reality: he was a man with no natural human feeling or affections and if he had them he would sooner kill you than let you see them.

She tucked her bag under one arm and held onto the straps of her shoes. She made her way to the hall and fumbled with the catch to open the door. Lucian was still in the living room; he did not bother to show her the way out or say goodbye. Clementine made her way down the brightly lit corridor. She hadn't looked in the mirror but her mascara was no doubt running down her cheeks. She did not want to put her ridiculous shoes back on now but she had nothing else to wear on her feet and she couldn't go through the lobby barefoot. As she was too unsteady on her feet to lean against the wall with one hand, she had to sit down on the cold marble floor in the corridor and concentrate hard on doing up the tiny buckles on each shoe. She then used the wall to steady herself as she got up. Walking was tricky now that her vision was steadily rotating. She clutched her bag and kept one hand outstretched as she made her way to the elevator.

She decided she would go back to the hotel, have a double espresso and maybe order a burger from the room-service menu. Hopefully that would sober her up. She decided that now she would just focus on getting to the airport and getting home. There would be plenty of time to think about her humiliation later, years in fact of dwelling on what Lucian had said and done. She had thought she had completely exorcised all her feelings for him but she had been wrong. She had found them, and even though he was no longer pretty and certainly not happy, she was nonetheless still infatuated by him. And he had just rejected her and made their shared past seem like it was nothing more than an amusement to him.

She thought about Tiny, and how Lucian probably missed her, because she was small, vulnerable and defenceless. I hate Tiny, she thought, and then and there she decided to cancel all payments to Tiny. No self-respecting person can live on the charity of others, she thought. It would be better if Tiny made her own way in the world. Clementine had, after all, done her a massive favour in buying her a ticket back home. She began to wonder if she should write to Tiny and ask for a reimbursement now that she was home and safe.

Clementine shuffled through the lobby, trying not to fall over into the tinkling water features that lined each side of the short flight of steps, running like miniature waterfalls to the double doors. She felt the eyes of the door attendant boring into her back – an ageing prostitute was probably what he thought, stumbling back downstairs at 1 am having done the dirty deed.

She hailed a taxi and clambered in, and once inside she took her compact mirror out of her bag and surveyed the damage. There was her face: blotchy from tears, red nostrils, red eyes, her mascara having slid down to her cheeks and formed ugly black lines. She was very aware that she smelled of vomit, as some had got onto her top and in her hair. She watched the taxi driver wind down the window to let the cool air in; he did this even though the AC was on. She did her best to clean herself up a bit in the back of the taxi. She scrubbed her face with a tissue, reapplied her powder and ran a gloss over her lips.

When she arrived at her hotel she felt a bit better and decided to go straight up to her room, order a burger with fries and a milkshake. She wriggled out of her clothes, eager to be freed from their confines, and dressed in the fluffy white dressing gown that smelt of fresh laundry. She started to run a bath, adding the hotel bath oil of lavender and patchouli. She made the call for the food and it was delivered within fifteen minutes on a tray, which was wheeled into her room by a smart bell boy. She tipped him generously and he slipped graciously away. She sat on the big, firm double bed with her meal and switched on the TV with the remote. She ate ravenously with her fingers, ramming the burger and fries into her mouth as if each mouthful could somehow restore her to health and happiness. The milkshake was vanilla flavour; it sat thickly, lazily, in its tall glass. She took out the straw and licked the ice-cream from its sides; then she gulped from the glass itself, the sweet viscous liquid leaving a white rim around her mouth, which she wiped off with her sleeve.

She lay back on the plumped pillows and opened the front of her dressing gown to look at her body. She saw the lack of definition on her stomach, and the purple stretch marks on her inner thighs. She reached both her hands down between her thighs to feel how wet she was. All evening she'd been turned on and she had expected some sort of gratification, but here she was alone in her hotel room, masturbating while watching a Cantonese game show where the prizes included sets of knives and pressure cookers. The game-show assistants were all dressed in red mini dresses, faces slicked with a thick layer of deathly pale foundation, lips rouged crimson. They were not large-chested as women in these types of show were in the West; instead, they were demurely petite, arms and legs slender as pre-pubescent girls.

Maybe he's right, she thought, allowing herself, for one of the first times in her life, to reflect on what another person had said. I should go back to London and find a guy who'll just be nice to me and love me. It was as if she had lost the thrill of the chase; she was no longer interested in being the hunter, the stalker; she just wanted to be known for herself. She laughed softly to herself. Was that what this had all been for, this humiliation? Maybe Lucian had done her a favour by just telling her what he thought, although no one ever knew exactly what Lucian thought. Even if he were madly in love with her, he would never say so, and he would probably act much as he had done, with cruelty and malice. She set the alarm on her phone and curled up beneath the duvet. Tears came freely, and she did not try to control them. She felt like such a fool.

CHAPTER 11

After Clementine had left, Lucian went to the fridge and took out the remains of a large chocolate fudge cake he had been given by the girls at The Junk to celebrate his thirtieth birthday. He had made sure to take the leftovers, as he hated the idea of food going to waste, and since it was his birthday cake he should be the one to finish it. It did not cross his mind to allow the girls to each take a slice home with them. He always assumed that they were watching their figures. He took the dark brown slab back to the sofa and tried to enjoy it while the smell of Clementine's vomit still lingered in the air. He was annoyed that she hadn't bothered to even try to make it to the loo; it was so typical of those stuck-up, bitch types that act like men in the way they drink and end up looking like hags by the end of the evening – vomiting or pissing in bizarre places. He had seen women act like this at university and at work so often and it never failed to disgust him. Women should always think about how they look and try to be as appealing to men as possible, thought Lucian. No wonder Clementine was all alone, trying to rekindle a non-existent former relationship with him in Hong Kong. What a sad, deluded bitch. He wanted to fuck her and then strangle her with her own tights. He would love to see the expression on her face when she realised it was all over.

Eating the cake was helping to take his mind off his erection. When he'd eaten it all, he wished there was more cake. He went back to the kitchen and looked in his cupboard for some cat litter pellets. He took the bag back to the living room and emptied the contents into the plant pot with the vomit. He didn't have a cat anymore – at one time he'd thought it was a good idea and he'd bought a Persian with white fur and yellow eyes. He thought the girls would like it when they came around. But the cat moulted on everything, including one of his Saville Row suits that a maid had left on the bed. So he promptly fired the maid and drowned the cat in the bathtub. He thought it would be easy to drown a small feline creature in the bathtub, but it made the most dreadful fuss. Twice his claws sank into Lucian's skin and as the cat's life ebbed away the bath water ran with his own blood. He wrapped the small, damp creature in an old towel (it looked about half its original size when wet) and stuffed it into a shopping bag. He then took the bag to the garbage disposal shoot just down the hall, opened the hatch and threw the cat in. He could hear the dull thud of its body as it made its way to the trash collectors thirty stories below. After that he was strictly anti-pets.

He thought about what Clementine had done to separate him from Tiny. It made him sweat with rage. It had been a lady that worked with Tiny that had texted him about her disappearance. Bad news travels fast, he thought. Although the woman didn't say, explicitly, he had known the disappearance had something to do with Clementine. He was furious when he heard and rang Tiny's mobile a dozen times, at first pleading with her to come back and then threatening her. Then he relaxed. She would most likely return anyway; it might take six months or a year but there was no way a girl like Tiny was going to be happy staying in a no-hope shantytown in Indonesia. He thought of what he would do to her if she came back. Unfortunately for Tiny, she had been the one woman who Lucian had got close to loving, and this, coupled with what Lucian saw to be her utter betrayal, meant that his thoughts turned to the most cruel, prolonged and savage way he could end her life. He was a god, and is it not true that when a god is angered, he rains down all his wrath upon those who have wronged him?

Lucian thought about his life and what had been going wrong. Tomorrow, he decided, would be the day he started to make massive changes. He already had a plan forming in his mind. He remembered a hardware store at the junction of Lockhart Road and Fleming Road. It was a small, neat store and he believed that within its walls there was everything that would make him satisfied and whole again. He had lingered on the sidewalk many times looking in at the beautiful display of garden shears, blowtorches and clamps. And now he realised that the fantasy would finally become a reality. He would go out the next day and get the supplies. His apartment would transform into his workshop. Great and wondrous things would take place, and finally Lucian believed he would come to know a type of peace that had long eluded him. A peace that one only attains when one confronts one's true nature.

Yes, he thought, it would be beautiful, divine almost. And in the process he would find himself truly elevated, satiated in a way that success at work never made him feel. He had left the holding email for all his colleagues to see. How he pitied them, for they would never ascend as he would. They would be destined to while away their earthly lives in mundane pursuits – in the pursuits that others prescribed for them. Only he, Lucian Dorsey, would break free of the cycle and become the ultimate alpha male – presiding over life and death, completely in control of another's existence. Imagine how a person might beg for their life, thought Lucian. He wanted to know exactly how far one would go to preserve their own life. To what depths of depravity could one sink before one actually asked for death rather than life. These were experiments that he was willing to conduct in the name of research, in the name of humanity. He now understood the angel of death, the dreaded Doctor Mengele. It was all in the name of science and now he too was a type of scientist probing the effects of pain on the human psyche. He would record it all for posterity. Others must be allowed to know the results of his research.

Lucian took a sedative and chased it down with a swig of Boodles London Dry Gin. Gradually all the tension of the day melted away. He lounged on the sofa, just remembering to set his watch for 9 am before his head sank back and he was no longer part of the conscious world. The strength of the sedative meant that he wouldn't dream and would wake up like one who had died and been resuscitated the following morning. Then, feeling like he had been pulled from the grave, he would inject something to perk himself up, before brewing a pot of strong Jamaica Blue Mountain Coffee. He was very particular about his morning coffee.

CHAPTER 12

When the newspapers arrived on her desk, Clementine remained transfixed on the pictures for some time. She read them over and again, glancing at intervals out of her window, at the cold, grey water of the Thames.

There was his pillow-soft face, porcine eyes, made tinier by strong lenses. His body loomed, massive behind the two prison guards that flanked him. His beige overalls were tight fitting where they should have been loose. The cardinal sins, sloth and gluttony, were what sprang to mind when she beheld him – and the waste, the catastrophic waste. It was as if his life had been a vat, into which all the talents, the opportunities, the hopes, the dreams, the money, had been poured, no one having noticed that the receptacle's material was poor and prone to leaks.

And now the world saw the complete degradation. But surprisingly, the prisoner was still alive and well. He wore a smirk, undimmed by the strobe lighting and paparazzi flashes. In fact, the upturned corners of his mouth were testament to how much he was enjoying himself. In his thirty years on earth, he had never derived such satisfaction.

Clementine had decided to meet up with Claudia for old time's sake at The Botanist in Sloane Square. They had kept in vague contact over the years. Claudia had continued to be a society girl who frequently graced the pages of *Tatler*, and Clementine, although a touch jealous, had continued to follow her style choices and bed-hopping (as they were reported). They were both reeling from the news and felt like they needed to see each other to talk about Lucian.

Claudia wouldn't shut up. There was the twitch, the annoying smoothing of poker-straight hair with lacquered fingertips. Her mouth left a sticky imprint on the martini glass, a pillar-box red smear. Her older face was nowhere near as symmetrical as it once had been. Her cheeks looked puffier and her forehead lines had already been paralysed by Botox.

It was all wrong, and they both knew it, but Claudia's way of coping was to talk about winters in Courchevel and summers long dead. Claudia had brought her friend from Cambridge; her name was Helena. Clementine recognised her but had never had a conversation with her before. She was annoyed that Claudia had brought along another person for this sensitive discussion.

Claudia had picked up the tabloid and now she held it like roadkill, proud to have brought this offering but suitably nauseated by the deed. There were always too many pictures, she complained. There is never enough focus. 'All I can say is it's lazy camera work.' It was her first comment.

They were asking each other how this could happen and kept repeating the same words: 'Isn't it awful'. They tried to fit together the pieces of a life that they had known both casually and fleetingly. Lucian always operated half in the shadows; no one could truly know what was on his mind. Claudia rambled on about the way he had gone psycho when he went to Senate House to find out his results and discovered he had a 2.1 instead of the promised First. He'd been so sure that the First was his, he took the news like a toddler, demanding to see his supervisor, taking a cricket bat to his supervisor's car, trying to get his work marked again. It didn't do any good. Yes, he was clever, but perhaps not quite as brilliant as he thought. As a result, he pushed to get one of the best-paid jobs so that he could at least brag about how much he earnt and sneer at the few friends he had who did achieve Firsts who didn't find, or care to find, such well-paid employment.

'Maybe it is a reflection on us as human beings,' the saccharine Claudia eventually offered up as her theory on how we are all essentially depraved individuals. 'We had a psycho killer in our midst all those years at Cambridge, and we just thought he was quirky and his behaviour idiosyncratic; perhaps we were all way too myopic.'

Helene looked semi-impressed by this theory.

Bravo, Claudia, thought Clementine, for summing us all up in one pithy statement; she even had to take control of this situation and get us all on her side, nodding like comatose little doggies.

What Claudia wanted to say, but couldn't, was that he appealed to her back in those days because he was aloof and sexy, and that was it.

Maybe that's all there was about him, thought Clementine. There certainly wasn't much of a personality there; if he'd been a twenty-stone scumbag with a face like a pizza no one would have looked twice at him. Ultimately, we were all brains, but beauty blinded us, as it always does.

Clementine didn't know why she had replied to Claudia's message to meet up after the news broke about Lucian. She had loathed the girl ever since that first audition they did together as freshers. Claudia had no idea (or so Clementine thought) that she had even slept with Lucian. She also seemed unaware of the long list of women Lucian was involved with at Cambridge; well, those women were not technically 'at' Cambridge, so Clementine wondered if they would count in Claudia's mind at all. To Claudia, Lucian was besotted with her; he loved her so much that it was her eventual rejection of him that made him turn to this life of vice. Clementine couldn't help but smirk into her pint, but one never knew with Claudia. Maybe she knew everything, down to the minutest detail, and this was just her way of making herself the centre of attention again.

Clementine never mentioned her trip to Hong Kong and her talk with Tiny. Although she was a nihilist and mostly without any feeling towards her fellow human beings, she was rather glad to see that, at the very least, it was not Tiny who had been murdered. Had she put the fear of God into that little creature? Mostly, she had done it to get back at Lucian; she could see how he had come to depend on that little waif and hated the idea that he needed her more than he had ever needed Clementine. It was too much. Buying Tiny's freedom was a small price to pay for the enormous distress it must have caused Lucian. It turned out that Tiny was not so swayed by emotion. Once presented with cold hard cash to take home to her family and the promise of monthly instalments (peanuts to Clementine) she had packed up her bags and left immediately. And it was so much better, thought Clementine, to have done that, than to give pennies to pointless charities that grow fat on the generosity of others. She had effectively removed one prostitute from the mean streets of Hong Kong and, despite her negative motives, she genuinely felt good about herself. Though she had toyed with the idea of cutting Tiny off, she had somehow forced herself to keep her word. Clementine was proud of herself for that; it gave her a sense of satisfaction.

'Why are you smiling like that?' Again, Claudia's annoying voice intruded on Clementine's thoughts, yanking them back to the present.

'I was just thinking how happy Lucian was at Cambridge; he was always so successful at everything he did and everybody loved him so.'

'Yeah, right,' said Claudia, pulling a face. 'He was a complete dick, and you know it; he fucked over everyone, but he was very sweet to me. He bought me all these weird gifts, like necklaces and earrings from Tiffany's – but I always felt he was like, y'know, trying to buy my affection.' Claudia feigned outrage that any man would ever try to buy her affection.

'Yes, it must have been tough on you,' said Clementine, trying to appear sympathetic through gritted teeth.

'I think he just couldn't accept that I was so popular

at Cambridge. I know he was, y'know, buff, but he really couldn't handle a conversation, or his drugs!' She laughed a little. 'And now, I just don't know what to do; I was his last proper girlfriend.' Again, Claudia seemed to disregard the extremely long list of young women that had succeeded her. 'And the papers were asking for interviews with me. I just don't know; my agent says it might not be bad publicity but perhaps it is a bad idea to have one's name associated with a psycho-killer.'

The choice about whether to sell the story to the tabloids seemed to be weighing heavily on her. Things hadn't quite worked out for Claudia in her acting career; she was getting small parts in films and theatre productions, but she had yet to reach the stardom of others who had graced the ADC Theatre stage as students in their year. What had gone wrong? Clementine often wondered about that. Most likely, Claudia had pissed off someone and they had blacklisted her, or maybe there was just an abundance of attractive blondes and as yet she just hadn't made the cut. Maybe it all went back to that night in the Pitt Club where she had flirted outrageously with Scheherazade's then-boyfriend, Simon Featherstonehaugh – everyone in the thespy circle at Cambridge had heard about that – and then of course Claudia had started dating Simon, and then broken it off, rather acrimoniously. Obviously, opportunities were running a bit dry and her agent was probably begging her to give the scoop on Lucian just so people would start mentioning her name again with interest.

'Look,' said Clementine, drawing in a breath and trying to look concerned. 'You shouldn't forget that two women were tortured to death and died; don't you think it might be deemed a little disrespectful if you make it all about you, I'm just, y'know, playing devil's advocate.'

'Well, yeah,' said Claudia, 'that's what I mean, y'know, it could have been me.'

Yes, thought Clementine, yes, that was precisely how she would play it. And why not? The opportunity was ripe for the picking, for a vulture like Claudia. She decided to have one more stab at undermining her confidence and added, 'But, y'know, as you've said, you never actually slept with Lucian; don't you think the press would prefer to interview someone who was actually, y'know, intimate with him?'

'Yeah, I know I said that, but y'know, we did stuff.'

This was news to Clementine, who had always imagined that underneath that sexy exterior Claudia was in fact a prude and completely frigid. The little bitch, thought Clementine, as she imagined how Lucian's attention would have wandered from her to Claudia while they were in his room doing stuff. But she was probably lying – she was an actress after all and the line between fact and fiction was always blurry for these arty types.

Claudia and Clementine sat in silence for a few minutes. Claudia pretended to read the paper and Clementine stared into her pint.

'I was just going to say, by the way, that your looks have really improved.'

'Thanks,' said Clementine, not knowing if this was a compliment or another subtle dig.

'Yeah, you were so gothic-looking at Cambridge; you really scared off all the boys. They did not know what to make of you.'

'Oh,' said Clementine, rolling her eyes.

'Lucian used to say you terrified him! Especially with all that stalker stuff.'

'He did?' asked Clementine, mortified that Lucian had told Claudia about her following him.

'Oh yeah.'

'Imagine that – I terrified a psycho-murderer!'

'Maybe you pushed him over the edge!' joked Claudia.

'Maybe I did!' said Clementine, a half-smile on her face. And as she said that, she realised that she had to see him again. That she herself had to be the one to get the truth out of Lucian. Clementine would be the winner in this game.

The End

ALEXANDRA STRNAD read English at the University of Cambridge and completed her postgraduate studies at the University of Oxford, as well as studying at Charles University. A Czech-British-Australian National, she lived in Prague for several years, and now spends her time between Africa, Asia, the Middle East, and the Czech Republic. Widely published as a poet, she was a Winner of the Jane Martin Prize. This is her debut novel.